Praise for

K a t e   B r a d l e y

'I was gripped by this fast-paced thriller with a unique and fascinating character at the heart'

CLAIRE McGOWAN

'Fast-paced'

C. J. TUDOR

'An addictive, original and brilliantly twisty thriller that asks how far we might go – and how much we'd be willing to sacrifice – to do the right thing'

T. M. LOGAN

'An original and addictive page-turner. Gripping, thought-provoking, tense and highly recommended'

KAREN HAMILTON

'A clever, chilling and compelling debut, well-paced and well-plotted. I raced through the book in a couple of days, but it will take me far longer to let the characters go! This is a well-written and cleverly-plotted debut in which Bradley explores some interesting themes with sensitivity and skill. The twists start coming from halfway through the book and they just keep on coming. Highly recommended!'

DIANE JEFFREY

'This story is built on shifting sand . . . every time you think you've got it worked out there's another twist waiting just around the corner. Kate Bradley has created a truly remarkable novel and I can't wait to read her next one'

JAMES CAROL

'A nerve-shredding ride through the most brutal layers of the criminal underworld, the story pulls hair-raising moves and unveils some truly shocking twists. The question is: who is saving whom?'

A. K. TURNER

Kate Bradley

to keep you safe

ZAFFRE

First published in Great Britain in 2020 by
ZAFFRE
80–81 Wimpole St, London W1G 9RE

A CIP catalogue record for this book is
available from the British Library.

ISBN: 978–1–83877–061–7

Also available as an ebook

1 3 5 7 9 10 8 6 4 2

Typeset by IDSUK (Data Connection) Ltd
Printed and bound in Great Britain by Clays Ltd, Elcograf S.p.A.

Zaffre is an imprint of Bonnier Books UK
www.bonnierbooks.co.uk

For my mother, Jenny.
And for my husband, Brad.
Both heroes.

Prologue

I hang my legs over the cliff edge and look over so I can imagine your broken body lying on the beach below. I never tire of sitting here. I come even in winter, when the storms seethe, forcing me to grip the scant grass, because I feel that I could die here too. I like that. I watch the crashing waves below, beating against the bluff, pushing and pulling the flotsam and jetsam, relentless, relentless, relentless.

Then I do my own falling. I uncork a bottle and for a while feel the raw pain of my loss.

Walkers have approached me in the past; they see my solo picnic of wine and the inches between me and certain death, and they think I'm going to jump. The police have been here too. Twice they've arrested me under section 136 of the Mental Health Act, determined to get me assessed, but my last psychiatrist intervened. He said that I push all of my grief and guilt onto the clifftop, as a coping mechanism. He's wrong.

As I sober up at home, I spend the night staring at my bedroom ceiling while the world sleeps. I think about my choices, questions writhing like worms in my mind. I replay everything: everything I did and didn't do. What it caused; about the people who got hurt. Who died. I remember blue eyes locked on mine, eyes filled with the pain and the nearness of death. Then the peace, after.

I know I am guilty.

And then when I tire of my self-hatred, I wonder what would've happened if we hadn't come together like a planet spun from its orbit into the path of the other. How different my life would've been. And that's what I can't get over – that's why I cannot know peace.

I turn over what happened to us in my mind, the memories getting no less worn through the constant re-examination. Relentless, relentless, relentless.

I don't need this clifftop to remember you or what happened that Friday afternoon in May, three years ago, when everything that I'd ever loved, would be gone before the sun rose on Saturday.

I think and I think and I think; thoughts of what I'm going to do next beating relentlessly into the shallows of my mind.

Friday
08:55
May, three years earlier

Jenni

'Quiet! I'm taking the register.' Fifteen minutes, twenty-six teenagers, one register. A sum I've done before, not a sum that should change my life. But change it, it did, because she was there.

I didn't notice her straight away as I looked out across the kids in my form group. I knew I should know them well by this point, particularly as some were also regulars in my maths class. But a year into teaching and it was clear that I was never going to find it easy. I still struggled with their names – there were so many of them. Finn Taggart stood out with his huge cloud of hair and permanent smile, and right then he was flicking balls of paper at the group of girls at the back. Jordan Shire I did know because at six foot four he was one of the few that stood taller than me and I watched him now threatening to punch his best friend. I still hadn't forgiven Jordan for last week, when halfway through teaching fractions, he put on a perfect Dalek voice and imitated me, saying: 'you will be mathinated', instantly creasing up the class. I threw him out, of course, but the thought of what he meant bothered me more and more – at night, in particular. I couldn't help wanting to know what he was insinuating. Was it that he had found me out? Could he somehow tell I struggled with certain things? Determined to let it go, I unscrewed the lid from my water bottle and took a swig, scanning the room, looking elsewhere so I wouldn't have to deal with him. I hadn't been sleeping well and I knew I wouldn't be fair on him. As it was, I had woken this morning with a head full of thunder and fresh concern that perhaps something was wrong with me.

Something more than the recent bad dreams.

My sleeplessness was now threatening my ability to train – normally a granite wall wouldn't stop me from a fifteen-mile run before work. Given I'd never seen a doctor in my life – except that spell in hospital prior to my discharge from the army – I wasn't sure what to do. The sleeplessness didn't shift with herbal remedies or any of the other advice I'd seen on the internet. I'd trudged to work this morning and with each footstep I thought *I'm a drum, I'm a drum*, over and over again. The thought didn't make sense but I couldn't shake it; I didn't know what it meant, what I was supposed to feel. I felt nothing and I couldn't stop the relentless beat of my life.

Then a child at the back of my classroom caught my eye.

Destiny Mills sat alone.

Destiny. How I worried about her right from the very start. But then, worrying about her was better than thinking about me.

In a year group where some of the boys were already bigger than me and some girls seemed like adults, there were just as many at fifteen that still looked like young children. Destiny was one of the younger-looking ones. With wrists so thin a glare could snap them, she tamed dark curls into plaits and stood shorter than average. She had large watchful eyes and a mouth that never smiled. If she didn't have to speak she wouldn't, not to her peers or her teachers. She was rarely in school and when she was, she sat alone at lunch, playing on her phone if she could get away with it or reading obscure novels. Her small, silent demeanour could've meant that she slipped into the sea of unnoticeable kids, but she didn't because she was exceptional.

She was exceptional for two reasons: the first because she was the smartest kid in school. She was in year ten, which meant that she'd be taking her exams in a year. When she'd joined the school three months ago, she'd achieved nines in every subject assessment. Teachers would rather not predict let alone award a nine, particularly a year early, but after her mock exams last month when we'd all assessed her at the same grade, we quietly relaxed, glad to accept that perhaps Destiny Mills was simply a genius.

Destiny was also notable because she was in care. Teachers have to know about vulnerable children and as her form tutor I had to know more than most. But unlike most kids in care, she wasn't tucked up with a foster family. Social services claimed that she was unplaceable. They said they'd moved her halfway down the country because they couldn't find another children's home that would take her – apparently, not only did she constantly lie about being sexually abused in every home she'd been placed, but at the last one she'd set fire to her room. Arson meant she'd failed risk assessment after risk assessment. The school had never had an arsonist before and we'd all had to be briefed. If George Danvers, the head, was right, if she failed her placement at either this school or at her new care home, then she'd be moved to a secure unit. She wouldn't get nines there.

If she didn't get great results, maybe she'd never climb out of the pit of her life. Since I'd retrained, I clung to the meaning-fulness of education – the fact it could change someone's life. It wasn't the army, it wasn't life and death, but it had purpose and I grasped on to that as a reason to stay. I was too new to teach the top sets, so I didn't teach Destiny, but I liked the idea that schools gave kids the opportunity to change their lives. We all wanted good things for this friendless, diminutive, damaged girl.

But a bright future was starting to look impossible. She often truanted, so I didn't expect to see her in registration. She was missing lessons too. The way the exams were now, if she didn't start attending it didn't matter how bright she was – if she didn't know the content of the curriculum, she'd fail her exams.

What a waste.

Glad of the excuse not to have to challenge Jordan and deter-mined to speak to Destiny about her attendance, I started to cross to the back of the room. Her demeanour now in this noisy classroom, the way she held herself so small, made me think of a frightened hermit crab. Is that what she was? Frightened? I couldn't be sure.

As I got closer, I noticed something new – Destiny Mills had a huge black eye. I crossed the classroom, put down my water bottle and sat on the table. 'Are you OK?'

She stared at her twisting hands, her bottom lip quivering as she shrugged.

'Destiny?'

'I'm fine.'

I paused, deciding the best way to build a relationship. The topics like black eyes and care and truanting needed time to work into, but there was never any time in teaching. Everything had to be done in a hurry because there were so many things to do. I'm not sure it made my alexithymia worse, but perhaps it didn't help that I didn't tell anyone. My dad said it didn't matter, it just meant I wasn't 'a people person'. He said lots of people aren't able to read what people are thinking, but I shouldn't let it stop me from being out in the world. I wished I could be bright and chatty like most of the other teachers. But I wasn't, I had nothing to say. I thought of the drum again; beating, yet empty.

Perhaps *I* was the drum.

Destiny bit her lip, her gaze darting anywhere but at me. The bell sounded for the first period. Everyone bundled out, but I paid no attention – I hadn't even asked her about her bruise yet. 'How did you get your black eye?'

Destiny jumped up, bag in hand, banging the table as she tried to get away. I moved quicker, standing in her way to stop her from leaving. Around us were crashes as someone knocked the door against the wall, the cacophony of noise from the corridor, scraping chairs and shouts as the pupils began their brief chaos of getting to their class on time.

I waited until the rest of the tutor group left. 'Your eye looks like it must hurt,' I said, taking a closer look: it had the green and yellow of an ageing bruise. I also noticed a cut near her eye.

Whoever had hit Destiny had hit her hard. 'What happened to you? Is this why you've been off school all week?'

She shrugged. Just as she edged again towards the door, a phone rang in Destiny's bag. She jumped. Finding it with shaking hands, she saw the number and gave a strange moan like a keening gull.

I felt a thump of disquiet. 'Destiny? What's the matter?'

'Miss, I've got to go,' she said, her voice a husk as the colour dropped from her face.

My condition meant that I couldn't feel things right and not knowing what the hospital doctor called 'the full spectrum of emotions' made it difficult for me to recognise some emotions in others. But I couldn't pretend that I didn't know what was going on here. I couldn't use my condition as an excuse this time. I'd only been teaching for two of my forty years, but I'd never seen any child before or since look like Destiny did right then, with unadulterated fear. I'd seen grown men look like that under fire, but that's different. War is difficult, adult. But real fear in the classroom? Seeing it made my own heartbeat quicken. 'No taking calls in school.'

I have to, she mouthed before turning away. 'It's me – Candydoll.'

Candydoll? Why was a child answering a phone like that? I sat down hard on the table and crossed my arms, so she knew I wasn't going anywhere. And I wasn't – I had a free period so this could take as long as it needed to.

She turned and looked at me with eyes like she'd been stung, before turning back to the window. I got up to look outside, but didn't see anything. Then I noticed urine puddled by her feet. Destiny had wet herself. But even worse – she didn't seem to know or care. She said something into the phone that I couldn't catch. She whispered something else, and I realised she was fearful. 'No, please, it's only Miss Wales.' Her voice was the whine of a kicked dog.

Why was she talking about me? The weeing on the floor, the fear in her voice, made my own bladder twitch in response.

I thought: *confiscate the phone.* As I reached for it, she spoke: 'She's nice, leave it!' She turned to me and pointed outside. There was a van outside of the school gates. She covered the phone with her hand and said: 'I'm sorry, Miss.'

Then, turning away again, she added: *Run.*

Friday
09:15

Jenni

I ran.

My brogues hit the empty corridor, *bang, bang, bang*. Everyone was in lessons and the school was quiet.

I covered the long corridor in seconds. I ran through reception, ignoring the receptionist at the front desk. Through the foyer. Pushed through the front double doors. Ran three steps down onto the front drive.

Cold wind smacked my face as I saw it: a large Ford transit. White. Clean. Two men staring right at me from the front seats. They had parked further down the drive, but now as I ran towards them, they revved their engine and sped towards me.

I jumped onto the grass verge. Just in time, as I felt the front wheel throw gravel on my shoes. Shiny hubcaps. It skidded to a turn and then sped out onto the street beyond. A large padlock swung from the rear doors.

As the van left, I only then noticed Aaron Vaughn from year eleven staring after it. The boy's mouth hung open. 'Miss! How bad was that! Are you all right?'

'Did you see that van's number plate?'

A shadow crossed his face. He shrugged, his usual insolence returning to his voice. 'I didn't see nothing, Miss.'

'Then get going, you're late.'

He glanced back over his shoulder as he went, our brief roles as comrades restored back to the status quo.

Jenni

Destiny.

I realised that Destiny still stood in her own urine in room 12.

I ran back past the reception, jogged up the now silent corridor.

Destiny was still in my classroom. Using my desk tissues, she was mopping the floor.

'Let me help.' I took the wodge of paper off her and finished wiping the floor. 'We better get you to Mrs Hodges.'

Terri Hodges was the nearest we had to a school nurse now that the school's welfare team had been cut from six to two. She was in charge of the school reception, but behind reception was a small room with the medical bed where kids went with temperatures, banged heads, bleeding noses. With the room came the responsibility. I didn't know her, really; I worked in the maths department and barely left it. I'd noticed that other staff who'd joined the school at the same time as me seemed to know everyone by now and were always in the staffroom, laughing and chatting at lunch. I kept to myself; it was better that way. That way I couldn't make any mistakes about what they meant, like when Paul Goods, the science teacher, had been saracastic about the deputy head and I thought he was being serious and everyone had just stared at me like I was from another planet. It hadn't been like that in the army.

I hoped Terri was kind.

I could leave Destiny with Terri, I decided, but I also needed to report the incident. Since we'd lost our protection officer, Mary Nightingale, one of the two assistant heads, had taken over the responsibility for safeguarding student welfare. But she might be teaching. I checked my watch; I still had twenty minutes before my next class.

Destiny had put on her coat. 'Where are you going?' I asked.

'I have to go, Miss. I'm sorry . . .' she cast around, as if to express her anguish.

'I'm going to take you to the medical room. Mrs Hodges might have a spare skirt you can wear.'

Destiny fiddled with her coat zip, then looked out of the window. I could see her wondering if she should follow me or make a break for it.

I turned and walked down the corridor, holding my head up with a surety that there could be no debate and her only option was to follow me. I remembered when I was a corporal and my command carried authority: it seemed like a distant memory now. In my chest I felt a pressure: I pushed it away. It needed to stay distant, the more distant the better.

We found Terri Hodges in reception dealing with what seemed like an anxious parent, on the phone. We waited but in the end

I was forced to mouth about Destiny's 'accident', even twitching inverted commas into the air to make my point and speed her up. Terri finished her call and primed up like an engine, large bosom puffing up in response. 'Come now, dear, you're safe with me. We'll let Miss get to class.'

Class. As reluctant as I felt to leave Destiny, I had to go. That was something teaching had in common with the army: you could never be late. 'Just one thing,' I added to Terri with a whisper, 'I'll write a safeguarding report, but I want you to know that I don't think Destiny is safe out of school. Could you keep her in sight? I'm worried that she's really . . .' I thought about the padlock on the back of the van. '*Really* vulnerable. Do you think you could do that? It's important that she doesn't make a bolt for it. If we lose her today, we might not get her back.'

'That bad?'

'Look at her eye.'

Terri did before she nodded at me and touched my arm.

I wasn't sure what she meant by that, but I could see her take an interest in Destiny so I decided it meant that she believed me.

Friday
09:54

Jenni

I took the east stairs two at a time; I could hear my class before I'd even reached the top. As I walked past a neighbouring classroom, my colleague Steve Fullers, the head of the maths department and the second assistant head, was at his door. Seeing me, Steve gave me a look that was long enough to mean something before he shut his door, closing the view of his already seated and silently working class. It felt like yet another punching reminder that I wasn't getting teaching – or perhaps at least *he* thought I wasn't.

I wondered if more than one whole class detention would be fair before I checked myself: it wasn't the year nines' fault if I was late.

'If I can't rely on you to behave . . .' I muttered five metres from the classroom door, already mentally in there.

It is *this* moment I remember, this one above the many that happened in the hours after, this one that changed my life and the life of those around me, because this one was a moment of chance. Everything else in this account was a choice; I accept that. Although, for me, it was a Hobson's choice: Destiny had wet herself in front of me, laid her fear out in front of me as clear as if she'd gripped my hands and begged me for help. Seeing something then deciding not to act might be a choice for the lazy, the dispassionate, the cowardly, but I am none of those things. But as much as I am the sum of my parts, I accept my choices are still choices.

But it wasn't a conscious choice to glance out of the window from the first floor, only ten feet from my classroom. If I hadn't turned my head to glance out of the window, the trajectory of my entire life would have remained unchanged. I would've kept my job, not have had my actions with Destiny been made public by the press and would never have been arrested. And poor Destiny would have continued on her sad journey, like thousands of kids who slip through the system destined for bad things.

I might not have looked out of the top-floor corridor window. But I did.

Friday
09:58

Jenni

I ran.

Back down the corridor, back down the stairs, three at a time. Down the lower corridor. Past Terri as I sprinted out onto the front drive.

'*Destiny*!' I shouted. 'Come *back*.'

Destiny walked towards the front gate. She didn't walk in a straight line, but weaved as if caught in a buffeting wind.

The van was stationary but I saw the exhaust, heard the engine running. They were ready to leave.

Destiny stopped at the sound of my voice and turned. As I got nearer, I thought she seemed upset. I wasn't sure, but her face was screwed up and her hands were balled into fists. She was still wearing the same skirt. And I saw in my mind's eye: Terri leaving to get the replacement and Destiny walking out of the door.

'What are you *doing*?' I asked her as I grabbed her by the shoulders. I looked up to see the passenger door open. A large tattooed hand gripped the door, then a grey tracksuited leg wearing a black trainer emerged. I didn't wait. I grabbed Destiny – harder than I would like to admit – and ran her, pulling and pushing, back towards the school. I remember she didn't exactly resist, but she whimpered and protested like I was hurting her by not letting her go.

I heard footsteps behind us, running faster. I learnt in the army to never look back. When I compete in Ironman, I only keep going. So I pulled Destiny harder, my grip clawed her shoulder and propelled her forward with my body weight.

As we got to the front steps, Destiny looked behind again and cried out.

I still didn't risk a glance.

With a heave, I pushed Destiny back into the school.

And then I dragged the big bolts into place, locking the front door.

A man was running towards us and came right up to the half-glazed door. He stood so close that his breath steamed the glass. He was pale-skinned, a big man, broad with the huge shoulders of a weight-trained bouncer. But he wasn't as tall as me, maybe only five ten. He had a large shaved head with small terrier eyes that stared unblinkingly at me. His neck was like an oak tree and there was a flattened bridge to his nose, like it had taken too many blows.

I stood against the door and lifted my chin in defiance. 'Get out of here,' I told him through the glass, staring down at him.

Behind me, Terri called out a question, but I ignored her. Instead I focused on him: our faces were only inches from each other, his face forced to lift up to meet mine. He glared at me and as if I disgusted him his blue eyes burnt into mine, it was as if I could read his thoughts because I knew that if the security glass hadn't been threaded with wire mesh, he would head butt his way to me. I banged the glass in front of his face – aggression for aggression. *Don't you threaten me, sunshine: I'm no Barbie.* 'Go on, clear off, this is school grounds. I'm going to call the police *right now.*'

His blue eyes continued to stare at me unblinkingly through the glass. Then he pulled up his hoodie and tucked in the waistband of his tracksuit bottoms was a handgun.

As I stared at it, he gently leant in, closing the small gap between us and slowly licked the glass with a thick slug-like tongue, leaving a spittle trail right in front of my face.

Later, after my arrest, as I explained my actions, I insisted I had been scared. This was important. This was my defence.

It was also a lie.

Yes, I had been disconcerted by the man. Revolted by the wink he gave me before walking away.

But scared?

No.

I think, for the first time in a long time, I felt alive.

Friday
10:10

Jenni

After I shouted at Terri, bawling her out in the corridor for letting Destiny go outside after I had been so very specific that she wasn't to let Destiny out of her sight, George Danvers, the head, came rushing out of his office. 'Ms Wales, please step into my office for a moment.'

'I can't. I've got a class waiting for me.'

George looked at Destiny who stood against the wall, head and body bent over; then he looked at Terri, red-faced and near tears, and inhaled deeply before speaking to her. 'Please send up whoever is on call and ask them to supervise Ms Wales's class.' He then turned to me. 'Ms Wales.' He stood to one side, his hand open to show me his office door. 'If you would be so kind?'

Where was I going to leave Destiny? I couldn't let her out of my sight – I could hardly trust Terri – but what I needed to say couldn't be said in front of Destiny.

Then George solved it for me. 'Destiny Mills, what lesson are you supposed to be in?'

'Geography.'

He addressed Terri. 'Mrs Hodges, would you mind . . . ?'

Terri put her hand on her hip, and with an arched eyebrow and a tone of voice I couldn't place, said, 'Ms Wales suggests I should change her skirt first. If I take her, I'll have to close reception and I'm not allowed to close reception.'

George's gaze lowered to Destiny's skirt, but he didn't react, instead he simply thanked Terri for her help.

As I stepped into George's office and started to explain, he held up his hands. 'No, not yet Jenni. I know you're new to teaching and I understand it's not been easy for you, but this really is unacceptable. You cannot – *ever* – leave your class unattended. Do I make myself clear?'

'I've just been threatened with a gun.'

George was well known for his calm handling of all situations. I'd seen a student hold a knife to another pupil, and even then George didn't fluster or panic, he merely talked the student down. Yes, George could take anything in his stride, but even his eyes widened a fraction.

He made a phone call to his secretary. He glanced at me as he said, 'Sylvia, contact Steve Wichard and tell him I've had an emergency come up.' There was silence for a moment, before he said, 'I can't. In fact ... tell him I'll need to delay until later today. Check his availability for me, will you, and reschedule against my diary.'

Then George turned his soft brown eyes to me and said: 'Tell me what happened, then we'll call the police.'

So I told him, then he pushed the desk phone at me and I rang 999, and the police came within the time it had taken for George to have his secretary to arrange cover for my lessons until lunch and make us both a sweet tea. I didn't need the sugar in my tea, but because of my height and my six pack, which outclassed any man I knew, it was rare for me to be treated delicately, so I accepted the sentiment as it was meant.

I'd always liked and respected George. Despite the fallout that happened only three days after I sat across the desk from him drinking the milky sweet tea, the fallout that put him in hospital, cost him his job and ended his career, I like to think that he didn't regret taking a chance on me and employing me.

But I don't know. I've learnt that there is often a big difference in what I like to think and what people really think.

As we waited for the police, he sipped his tea. 'Exactly what is it that you think is going on, Jenni?'

'I don't know. Something weird. Destiny is really scared. And she's vulnerable.'

'We haven't rung social services yet, we should do that now.'

And he did.

Friday
10:52

Jenni

Two police officers turned up, a PC Hollinge, a red-haired copper who looked as if he should still be wearing braces on his teeth, accompanied by a woman about my age, PC Glad, with eyes that stared without blinking.

George introduced me and let me tell them my story. At the end, he told them that he was waiting to hear back from social services after ringing Destiny's social worker. We'd also made a safeguarding alert through the MASH call centre hub and properly followed it up with the relevant online form.

Glad had a look at the safeguarding form on George's computer, while Hollinge took my statement. At the end of each laboriously handwritten page, I had to sign to say it was accurate. When I got to the gun, I was already three pages into my statement. 'It was a Glock, probably a nine.'

Hollinge and Glad exchanged a look.

'How do you know that?' asked Glad.

'Well, I can't be sure. It could've been a seventeen, obviously.'

'No, how do you know about guns?'

I explained about my firearms history. 'I was a serving corporal in the British Army for many years; I've completed tours as both a frontline medic and in combat, including Northern Ireland and Iraq. Although I carried a SA80, guns in general have always been an interest of mine.'

George started to say something, then he stopped. I thought he looked as if there was something he wanted to ask. The same question everyone asks.

'You're going to ask me if I have ever killed someone? Yes, I have, but only in the service of my country.'

George blinked and drew air in audibly through his liver-coloured nostrils. 'I was actually going to ask if you wanted another cup of tea. I . . . was worried that you were shocked by seeing the gun, although . . . I realise . . . now . . .'

'No, George, I was not shocked. I've been shot at many, many times. What I did think was that his choice of where to store his weapon wasn't very sensible. The Glock is a heavy piece of machinery; it could've easily fallen down his tracksuit bottoms. I rather thought it showed he wasn't very experienced. Even if,' I thought again of the slug-like tongue, 'he was an enthusiastic adversary.'

They looked at each other and I continued my statement without further question. When I got to the end, I asked them what would happen now.

'We will need to speak to social services ourselves,' said Glad. 'If you get hold of them first, ask them to contact us.' She passed a card to me and George, writing down the incident number for us. 'Obviously, we are concerned. We'll put out an alert on the van now, but without the number plate, it could be difficult to trace a white transit. We'd like you to pop down to the station today or tomorrow and we'll get you to do a photofit of the person you saw. We can put it through our computer and see if it pulls anything up.'

'But what else? Surely Destiny needs some protection right now?'

'We'll contact social services, as I said.'

'She doesn't need you to contact someone, she needs your protection.'

'If you're thinking we can offer her around-the-clock guard,' she said, 'you'd be wrong. Obviously, we need to interview the girl herself, but her social worker can come down to the station with her or arrange for an appropriate adult. We need to hear her side of it. Right now, that's all we can do.'

Glad stood to leave and Hollinge followed her lead, thanking George for the tea.

'There must be something else?' I pushed. 'Something to help her after school?'

'Destiny probably knows their identity. When we hear from her, we can get an ID, we can pull them in for an interview, maybe even get a search warrant for that gun.'

'But what happens today?'

Glad sounded firm. 'Let's wait to hear from social services.'

Friday
11:50

Jenni

I dismissed my class a few minutes early so I was at George's door as soon as the lesson bell sounded. Before I knocked, I checked that the police car was gone from the driveway. Although I knew they wouldn't linger, I still didn't want risk seeing them again. I didn't like the way Glad looked at me. Maybe being a copper made them suspicious of everyone; maybe it was habit to scowl at people as if they were about to lift your wallet.

He opened his door and sighed. 'Jenni.'

'Is the social worker here yet?'

'Not yet. They won't give me an appointment; they'll turn up when they can.'

'When they arrive, can I see them?'

'You'll be teaching.' He checked his watch. 'I thought you had a lesson now.'

'Can't someone cover my lesson?'

'Jenni, you are here to teach, not run round like you're in charge of crisis management.'

'But if you got cover for fifteen minutes I could—'

'More cover from where? You've had a free this morning and you've got a free period six and that's your lot. Besides, Sal is already broken by arranging cover today – did you know she ended up covering your period two and three lessons herself? We've got three staff off on long-term leave; two more called in sick today – there is no one else. I've already got two agency teachers in murdering my budget. *You* will teach your lesson and *I* will oversee the social worker. I'll make sure they know everything that has happened.'

He held up a hand. 'In the nicest possible way, I'm going to shut my office door now. I don't know why you're not getting it, but I need you to go. I've got to make a grovelling phone call to my boss, who I cancelled on today, because of this debacle. Now, if you would *please* let me do that, because some of us value the relationships of our managers and will do what we can to keep them sweet.'

He gave me a warm smile and then very slowly, but very firmly, shut the door.

Friday
12:41

Jenni

I was back at George's office, but this time I'd made it inside.

'No. Now Destiny's social worker has been in and seen her and met with me, you have to accept that there's no more to be said on this,' George said, calmly. 'Enough, Jenni. *Enough*.'

'*Not* enough,' I insisted. 'That man had a fucking gun!'

'So you've said. I'm not going to go through all this again. I've done everything I can. I need to have something to eat before I catch up on a billion other things that need my attention.'

'But—'

'No buts. What with you, then the police, then meeting with Destiny's social worker, I've already put most of my day to this. And this school, despite what you might think, still has to run for the 1,108 other children that we've got here.'

'Where is Destiny now?'

'She's being supervised by Mary.' He held up a hand. 'No – don't say it. If we can't trust the assistant head to keep one pupil under lock and key, then this school is sunk. Now, go and have your lunch knowing she is in safe hands.'

I crossed my arms and stayed put. 'I cannot believe that social services have been here and are writing her off. I've never seen a sign that she's a . . . what did you call Destiny?'

'Not me,' he said carefully, 'social services. Their word was "fantasist".'

'And you believe that?'

'You've already asked me that. Despite you being her form tutor and already knowing about Destiny's history.' George sighed and ran his hand through his greying hair. 'All right, you've beaten me down. I'll give you one minute, so come in but don't sit down.' He shut the door and sat behind his desk. 'Look, it's not up to me. I've told you, it's their view. And, Jenni? They know her better, love.' With the endearment and the gentling of his voice, I heard the hint of his almost gone Yorkshire accent. 'Destiny's been in and out of care since she was six. It's understandable she's got problems. And that's how these problems come out – she makes things up for attention.'

'But I saw them! This is what I keep telling you! She hasn't said anything to me. In fact, she was going to get in the van. It's not her fantasy, and I know damn well it isn't mine. Don't they care about the fucking gun?'

'That's in the hands of the police. Stop shouting, Jenni, you're starting to sound like you've lost the plot.'

'No. What did the social worker think about the gun?'

George did not look happy. 'He asked about you. I told him you'd been in the army.'

I felt like I had been dunked in freezing water. For a moment I couldn't breathe. 'Is that what you think? That because of that I see guns everywhere?'

'It doesn't matter what the social worker thinks. The police are looking into the men, since that bit is their job, and the social worker's job is looking after Destiny. Everyone is doing exactly what they should be – except you, it seems.'

I ignored him. 'But it *does* matter what her social worker thinks. It matters a *whole lot* because it's him who makes the judgement about whether Destiny is at risk. And it's the presence of a gun that puts her at risk.'

'Destiny was at risk yesterday, the day before that and the day before that. She's had a caseworker since the day she was born.' He sounded tired.

'That doesn't mean she's not at risk now.'

George took his glasses off and rubbed his face. 'He came and saw her within the hour.'

'I think you're being blasé about the danger of an armed man.'

George gave a dry, humourless laugh, 'Oh Jenni. I don't think anyone accused me of that before. Are the police not good enough for you?'

'How well does the social worker actually know her?'

'He wasn't her case worker, but the one dealing with emergencies today.'

'So he doesn't know her at all.'

'He'd read her file and he certainly seemed very knowledgeable about her case. He even offered to take her home there and then. She's only still here because her attendance is low and I thought it was better that she didn't miss any more lessons. He'll also update her file and has promised that he'll keep a closer eye on her. Tell me, what else can social services do?'

I stared out of the window, barely seeing the oblique view of the schools fields, the distant trees and gathering storm clouds. It all felt so lame, so not enough, given the situation.

'Look, teaching is hard. I should know, I've been doing it for thirty years. You've come in at a very difficult time, resources have never been so stretched. When we took you on, you might not realise, but I had to cut the drama department by fifty per cent to keep the core subjects with enough teachers.' He must've seen my wince: 'Sorry. I didn't want you to know, but if you're angry with how things are, good. Be angry. We should all be bloody angry with how things are.

'You're in the middle of what an esteemed colleague of mine calls a "headteacher spring" – there's an uprising of headteachers and they're angry and political. You know this. You know that we can no longer use the netball courts because they're no longer safe to do so. We have thirty-five geography textbooks for ninety-eight students doing GCSE geography. The school is falling apart. I have one headteacher friend who can't sleep at night because of the stress and has developed IBS. Another has quit. Another hasn't had a day off in six months because they spend their weekends coordinating the campaign against government cuts.' He opened a drawer and plonked a bottle on his desk. 'This is how teaching has changed. When I was a kid it would have been a malt to drink with the parents. Not now.' He tapped the lid of the Gaviscon bottle. 'I don't even dare admit to my doctor how much of this stuff I get through. And I can tell you, since I had to cut the SEN worker to part time and take on some of her work, my job has now about topped out as manageable and I'm up an extra bottle a week.

'So, as much as I share your concern – and I do – I'm just relieved a social worker turned up to see her so quickly. With the way the cuts have been for children's services as well, I can count on two hands the arguments I've had with overstretched social workers telling them that I'm going to stay with at-risk kids until they come in and take them. With Destiny, he was here within an hour, spent time with her and was even keen to take her home, plus she lives in a secure unit. I don't know why that's not enough for you. It makes me feel like you're looking for a fight.'

Shame and anger burned my cheeks. 'It's not enough.'

'Destiny has to make better choices about the people she chooses to spend time with.'

'What's that supposed to mean?'

'They are her cousins, apparently.'

'Her cousins?' I couldn't keep the incredulity out of my voice.

'That's what Destiny told her social worker. The social worker says Destiny encourages them. The staff at her home have had problems keeping them away, but she continues to hang out with them. A month ago, she was found climbing out of the bathroom window to see them, so now they keep it locked.'

'No, she wouldn't go with them out of choice. She wet herself, George. I saw her shaking. She's got a black eye. Why does a young girl go off with men when she's covered in her own urine and clearly frightened?'

'Look, Jenni, this is the end of this discussion.'

'Because she's more scared not to, that's why!' I banged his desk. 'Because she doesn't have a choice.'

George didn't react. 'All the right things have been done. You're not the only person who cares, Jenni. We all care. But we have a lot of kids that need our attention. Milly Davis is self-harming again. Jack White is having hassles in the community because of his dad; Janie Matthews' mum died yesterday, out of the blue. CAMHS is concerned that Lacey Jones is being abused at home. I've got a boy starting from the behaviour unit who is going to bring his own set of joys. One of your colleagues found out last week that they've got stage three cancer; another is going through a divorce; one of the staff who phoned in sick this morning is now refusing to come in having made serious allegations against another staff member, and a supply teacher walked off the job on yesterday because they say the behaviour of the students is so bad they can't teach here and the agencies we use haven't got anyone else. Year eleven are taking their exams soon and half of them are freaked out and their teachers are exhausted. Ofsted are due. So what do you want me to say, because trust me, I could go on. Please accept it when I tell you that the social worker was very nice and very concerned. He says he'll continue to keep an eye on her. So he'll do that; you'll play teacher instead of social worker and I'll finally get to my meeting.'

'What's the name of this visiting social worker?'

'Karl Bright. He assured me that the team always looks into every allegation Destiny makes. He seemed a good man. But this is how it is, Jenni. There's nothing anyone can do to stop the drama: Destiny's just too damaged.' He checked his watch again. 'Your time is up. Now – please – go have lunch and let me have mine.'

Friday
12:53

Jenni

If I walked fast, it took me exactly three minutes from the school gate to reach the terraced two-up two-down that I had grown up in and where my dad still lived; being able to visit my ageing dad every lunchtime was one of the attractions of accepting the job at Northshield Academy.

Every day was the same – I left the school around three minutes after the bell for lunch sounded and then it took me another three minutes to walk the long road that both my dad's house and the school shared, dodging crisp packets and dog poo on my journey.

I used to live on this street, but I didn't go to the box-like school that occupied the Northshield Academy site – not for more than two weeks anyway. My dad wouldn't tolerate any more of the bullying that I barely recall now and packed me off every day to travel by train to the all girls' school five miles away. It was probably a good decision because I ended up enjoying school. But after two years, I think my dad decided that I wasn't getting enough exposure to boys, so he marched me to the Territorial Army barracks a mile away and signed me up for the evening youth squad. I was the first and only girl there for a long time, so for a couple of years my days were all girls and my evenings all boys. I soon realised whose company I preferred, so when I left school, I joined the army the next day.

When I was in the army, I rarely saw my dad. When I got back, I felt I should. Twenty minutes a day, for the four days a week I worked at the school. It worked for us. For those two years, it was a good thing and the memories of it kept me going in the dark nights that followed.

I'd always arrive at my dad's at exactly 12.46. He'd always be sitting at the table with a pot of tea and a sandwich for him, and a pint of tepid water and four hard-boiled eggs for me. I was on a high-protein diet for my Ironman training and the next UK event was in July. I planned on being the winning woman again – now I'd turned forty, the stakes felt higher than ever.

But today I was late. With the sound of blood pounding in my ears, I let myself in.

The hall was tiny, but I could see into the dining room and small kitchen at the rear. One step in and I could see my dad, standing, watching the front door. I noticed he was holding himself up against the worktop, for despite his thick hair and strong jaw, his knees were becoming increasingly weak. On a different day, I would've worried about him.

'Love!' he said, sounding like George, because they were born and raised within ten miles of each other but twenty years apart, 'I was worried!' My dad was also ex-military, so he too observed the clock like a master.

I had never been early or late. My dad joked that he could set a clock to me. And it was true: I never let the kids out a minute early, but nor could anyone keep me late. No one could delay my visit to see my dad at lunch – the kids knew it, my colleagues knew it and if anyone, even George, tried to ask me something in the corridor, I would keep going, calling back without stopping that I'd catch up with them later. I worked hard and the forty minutes I had at lunchtime, was my lunchtime.

'I have a problem,' I said, frantically shelling a burning-hot egg.

'Love, I'm sorry if it's overcooked. I know you don't like grey yolks. It's been sitting on the plate, though . . . so it might be.'

I bit into it; it was fine. My dad fretted about pointless things. I often thought that he needed more to worry about than daytime TV. I told him about Destiny and he listened as I knew he would. Twelve years of service and then thirty-six working on the Newhaven docks as a foreman meant that not much surprised him and if it did, he'd learnt not to show it.

'Where is the girl now?'

I shrugged. 'Hopefully still in school having her lunch somewhere.' I peeled another egg. 'But what can I do?'

'What can you do?' That was my dad: not a man of rhetorical questions or inflection, just a straightforward talker. When I was small, his best friend, Reggie, would always lean across the table at the local Labour social club and tell me: 'Your dad is the straightest man I've ever known. He'd give a dropped ten pence back to Richard Branson if it were his.' And my dad would've done, too. He would chase Branson down for a mile if it meant he returned something near worthless to the man who owned it. But that was my dad: completely reliable, a man who would always put himself out to do the right thing. And as I sat there and looked at him across his uneaten ham sandwich, I knew that he was thinking about the right thing to do now.

'She's still in danger, I know it.' I bashed another egg with a satisfying crack.

'What exactly did the girl tell you?'

'Children are rarely explicit about their fears. But her body language! She was shaking and had eyes like dinner plates. But the biggest thing was that she wet herself. She peed on the class-room floor.' I rubbed the smooth shiny surface of the egg. The wobble and shine reminded me of how guts look when someone has been disembowelled. I put the egg down.

'Are you sure . . . ?'

'Am I sure what?'

'You know?' His head made a small dancing movement. 'That you read it right?'

'You tell me? If someone shakes and wets themselves, what does that usually mean?'

He nodded thoughtfully. 'OK, yes. I see your point.'

Good. I believed my dad on all matters concerning the emo-tions of others.

Despite how I felt, I forced myself to eat the egg; my diet was carefully worked out and everything was about staying at the maximum level of athletic performance. Nothing I ate was ever about hunger or emotional responses. 'I wish I'd had a chance to speak with the social worker. If I'd heard from him, his thoughts, his plans, I'm sure I would feel better, but I'm in the dark and I hate that. It means I have to trust them, trust the second-hand info I get via George, and as much as George is a good guy, he's overworked and is not a details man.' I met my dad's gaze; in his watery eyes I saw something. 'I guess I need to know that the social worker isn't going to forget all about this, but is actually going to do something tangible about keeping Destiny safe.'

'Do you have his number?'

'No, but I have his name.' I paused, thinking it through. 'Mind if I use your phone?'

I went through to the MASH. I hadn't had to ring social services before, but our training at school was pretty good. MASH was the multi-agency social care hub, and they took Destiny's name and the social worker's name and then patched me through to the appropriate social work team. After two minutes of Handel's *Water Music*, there was a click and then a woman's voice thanked me for calling before asking me to leave a message after the beep. Then the voice changed to an automated voice, saying the voicemail was full.

I rang back. After getting an engaged signal, I had to try three further times before I got through again. This time I got a man answering the call, who told me that they couldn't do anything to help me as I wasn't reporting a fresh concern, and instead suggested I email a general inbox with my query. 'No, I want to speak to a particular social worker.'

'Which is who, madam?'

'The visiting social worker who is dealing with emergencies today, Karl Bright. Or Destiny Mills' case worker – either.'

'I'll check.'

I listened to Handel's *Water Music* again, and with every passing second, I became more irritated. I checked my watch: I had to get back to school, and just as school could never keep me from leaving for lunch with my dad, nothing would keep me from getting back. I decided that if I got dumped through to a voicemail again, I would leave a terse message and call back when the kids had left school for the day. Perhaps, I decided, I would even take a trip up to wherever their office was and talk to them there.

Then the music was interrupted. 'Sorry.' It was the same man again. 'I'm back. So sorry for the delay. Could I check your details again please?'

Relieved not to have my call dropped, I answered his question before adding what Karl Bright had said and done.

'Hold the line, please.' He paused. 'Don't hang up.'

No music this time, then a woman came on the phone and gave her name as Janice Strong, adding, 'And I'm the team manager.'

'Are you Karl Bright's boss?'

She paused. 'No.' Then, as I felt irritation clench my chest and was about to ask to be put through to Karl Bright or his boss, she said, 'Karl isn't Destiny Mills' social worker. Her social worker is Madeline Watts, but she is on extended leave at the moment; her cases are being overseen by the team.'

'I know that, but he was the one dealing with her case today. I want to speak with him because he came to see Destiny earlier and I'm not happy with his decision. I think Destiny is in trouble and I want him to do something more constructive to keep her safe than the bugger-all he's done so far.' Many people found me too blunt, but I didn't care. If something needed saying, I didn't know how else to do it other than say it.

There was silence for a long time. I thought I had blown it and she was considering hanging up on me, when she said, 'Actually, I wanted to ask you about Karl.'

'I think we should be talking about Destiny.'

Pause. 'We are concerned about Destiny too. She is scheduled to be visited this afternoon at her residential.'

'Why are you seeing her again?'

'We're not seeing her again.' Her voice was careful, but I couldn't read it. It was the thing that most frustrated me about myself: the difficulty to understand people's tone of voice or facial expressions easily. It was like being dropped into an unknown land where everyone else had a map and I did not.

'What are you saying?'

'That if you are confirming that you had a social worker visit Destiny today, then we potentially have a problem.'

'There is a problem. I've been telling you about that—'

'*Please.* The problem isn't Destiny. The problem is the social worker.'

When I sat back at the table and pushed aside my water, my dad must have seen something in my face because he raised an eyebrow and asked: 'You OK, Jenni love?'

'I don't know,' I told him and I didn't.

Friday
13:12

Jenni

My dad got up, found his rolling tobacco and slowly rolled a cigarette. He wasn't supposed to be smoking since a recent bronchial infection, but I didn't comment. I understood.

'Let me get this right. So that man, Karl Bright, walked into your school and pretended he was a social worker?'

I nodded.

'How did he get in? Don't they have to show identification?'

'Yes, they do, but I'm not sure as I wasn't there.' I thought for a moment. 'But you're right, it's not possible. We're all super tight on safeguarding – there's no way anyone could get into our school who isn't a social worker.'

'Yet this woman from social services said they hadn't yet sent out anyone and that this Bright man couldn't have been who he said he was because she'd never heard of him?'

I shook my head. I didn't understand it either.

'So what did happen?'

'All I know is that George met him. They had a chat ...' I tailed off, seeing it all now, anger tightening my grip against my mug. 'Then Karl spoke to Destiny on her own – of course he did,' I added bitterly. 'Then Karl repeated their conversation to George.' I shook my head. 'He even offered to take Destiny home. I bet he did, the scum. You see Dad, those men are not her cousins at all! That Karl man would've forced Destiny to say that, to throw George off the scent. And that,' I said as I thumped my mug down, slopping tea, 'makes me all the more suspicious as to what is going on here.'

'So what did this woman say would happen now?'

'They said that now they knew someone had been acting as an imposter, they would reassess the original safeguarding alert as more urgent.'

Dad was silent for a minute. 'But is that urgent or just more urgent than before?'

'Exactly,' I spat. 'How could it not already be urgent when I saw a gun?' Even as I said it, I understood. I stood up. 'Of course, they don't believe me.' I felt sick, knowing it was true. 'They don't think there was a gun.'

'Jenni?' my dad's brow furrowed further.

I started pacing the small room. 'What they *actually* said was that the police have contacted them to say they've picked up my report and because Destiny's known to them and is already living in a children's home, she is – and I quote them here – in a "low-risk environment" so she's not their priority.' I rubbed my eyes, exhausted. 'I guess their top worry is about children not known to them, kids not already labelled as fantasists, because it's clear that whoever Karl really is, the view he gave of her was the correct one as far as social services are concerned.'

'What I still don't understand,' Dad said, 'is how this Bright – or whatever his name is – knew to turn up?'

I thought for a moment. 'I told the man with the gun that I was going to call the police. It's not a stretch for them to assume that either we or the police would also ring social services.'

'Must be a crime, that, impersonating a social worker. I reckon that social worker manager lady will be straight onto the police to report what's happened.'

'You're right,' I nodded. 'I'll ring them now.' The landline was in the front room, a modern copy of the dial phone we had when I was a kid. I'd bought it for my dad for Christmas, thinking he would enjoy the nostalgia; I think he would've preferred a bottle of whisky. I picked up the receiver, and dialled nine.

Then I stopped.

I knotted and unknotted the curled wire. Right or wrong, I couldn't shake the feeling that calling them wasn't safe *enough*. I had read the papers. I knew how bad things could be. What if this was part of something bad, something corrupt? The fake social worker, the uninterested police, perhaps even George himself?

No, that was crazy. The police worked effing hard; like us teachers, they grind away for the public good for little money and no applause. And George had to be one of the good guys – if he wasn't, who was? I had to believe that the police would help Destiny. After all, there was no one else.

I dialled another nine.

Then paused.

Maybe I should talk to Destiny first. *Just* in case. I checked my watch. I had to leave now. What harm would it do to check things out with Destiny? After all, what could happen in the two hours left of school time now people were keeping a close eye on her?

I returned to the kitchen. My dad sat at his small table and smoked, watching me. I didn't tell him that I didn't make the call, but I think he knew.

This was the first time he didn't say goodbye. All he said was, 'Of course, this news about this Karl Bright means those men are very determined to get hold of her.' He ground his cigarette out as if it disgusted him. 'Means there's nothing good that's gonna come of what they want this poor wee girl for. Nothing good at all.'

My head was so full of concern for Destiny, I just nodded and left, without saying goodbye either.

I wish I had, because I could never have guessed it was the last time I'd ever have lunch with my dad and he deserved more than that.

He deserved a thank you and a proper goodbye.

Friday
13:40

Jenni

I continued to think about Destiny at my computer while my year sevens dutifully worked through a long list of problems. I wanted to speak to her, but wasn't sure how I could before the end of school – and then it would be too late. I didn't know what to do, or who to seek out for advice. I didn't do indecision and now I had been left unsure, nails chewed, as I tried to decide what was best.

While the class worked, I mooched through the computer system checking up on various children that I taught. I tried to settle into acceptance that social services should be allowed the time to resolve it and, when recalling my earlier conversation with Janice Strong, started to feel a certain confidence that they would.

For some reason, it was then that I started thinking about Billy Dawson again. It was a puzzle in itself that Billy had recently jumped back into my mind, when the door had been closed on him for the last two years.

Now he was back, he was back all the time. All my life, I have rarely dreamt of anything and when I did, it was very straightforward, like going food shopping. But the dreams I'd started having of Billy were different. And there were so many of them. It was strange when I hadn't thought about Billy in such a long time. Except the other day – which thinking about it now: yes, yes, I'm sure – was the start of it. Yes, it was because I saw that royal prince in the news; the younger one, who has the same hair and skin colouring as Billy had and there had been footage of him in his fatigues. But the prince came home, got married, had a family and did lots of other things and it started me thinking about all the things that Billy didn't get to do.

He should've done things; he should've had a life. I sighed staring at the computer. Billy didn't and it was my fault.

Private Dawson. Not handsome, nor an officer like the prince. He had a doughy face despite being skinny. And he wasn't prince confident either; he was too nervous, too afraid.

I rubbed the back of my finger across my top lip; my skin was leathery, tough. It occurred to me that I was getting older; time was running out. My mother was forty when she died. I don't miss you, I thought, thinking of her, I don't feel sad that you are gone.

Billy was gone, too. There was no point trying to feel sad about that either – although I think I understand what sadness might feel like to other people because my dad did a painting once with watercolours using violet, dark blue and black and he told me, pointing at it with his paintbrush: 'Jenni, love, *that* is sadness.'

I wish I could feel things, rather than just irritation or agitation. I wish I knew what others felt. Real things, like love or hate. Happiness or sadness. Big feelings – important feelings. But even if I can't do the feeling, I can do the knowing, and I do know

Billy was my responsibility in every way: I was his corporal; he was in my section. And yet . . . he was gone. And it was my fault. And the trouble was, I didn't like thinking about him, about what had happened and about the effect it had on my career, but I didn't know how to get him out of my mind again.

About then there'd been a knock on my classroom door. When Destiny stuck her head in and had asked to speak with me, it was the answer to my problems. Now I'd be able to speak to her like I wanted and I'd be distracted from Billy Dawson. So I'd gladly got up from my desk, cautioned my year sevens to continue working, and stepped out of the classroom and pulled the door closed, just enough to give Destiny and me privacy, but open enough that the class would know I would hear them if they were talking.

We stood in the empty corridor and she twitched her pass at me, which meant she'd been given permission to leave her lesson. She'd told me that she was supposed to be in the toilet. I understood the clear message – she didn't have long.

Then she'd delivered the killer punch. She told me she was running away and that she was going to leave before the end of school. Today? I'd asked her, and she'd nodded: today. I'm leaving for good. Before they come and get me, she added. Even as she stood in front of me, I imagined the men from the van pushing her into the back and padlocking the doors behind her.

Somehow, instinctively, I knew this was coming. After all, all any of us want to feel is safe – why would a fifteen-year-old like Destiny be any different?

But I didn't want her to run away. Where would she go? How would she live? To delay thinking of a careful response, I played for time and asked her about her social worker. Although I knew, I wanted to hear it from her. When she confirmed it wasn't really her social worker who'd visited her, I realised how real this was. To hear how she'd been forced to play along in front of school staff, to think of how frightened she must've been, how helpless, made me understand that the system wasn't safe enough.

Was he one of the gang from the van, I asked. When she confirmed he was, I knew I had crossed a line. When a child makes a statement of harm, it's important that the teacher doesn't start asking questions. Children mustn't be led and investigations mustn't be started by someone without the proper authority. That was procedure. But now Destiny was in front of me, it was easy to revert to no longer trusting the procedures. Just like that, I'd changed my mind. The police had been here, and social services had been contacted twice. It was now less than two hours before the end of school, and even if I'd made peace with the slowness of the system and trusted that they would follow up with Destiny before the end of the day, it seemed that Destiny could not. And if the child doesn't feel safe in the system, then the system has failed.

Destiny's safety had to come first. *Had* to. And she had to come above every other consideration.

Now she'd gone back to her classroom, I was left trying to decide what to do. It wasn't that I couldn't help her – period six was free for me. I realised then what I had to do to keep Destiny safe. It meant putting myself into a situation that might change everything for me. For ever.

I have always been decisive. I made my choice and never looked back and hearing that the gang had bluffed their way into the school, made it easy for me. I knew that she had to come first but it was still difficult.

I wished social services had acted more decisively. If they had, if they'd been able to, it would've been a different story.

I never blamed them for this. I never felt that there was a lack of concern from them. But I knew how it was in the public sector. I knew that they didn't have the resources they needed to make the decisions in the way that they wanted. Having spoken to them, I was sure they were concerned for Destiny. I was also sure that they'd make a visit to see her. But it was like teaching: there was more demand than supply and that might limit what they could do for her.

I knew that these men would stop at nothing to get Destiny. If she believed they would simply pick her up as soon as she left the building at three o'clock, then I believed her.

I did try to reassure her. I did try to do the right thing. I did.

I told her that I had reported the fake social worker to the real social services. I told her that they took it seriously and would treat her as a priority. She laughed.

I looked at her: small, pretty, young-looking. What *had* she been through? I'd had a tough childhood losing my mother at such a young age, but I had no concept of what Destiny's experiences had been. She was vulnerable and I knew from my child protection training and watching the news, that already vulnerable children were at risk of exploitation. Was that why they wanted Destiny? My suspicions threw new darker shadows in my mind. I thought of my dad, who said so little about anything, saying that nothing good was going to come out of what they wanted from Destiny. The feeling that I had stumbled across something more sinister returned.

But as I worried, she'd brought me back with the simple statement: *Miss, listen, because I haven't got much time!* She spoke sharply. I didn't allow my students to speak like that to me, but Destiny was right to get me to concentrate.

That was the point where a subtle change happened in our relationship. In a way, Destiny was *my* teacher: she was the shuck knife forcing me to see inside the oyster. Inside I saw the rotten flesh of a society gone wrong, but despite all that followed, all that I lost, I have no regrets, for I found Destiny, who was a rare and precious thing.

And when it came down to it, she only wanted just a little help.

She wanted a lift in my car four miles up the road. My aunt lives there, she told me. She's already agreed to take me in. She has a spare room and she said that she's always wanted me to stay. They won't look for me there. The gang aren't even from round here. They'll think I've run and they will forget all about me.

Miss, she said, I've given up on the social workers and the police. I just want to leave. Wouldn't you want the same?

And I would, I would want to be able to run.

I thought about the month I'd joined the school. There had been a huge row about a teacher, Daisy Ruthborn, who'd picked up a student in the middle of a storm. Daisy had driven past the boy when it had been hailing; there had been lightning and gale-force winds. She'd given the boy a lift home to his parents, rung the door, deposited the child, received grateful thanks from the boy and his family and that should've been it. But somehow the school had found out and there'd been an enormous row and if the teachers' union and the family hadn't intervened, then Daisy would've received a warning.

This felt like exactly the same thing, where rules seemed to take precedence over good sense. But, in this case, the danger was more real – a van, a gun, a gang who clearly wanted to do harm to their 'Candydoll'. If I didn't take Destiny to where she wanted to go, they would get hold of her. Whatever they had in mind for her was far worse than hailstones. And the awful truth was that I would never know if I'd been right to refuse her. I would never know if she ran and got to her aunt's or if she ran and they found her. All I would know was that she'd disappeared. I would never see her in my form again. Her empty chair would remain there, reminding me of how I put my own reputation ahead of her safety.

The only advantage of not taking her was so I could say to myself that I had done the right thing professionally. But no one would ever know that I did. All they would know was that Destiny would not turn up to school any more, and they would contact her care home and they would confirm she was missing. How much was a missing girl in care looked for? I wondered how many kids went missing every year.

I did a quick Google check. I gasped loud enough to draw glances from some children near me. A narrowing of my eyes was enough for them to bow their heads and carry on. Two thousand children living in care went missing every year. Many were the target of gangs. The report said that one in five would suffer from sexual abuse. I thought of that slug-like tongue and remembered a missing poster put up for a girl last year. Now, instead of the girl's face, it was Destiny's I saw looking back at me.

Where did all these missing children go?

Daisy was right: it would've been cruel to leave a kid out in such weather, alone.

This was the same thing. To refuse to help Destiny, to turn my back on her, would be cruel. I understood that leaving a child defenceless was the most dangerous action of all. I had no choice. I would take her, I decided, to keep her safe.

Friday
14:35

Jenni

I sat in my car two streets away from the school, watching the empty road behind me in my rear-view mirror. I'd parked next to the recreational ground so I could leave my car running and not draw attention from curtain twitchers.

I still couldn't believe that I had agreed to this.

We'd agreed that I would meet her here after she'd assured me she could climb over the gate. Her aunt only lived a few miles away, and I would be able to drive her there and still be back at my desk by four o'clock. I would make a point of speaking to some colleagues around that time so they wouldn't think of me, if there was some trouble about it. Unless there was a fire alarm, I wouldn't be missed. Even if there was an alarm, I'd say that my dad had had a fall and that I'd forgotten to sign out.

But as I sat in the car, engine running, I still felt torn. I knew I was letting George down. He had always been good to me. He'd given me a chance when my second teaching placement had threatened to fail me because my awful mentor didn't understand me. He'd rescued me by giving me the opportunity to repeat the placement with him. Yes, he'd been desperately short of maths teachers, a single vacancy unfilled for months, but still . . . he would be so disappointed in me.

Again I longed for another's opinion. Then it occurred to me that people's circumstances controlled their choices. Most of the teachers I worked with were hugely devoted to their roles – that had impressed me when I joined, a factor that made me think that I could relate to teaching. I was used to operating with hugely dedicated professionals. The teachers I worked with gave their all – and then more on top. But they also needed their jobs to pay their bills, or perhaps they had children or a spouse at home that meant that they couldn't risk being fired. But what did I have? I didn't have anyone who needed me to do anything or not do anything. I had a generous pension from the army; I didn't need my teaching salary. I never went anywhere, I never did anything other than train and compete and I was still making money from competitions. I could walk away from this job – or worse – and it wouldn't really change anything for me.

I was a free agent. It occurred to me that the only person's permission I needed was my own.

Besides, a little voice whispered, I wasn't even sure I liked teaching: I could always try the army for employment again. They might let me back in if I did a desk job.

I looked in my rear-view mirror at the empty road. And I remembered what Destiny had said that sealed the deal: *If you don't help me, they will take me.*

I continued to watch the rear-view mirror, heart pounding. I needed to be careful. Part of me enjoyed the thrill of the operation: it was like being back on the squad again. Watching, waiting; a mission to complete. I was ready. Now all Destiny had to do was to climb the six-foot fence and bunk over the top. I knew she could do it because my classroom overlooked the fence and I'd seen kids leave school early time and time again.

I glanced at my watch and when I looked back up, I saw her walking down the road. I checked all my mirrors again – in half an hour this road would be jammed with kids flooding out of the school, but now no one was around.

I watched her walk towards me, steady as a heartbeat.

And then I saw the van coming from behind her. They were back. And they were closer to her than I was.

Friday
14:45

Jenni

I didn't hesitate: I threw the car into reverse and hit the accelerator. I reversed, gearbox screaming at the speed.

My arm locked over the back of the passenger seat as I craned to see the road. The backwards steering only caught me for a split second, but I didn't let it throw me: I drove straight for Destiny.

She saw me and her eyes widened. She glanced over her shoulder at the van. She obviously saw it because she stood, frozen to the spot, with, I think, horror on her face. I reached her first. I threw open the car door. 'Get in,' I said, my voice quiet and low.

Her eyes were wide; she stared at me before looking back at the van. 'Help!' she said.

'I will – don't worry!'

I realised she was too traumatised to move, so I unclicked my seat belt and got out. I ran round to her side. The van had stopped and the passenger door opened. I could see a man getting out. It was the same man who had the gun. For a moment we simply faced each other in the street, like gunslingers. I wished I had my army rifle. I had never felt like that before or since in civilian life, but I remember how much I'd wanted to kill him. Even though we only stood facing each other for a few seconds, it was enough that I could feel the weight of my rifle in my hands as I lifted it up, the butt nestling into its familiar spot by my shoulder joint. I imagined raising the scope and seeing him through it, his heavy features that of an abusive exploiter of children, before squeezing the trigger. I could hear the *crack*. I could feel the recoil and see the surprised look on his face as a black mark appeared on his forehead, between his eyes. I could see the spray of blood burst outwards from behind him like a plume before he fell to the ground.

But he was still standing there, because that was then and this was now. And I didn't have my rifle. There's a big difference between wanting and having.

He still stood there and pointed at us. 'You're dead,' he mouthed at Destiny, drawing a finger across his neck. I heard her whimper. She was holding her school bag, but she dropped to the ground.

He started to walk towards us; cocky, he didn't rush. His arms were held out to the side of him, as if his overworked muscles meant they couldn't lie flat to his sides. He raised his chin and pushed his shoulders back as if he was bracing himself for action, an overmuscled fighting dog squaring up to another. He might have been a big man but I remember thinking that he was short-limbed and, typical for endomorphs, slow. All those muscles for strength didn't mean he was built for speed. I was built for speed. I haven't won three Ironman contests for nothing.

I opened the car door and picked up the bag Destiny had dropped, throwing it in before I helped her get into the passenger seat. I slammed the door and had made it to my side as he picked up speed and was only ten metres away.

We were gone just as he reached us.

Friday
14:51

Jenni

Despite his proximity, I drove away carefully; we were in suburbia in a thirty miles an hour zone. I stuck to twenty-eight miles an hour – the last thing I needed was the police stopping me.

Destiny then had a panic attack. She went crazy, screaming that he was going to get us. She was hyperventilating, pulling on the locked door handle, yelling that we weren't safe. I found a carrier bag, got her to breathe into it. Eventually she calmed down.

We passed through quiet streets. The houses were mostly small semis built in the fifties, punctuated occasionally by a run of bungalows or a short parade of shops. Here, grass verges were kept mown, front and garage doors kept well painted and there was very little litter. This was not the neighbourhood to drive the car at sixty and not expect to gather attention.

Instead of attempting to outrun them, I was content to watch them in my mirror. Every time I took a turn, they took a turn. I thought they would; I wanted to test how close they would stay. I wanted to see what I was dealing with. Know thy enemy.

It took only minutes for me to make a series of judgements about them. They were patient, which suggested confidence.

They were also smart enough not to try anything that might draw attention to passers-by, like ramming me or trying to pull in front of me to stop me in the road. They didn't even get too close, which suggested they weren't just trying to harass me, they were prepared to play a longer game of cat and mouse. For whatever reason they wanted Destiny, they obviously *really* wanted her. They were a difficult enemy. A bit of me felt the thrill that I was fighting for good again.

I would win this, I decided there and then.

I will win.

'They're following us, Destiny.'

Her voice was so small, I could barely hear it. 'Speak up.' I gentled my voice. 'I need to know as much as I can so I can' – *win* – 'deal with this.' I indicated again, slipped down to second gear and took the turning. As I did, I watched them indicate too, and equally slowly, they then followed me round the corner. 'Do you have anything they want, something perhaps that you took – and I won't judge you even if it's drugs – or is it *you* they want?'

'It's me.'

I accelerated gently, hitting no more than twenty. A black cat ran in front of my car, but was gone before I was even too close.

I passed house after house, reaching the end of the road, I indicated left. So did they. 'How long do you think they'll keep this up?'

'For ever.'

I accelerated gently away from the corner. I thought through my options. There was a police station nearby, and I considered driving to it. But I thought again; the local town police stations always seemed to be closed these days, and if I pulled in, I'd be in a car park and we'd be trapped. Besides, I had no intention of seeing the police.

I considered different ways of throwing them off. When I hit upon my plan, I decided it was brilliant. I gave a tight, private smile: yes, I *would* win.

I drove towards the centre of town.

The town was busy but I wasn't heading for the high street. I headed for the railway crossing. The railway line crossed the town's roads in two points: one I had considered and dismissed, because the approach didn't have a turn-off, which meant that we would be committed if the gates were down and right now, I didn't want to stay committed on any road. I'd picked the second crossing because it had what I needed – a turning I could take if the gates were down. And I could see right now I needed it because they were. With London trains coming through here, the locals complained about the amount of time the crossings shut the roads, but now I was determined to make it work for me. I indicated right and moved away from the crossing.

The van followed.

I went round the block.

Destiny hunkered even further down into the seat.

I felt the beat of my heart, but with my hands planted firmly on the steering wheel, I felt safe. The doors were locked, I was in a public place in broad daylight, and if they came for me, I'd give as good as I got. My wheel-jack was under the seat and with that, I reckoned I could defend myself.

Bastards, getting hold of young girls for goodness knows what. I remembered Destiny standing in a puddle of her own urine and thought the wheel-jack was too good for them.

I cruised down the road, turned left again and went round the block. This time the gates were up and traffic was flowing. As I approached the crossing, I slowed. 'Come on,' I hissed to the gates under my breath. But nothing. The gates stayed up. I was forced to keep up with the flow of traffic and move over the crossing point to the other side of the road. I indicated left and went round the block again.

They must have known what I was trying to do.

After turning down two more streets, I was back facing the crossing. The streets were fairly busy, but suddenly there was a lull in traffic with only the van behind me. It wouldn't stay like this as soon the school run would mean too many cars on the road.

I needed this to work now. I moved the car slowly towards the crossing. 'Come on, *please*,' I urged. As if in answer – third time lucky – the lights flashed orange and the beeping started. The gates started to come down.

I held my position, stopping directly over the tracks. I was now in the yellow hatched-box section in the middle of the crossing.

'Miss!' Destiny cried out.

I didn't answer; instead, I concentrated intently, desperate to judge the right moment.

'Miss! We could be hit by a train!'

I didn't plan on waiting that long; I just needed to block the van pulling onto the rail track behind me. But it was an intense moment. Destiny started screaming and trying to pull the wheel, a taxi driver from the nearby rank got out and started yelling, a few cars nearby started sounding their horns and two men sitting in front of the nearby pub ran over and tried to hold up the dropping gates.

With the gates only two metres from the ground, I pressed down hard on the accelerator. My little car shot forward. As I passed underneath them, the gates scraped against the roof of my car. I watched the faces of the men holding them as they shouted at me. I looked down; I didn't want to be seen. I didn't want to be caught on the CCTV that I knew would be watching me, but I also didn't want this van to be following me any more.

Behind me I heard the van beeping. If they didn't know what I was doing before, they certainly did now.

I sped off, seeing the van trapped on the other side of the crossing gates. Ever the professional, I resisted giving them the finger.

Friday
15:22

George

Despite the initial lightness George Danvers had felt as he'd pulled his office door shut, it had begun to dissipate as he drove out of the school car park; he realised that he would soon be apologising face-to-face to Steve Wichard for the delay to their meeting – an apology that would make that bloody, smug, little twat with his rising results and growing budget even more super smug.

George fiddled with his car radio – he only had a fifteen-minute journey, but he needed some music to unwind first.

He found Classic FM and the sound of Bach filled the car. Determined to feel a bit better, George rolled his shoulders against the tension in his muscles. The meeting wouldn't take long, he told himself. Perhaps only a couple of hours. George liked to be out of work at five-thirty, but Steve would probably want him to stay late. That would be so bloody like Steve to force the meeting to go on and on, waiting for George to be the first to say that he wanted to go home. 'I'll just say it,' he murmured. 'I have no shame.'

But George did. And he still had the ability to feel it. Ten years ago, his job only made him feel proud. How times had changed.

It took a lot of energy to deal with the likes of Steve Wichard. If only he didn't have to go to these meetings where he had to suck up Steve's so-called mentoring. He was sick of these monthly humiliations. Just because Steve's academy was an outstanding school and his was not. The organisation that ran both academies insisted George did this – so what choice did he have? George's knuckles paled as he gripped the steering wheel.

As he sat at the traffic lights, he realised that Steve would find a way to imply that George having to delay their meeting was a sign that he wasn't truly in control of his school: Steve bloody Wichard would never have an emergency. But then, Steve bloody Wichard didn't say yes to taking in children such as Destiny, those who had already failed at other mainstream schools. The man was a control-freak who got every child who so much as sniffed at the wrong time out of his school and into the local alternative education provision. He didn't care that he wrecked young people's lives – those who were often struggling with terrible home environments. He'd often heard him say: 'It's the Wichard Way or the highway.' But George didn't believe that the Wichard Way was the road to success. Just the mention of the Wichard Way made George, who'd walked away from every fight he'd ever had in his life, clench his fist in irritation. Just because Steve bloody Wichard had an intake with a middle-class demographic; had received a national teaching award and his wife had a narrow waist and small, white, even teeth, didn't mean that he was right.

George flexed his shoulders again and told himself to buck up. Even if he was seeing Steve, it was still great to get out of school. He'd just looked at the budget report and knew the only way it was going to work was if he resisted about 50 per cent of the staff getting a pay rise next year. It wouldn't matter to anyone else if he told them that he hadn't given himself a pay rise for the third year in a row. It would only matter to his wife, Sal, who'd have to keep doing her admin job for another year, but she'd understand without him having to explain.

Anyway, Sal didn't care about money, she just wanted him to quit. She'd started to talk about retirement. She wanted rid of their house with its mortgage. She'd started to point out smaller properties on Rightmove near her sister in Wales. 'Look, George, this one's got over an acre of land. Think, George, we could spend our time gardening. We could get chickens like you've always wanted.' If he had a yen for apple crumble, she whipped out the iPad and showed him a property with an orchard. If he patted his stomach and rued his lack of exercise, she showed him a property with a pool. If he complained about the traffic, she showed him a house with six miles of uninterrupted bucolic views.

The mantra 'think of your health' had now become an almost daily statement from her. No wonder he'd started to throw his empty Gaviscon bottles out in the large bins at work, the clinking making him feel like a secretive alcoholic. The last time she saw them in recycling she'd started crying. 'But there's so many!' she'd sobbed.

George had held her tightly, just as he hugged the truth to himself. He wanted the house with the sweeping gardens and idyllic views. He wanted to be free from the responsibility of the school that hung round his neck with a mass that defied the laws of physics. He wanted to tell the staff he was leaving. Sometimes, sometimes, he allowed himself to think of it. Sometimes. But he couldn't most of the time because it hurt even to think of it.

The truth was he wanted to go: he was tired. But George couldn't set himself free. He had to look after the school, he had to protect the staff and the pupils from the Steve Wichard clone who would be hired in his place. A clone who would take pay rises, who would get rid of any poor kid with an aura of trouble, and who would drive the unions out, leaving the staff with no protection. It would happen. He doubted if he could lean on a garden fork and look across the scenic Welsh countryside knowing that back in Hastings his school was unhappy without him.

He'd loved having his own children, but now that Caitlin and James had grown and had families of their own, the truth of it was that his school felt like his third child, just one that had refused to grow up and leave. Instead of getting stronger over time, each year saw it ailing a little more. The reducing of year-on-year budgets was like a reducing bloodflow cutting supply to vital areas. While a heart attack was inevitable, it still wouldn't be right to euthanise. Better that he stayed, held on, cherished and fought for his school as only he could.

No one else understood.

Only last week his daughter had intervened on Sal's behalf. She and her family had come round for Sunday lunch, and as soon as it finished, everyone else suddenly disappeared. Caitlin had cornered him as he dried up, taking the tea towel before begging him to 'Think of Mum. She's worried sick about you – she thinks your ulcer is going to perforate again.'

He hated being reminded about the emergency surgery last year. Everything about it was horrible. The pain had been intense. He'd collapsed at work, the ambulance carrying him off site. He'd passed out and didn't remember anything until he'd come round in intensive care. It had been the middle of the night and the smooth white walls and the wires attached to him scared him. No doubt high on drugs, he'd been confused, afraid he was in a space ship. He'd never confessed that fear to anyone. That moment of intense pure fear. Only the nurse who answered his cries knew how he felt. He never wanted to go back there again.

He'd had three weeks off work and the academy management had started to circle like crows around carrion. They smelt the opportunity to get rid of him, so he'd come back before he was ready. Sal had cried more from frustration than fear. But there had been fear in it too, he knew. Her own father had died at sixty and Sal feared the early widowhood that had curdled her own mother into bitterness.

Caitlin moaning on just heaped more and more pressure on him. Everyone needed him to do something. 'I can't help it if I give a damn,' he'd said, uncharacteristically snapping at his daughter. And although much of what she'd said, he'd heard from Sal's own mouth, Caitlin's parting words spat with frustration continued to resonate: 'Then what will be the change that will set you free?' George had never thought of it like that, but now he couldn't help think, *what would be the change that would set him free?* What would stop him from caring, so much – *too much*? No one ever told him when he trained how much each and every child would mean to him. And he knew it wasn't just him who felt like that: almost every single one of his colleagues felt the same. That's why they all ended up working so damn hard: it was because they cared so damn much.

And that was never going to change.

Nor would his student demographic, nor would the academy company and nor would any future government find meaningful differences in cash, whatever their rhetoric.

Nothing was going to change ever.

Ever.

This was it.

His indigestion burned in his chest. He clutched at it; it felt so painful, it often felt like a heart attack. Sal was right: his misplaced paternalism would see him into an early grave.

He drove towards the railway crossing with his earlier feeling of lightness now completely gone.

He pressed his foot down; he decided it would be better to speed up before the gates came down. The sooner he got there, the sooner he could say he was going home.

The urge to turn his car around came across him as quick and as powerful as an electric current. Fuck Steve Wichard. He could imagine Sal's face lighting up as he walked in the door, early and unexpected. He'd kick his shoes off at the door and leave his worries there too. The image was so clear, the urge to go home so powerful.

'For fuck's sake, George,' he told himself angrily, 'it's only a meeting. A meeting you've done loads of times.'

What would be the change?

He grated the gearstick into second as he approached the train crossing, angry he could feel the cold trail of a tear ease its way down his cheek. He swiped at it. It shouldn't be getting to him. He wasn't old. He was only fifty-six. He should have years left in him. Fighting years; years of being at the top of his game.

Then why did he *feel* so bloody old?

The lights of the crossing first flashed red before the warning alarm that the gates would be closing sounded. He thought of Sal's father. He thought of his own dear dad dying three years ago.

George pulled up, the first car to reach the crossing as the gates came down.

What would be the change?

The ulcer his GP still chided about?

His wife's happiness? Surely Sal was what mattered?

His daughter's slammed doors of frustration?

I can't help it if I give a damn, he reminded himself, digging in.

'Bloody, hell,' he said, something breaking his line of thought. His eyes widened at the sight of the oncoming car on the other side of the railway crossing still going even though the gate was coming down. 'Poor sod must be late for a meeting with Steve Wichard,' he said with a bolt of humour.

His eyes narrowed and the laughter died as he watched the car stop in the yellow box, right across the train tracks. Horns from nearby cars started sounding and George pulled on his hand-brake as the queue of traffic stopped for the crossing. Expecting the car to reverse, he watched goggle-eyed as two taxi drivers legged it over from the nearby rank and started to hold up the gates. What the hell had happened? Had the car broken down at the wrong time?

George deliberated: should he get out and help? Why wasn't the driver getting out?

Nearby people excitedly gestured at the car; it was crazy behaviour. A train would be along any moment and would slam into the side of such a small car and kill the passengers. Then, finally, the car drove forwards.

The gates scraped the top of the roof.

What the heck was going on? Were they nuts? He leant closer, keen to get a sight of who it was.

The car was travelling in the opposite direction to him but in anticipation of wanting to see who was driving, he wound down the window to lean out and get a better view.

'I don't believe—' He faltered, feeling a squeeze of urine escape, a hangover from his prostate troubles. Normally he would've grabbed his groin, a reflex of shame and alarm, but instead his hands simply gripped his steering wheel even tighter.

'Bloody, bloody,' he said in his soft Yorkshire tone, '*idiot*.' The driver was Jenni Wales. And, next to her, was Destiny Mills.

Friday
15:38

George

The railway gate stayed down and the crossing alarm continued to sound. George sat staring at the flashing lights.

Why was Destiny in Jenni's car? Why? His knuckles were white. His breathing that of an exhausted runner.

Instead of the usual nothingness of waiting for the train to pass through, the pedestrians who had gathered at the gates were animated. Mothers had let go of the hands of young children and dogs fussed each other unchecked. George vaguely noticed the confused looks and the questions on their lips. But he couldn't take it in. All he could do was desperately think, his mind speeding through the options, what *was* Destiny doing in Jenni's car?

There had to be a good explanation.

Had to be.

George sat, jaw clenched, breathing still rapid, turning it over in his mind, trying to figure it out. It kept coming back to the same thing: pupils never got in the cars of teachers. *Never.* Even on school trips, there were mini-buses or coaches. Risk assessments and common sense protected them all. If a child needed a lift somewhere, no matter how urgent, careful consideration had to be made, and two adults would always accompany a minor. And there had been no one in the back seat. His eyes flicked to the dashboard clock: because it was after three, was there any way this could be nothing to do with school? Rubbish, you snake George, he told himself. Accept it: this has everything to do with the school.

Jenni had decided to take the matter into her own hands. She was driving Destiny somewhere – but where? The train thundered out of the station. The gates rose. George stared at them dispassionately as he tried to remember exactly what it was that he saw. Destiny had looked anguished; Jenni determined.

His bladder twitched and his hands suddenly ached. He released the handbrake.

As he pressed the accelerator, he was still moving towards his meeting with Steve Wichard, but somewhere between that decision to go forward and realising that he couldn't – no, *mustn't* – do anything else other than check on Destiny to make sure she was all right.

He decided to turn round.

The gates were half up and moving upwards still. Before the oncoming traffic made it across the crossing, he yanked hard on his steering wheel. Doing a U-turn in the middle of the road, he found himself almost surprised to be travelling in the opposite direction. Now he was going after Destiny.

What would Steve Wichard say?

Fuck Steve Wichard.

George Danvers still gave a damn.

Friday
15:45

George

George kept to thirty-three miles an hour, which was as fast as he dared. He wanted to catch Jenni, needed to, but he didn't want to be stopped for speeding.

He scanned the road ahead, trying to spot her car. He felt sick. This was no good, he knew it. Why did Jenni have to do this? His shoulders ached as he hunched forward trying to spot her.

There she was!

Her blue Peugeot was up ahead.

He kept one hand on the steering wheel and, without taking his focus off the road, he patted around the passenger seat for his mobile phone. He would never normally consider making a phone call when he was driving, but what should he do? His fingers closed on his phone. Now, should he call the police or would that seem a touch hysterical?

George paused. No crime had been committed. This was a huge breach in protocol, but it was just a school matter. And if he didn't handle it right, he knew that Steve Wichard would see it as a damning indictment of his leadership.

Yes, George decided, better to assess the situation and take his time, before doing anything rash.

He followed the Peugeot through town. Perhaps Jenni was simply doing Destiny a favour. Perhaps the incident with the crossing was simply because she was a terrible driver or there was something wrong with her car. Perhaps Destiny wanted to get somewhere in town. Perhaps she'd hurt her leg or something and Jenni, being typical Jenni, had decided to do what she wanted in the way she wanted and this meant driving Destiny somewhere. But it would be harmless – very unprofessional and clearly unwise – but ultimately harmless. Perhaps this was nothing to do with the man who Jenni had claimed had a gun.

George glanced into his rear-view mirror. Could he see a white van anywhere?

No. He relaxed; this was clearly Jenni being her typical gung-ho self again.

George drove, waiting for the car to pull over and Destiny to get out. But as the seconds and minutes past, he felt his irritation rise. His hands tightened against the steering wheel. Jenni better have bloody good union representation, because after this little episode, she was going to need it.

In fact he decided, so outrageous was this, that he'd personally instigate the grievance against her today. Enough was enough; he would send this all the way up. And when he did, Steve Wichard would want to know how he, George, had contained the situation. George knew he had to consider very carefully how best to handle it.

He thought about it. He'd follow her for as long as necessary and then, as soon as he could safely pull over without losing her, phone it in to the police (which surely wouldn't be needed?) and to Steve. For now, he should see where she was going, stay with the car, so Destiny was safe. Yes, it wouldn't do to say he'd let them drive off without keeping an eye on them.

Jenni indicated right at the roundabout – George realised that she was heading onto the bypass.

Jenni was taking Destiny out of town.

He watched her pick up speed. This was not a lift up the road – this was something else. His temper flared from a simmer to a rolling boil. Enough was enough: she was out of her job. 'Jenni!' he yelled, leaning over his steering wheel. 'What are you doing?' And then he banged it in frustration. 'You're not—' *bang* '—the only one—' *bang* 'who cares about the ruddy students.'

George imagined news headlines if he handled this wrong; he imagined having to prepare a report for the board of governors. He imagined the humiliation of briefing Steve Wichard.

He needed to get this right. He would have to stay on her tail for as long as it took. He had a full fuel tank, he just hoped he didn't need it.

George had had many dark moments as a headmaster, not least dealing with the nasty sink hole that had developed in his budget. Two years earlier, there was the stabbing of a year-ten boy by another boy in year eleven. The victim had made a full recovery but the incident had reputationally hurt the school, and someone – probably the parents – had leaked photos of the victim when he was in intensive care. George had been very rigorously looked at and he'd come very close to resigning, thinking he was about to be pushed. But somehow he'd survived.

But now he had the nightmare situation of a rogue teacher – one he'd never been fully confident of but at the time filled a desperate recruitment need – with arguably the school's most vulnerable pupil in her car after school hours.

His eyes momentarily squeezed shut. He wished he could keep them closed. He didn't want this. Self pity ached and a tear leaked out again. He felt ancient. If only he'd not filled up his tank at the petrol station. If only he'd taken another route to his meeting. If only he'd left a minute before, he would have been under the crossing gate and away and would've been unaware of Jenni's crazy driving happening behind him.

He didn't have the capacity for a crisis. He knew he couldn't come back from another one. He wouldn't have the fight and he knew there was no one who would want him to, not his bosses, nor Sal, not even himself. He was so tired – when did it get so hard?

The phone lay on his lap with the weight of a stone.

When he got the chance, he would have to use it, and when he did, the situation would catch like compost in the August sun.

A thought occurred to him: he'd already taken the same turning off the roundabout. He had already started to follow Jenni onto the bypass. But he could fall behind. He could take the first turning off and head back towards his meeting.

Suddenly, he wanted to be in Steve's office. He wanted to be drinking the mug of weak Earl Grey he was always served. He wanted the dull lecture on improved performance.

And he could go there now.

He could pretend that he had never seen Destiny in Jenni's car. He could.

Friday
15:50

Jenni

We drove in silence, Destiny slumped in her seat while I concentrated on getting out of town as soon as I could. I took the nearest turn onto the bypass and drove as fast as I could without breaking any speed limits.

As we drove, I thought about what had happened, what it meant. My noisy reversing up the road by the school may have drawn looks in such a quiet neighbourhood and I had to accept that I might've been seen. More so now after the railway-crossing incident. I realised that my options were narrowing. But inside, when I thought about what I had done, what I had achieved, a small ember glowed.

I was pleased with my choice, of standing up for what I believed. I was used to standing alone with my opinions. I am not the same as other people. In staff meetings I often thought differently to others. I realised that my colleagues might cast me adrift when they found out I had taken Destiny. But if I stood apart, it was because I had dared to do the right thing.

They would not risk themselves for Destiny.

I would.

I lifted my chin. I decided then that I wouldn't lie about taking Destiny if asked. For starters, I was sure about what I had done. The fact that armed men were trying to take her in a van only backed up that I was right to do what I did. Of course, it would've been so much better if social services could've acted, but with the cuts going on in public services I was like any other teacher, nurse, or police officer. With reducing resources, how could they do anything *but* fail to do everything required of them, when the everything was so overwhelming? Who could forget those poor girls who suffered at the hands of gangs in the north of England? Who wouldn't go back and take strong action against those men, if they could?

In my heart, I am still a soldier: I can do what others can't.

I cast a sideways glance at Destiny. She had pulled her knees up to her chin, making herself even smaller than she was. Her hair fell across her face. It was a shame that I'd had to scare her in order to keep her safe. 'Destiny, I need your aunt's address in Battle.'

Destiny jumped as if stung by a wasp. She sat forward, covering her face and moaned again.

I felt a flutter in my chest. 'Destiny, what is it?'

Her shoulders were shaking and I wasn't sure, but thought that she might be crying. This went on for a while and I realised we had a problem. 'Destiny, you can tell me anything. But you do need to tell me, so I can help you.'

Finally, pale faced, she looked at me. 'I don't want to go to Battle.'

'Where do you want to go to then?'

She bit her lip and started rummaging in her bag. She got out her phone and flicked through it. 'Hull.'

'Hull? Are you joking?' I took several deep breaths before I spoke. '*Hull*? Please tell me you're joking?' Silence. 'Look at me, Destiny. Look at me!'

Big blue eyes looked at me and I could see the tremble in her mouth.

'You know what you've done, don't you?'

Destiny didn't say anything.

'You've purposefully misled me, haven't you?'

Destiny mumbled something I didn't catch and turned away.

I banged the steering wheel in frustration. 'You said Battle,' I said to myself more than anything. I didn't need to say it to her, because she knew exactly what she was doing, I was glad she didn't deny it. I gripped the wheel. 'You realise that is a four-hour drive each way? It's Saturday tomorrow, I'm supposed to be up and training at first light.'

Destiny tipped her face forward, her shoulders shaking again. When she spoke, I could barely hear what she said through the curtain of her hair. I only caught *no choice*.

She stared out of the window and told me that she didn't think I would've taken her to her aunt's if I had known it was so far away. I'm ashamed that I nearly told her, that no, I wouldn't have done, but I didn't and I'm glad. I thought it through as Destiny lapsed into an uneasy silence, her face still turned away.

I didn't feel angry, just duped. When you're a teacher, you get used to the duping – kids trying not to hand in their homework, trying to do as little as they can in class. It's a game: they try and get their way and we try to get ours.

It's like that on a tour too. Although it can change and change fast when your friend is injured or killed, it doesn't feel personal. It's more like a game of us trying to get our way, while the insurgents try to get theirs. A battle of wills. Just business; not personal.

I thought again about the gang. Perhaps it was fair that she did what she could to get away from them – even if it meant tricking me. After all, it was her life on the line. Who wouldn't twist the truth in that situation?

It will be all right, driving to Hull, I decided. I told Destiny that I wasn't angry. She didn't say anything, but I added that while I didn't mind driving to Hull, because I didn't have to work the following day, no one should try to trick other people into helping them. She didn't say anything, but she was still and I figured that at least she wasn't crying. She was just a kid after all and a hurting one at that.

I listened to the road for a bit, and found the sound of the engine soothing. I usually relax when driving and although my gaze flicked to the rear-view mirror more often than it normally would, I realised I was enjoying the drive, enjoying the mission of taking on danger to make the world a little safer for those who need my help.

Destiny's face was still hidden so I wasn't sure about how she was feeling. I'd never cared when they told me in hospital that I had alexithymia; I only cared about Billy being gone and everything else was just noise. The doctors' voices and the nurses' smiles were aimed at being reassuring – but I didn't notice. They

told me that one in ten have it, this inability to read other people's emotions and to understand my own, but why did I care
when it had never harmed me? There had only been my dad
and me and he never needed a fancy name to help me, and then
there had been the army and it never seemed to matter. I took
people on their word: if they told me they were tired, I believed
them. If they told me they were pissed off, I believed them. There
was no need to second guess.

But now, looking at Destiny's face, I realised what a disadvan-
tage it was not to be able to tell what someone else was thinking.
I knew I was doing the right thing in supporting her getting to
safety, but I felt the weight of the responsibility of having her in
my care. Despite having a classroom full of kids every day, I'd
never, ever, had sole responsibility for a child before. I wanted
to be sure she was still certain of her choice to run away, but she
said so little, I couldn't be sure.

And the truth of it was, I hadn't been terribly good at understanding teenagers. I thought teaching would be a good second
career choice for me: I am good at maths and good at telling
people what to do. I am resilient and hard-working. But I'd
learnt that there's more to teaching than that, and it was becoming clear just how little I understood the skills that my new job
required of me.

Given how badly my last review had gone, I wasn't even
entirely sure that I would have a job next year. I thought of
George shutting his office door.

I glanced again at Destiny. 'Destiny . . . can I ask you
something?'

She turned her face a little, and I returned my eyes to the road.

'Am I . . . a good teacher?'

She didn't say anything.

'Honestly, tell me, because I need to know.'

'Are you sure you're not asking me to blow smoke up your arse?'

I gripped the wheel. It wasn't right for Destiny to talk like that – it didn't suit her. But I wanted the truth: it suddenly seemed to matter. 'I want to know what you think.'

'OK, but remember, you asked. You know your subject, but . . .'

'But?'

'But the best teachers are the ones who care about their kids.'

I blinked. 'You think I don't care?' I felt like yelling: *what is this then?*

But she didn't answer, instead she turned herself further away from me. And I was left thinking questions that I didn't have an answer to.

Friday
15:59

Jenni

We had returned to silence. Destiny possibly sleeping – or pretending to – and me putting all my mental energy in making sure that the distance between us and the van grew bigger every minute.

It was only when I saw a police car pull into my lane that I realised it wasn't just the van I had to watch out for. Startled, I pulled into the inside lane and held my breath as I saw the police car copy my move.

It occurred to me for the first time that if the police caught me with Destiny in my car, I could be breaking a law.

Friday
16:13

Jenni

'Destiny,' I said in a low voice, 'you're safe, but we need to take action.'

I couldn't see her reaction because I didn't dare take my eyes away from anywhere but the road and my rear-view mirror. The police car was still there, with only one car between us.

'It is possibly nothing, but I realised I've failed to do a proper recce with you.' I took a deep breath, checked my speed – a steady and unremarkable sixty-five miles per hour – and told her about the police car.

When I swallowed, I realised my mouth was dry. Come on, Jenni, I told myself, you've handled worse than this. But this was different. In the army I was used to being on the right side of the argument. I was used to being in a section. I was used to giving orders to my section, following the orders of my sergeant. Look how it ended for me – how it ended for Billy – when there were no orders for me to follow. I felt an ache develop in my temples; I didn't want to think about the past again. Looking after Destiny had given me a few hours' precious peace. Destiny needed me now.

The police car was still behind us. On the long motorway, it could stay like that for a while. I was talking to myself when I said, 'We can't risk getting caught.'

Destiny squidged further down into the seat. 'Are the police going to catch us?'

'Don't worry. If you stay low, they won't see you.' *You're too small.*

Just then, we heard the sirens. I swear the sound stopped my heart for a beat. I glanced in my rear-view mirror and could see blue flashing lights.

Friday
16:15

Jenni

The police car pulled out into the outside lane.

I was aware as it moved from being behind me at six o'clock, then to five o'clock, four o'clock and then right next to me. I wanted to keep looking dead ahead but, like unruly children, my eyes ignored my determined direction and looked at the car.

As I did, the uniformed policeman in the passenger side turned and stared straight at me. For the briefest of seconds, our gazes locked.

I held my breath. Someone had seen us. Someone at the school or a neighbour had called it in and the police were looking for us. I remembered the roof dragging under the gates and wondered how I could've been so stupid. The taxi drivers had seemed so concerned and then so angry and, of course, it would've all been caught on CCTV.

The blue lights flashed and I looked at Destiny, her face cast in blue showing an expression I couldn't read.

Jenni

The police car slid past.

I got ready to apply the brakes as I knew they would apply theirs, forcing me to slow down.

But they sped up. For a moment I was confused.

Then they were gone.

They weren't after us.

We were in the clear.

For a long moment, neither of us said anything.

I tried to be reassuring. 'It's fine, Destiny, they've gone.'

She didn't say anything, but from the corner of my eyes, I could see her shoulders were shaking. 'Are you laughing? Did you—'

A strangled, sudden sound from Destiny cut me off. I wanted to be able to see her, but I couldn't take my eyes off the road. 'Are you . . . all right?'

'I thought they were going to arrest us, Miss.'

I've never been given to great affection – perhaps that's why I've been single for so long. My mother died when I was three

– she's left a crease –

and I was an only child growing up with a kind but physically distant father. Now it felt awkward to do anything to reassure her.

I thought about pulling over, but there was nowhere other than the hard shoulder. I reached out and patted her arm, hoping that was appropriate. Without the framework of school, nothing felt very sure. I couldn't offer anything else – I didn't have anything else.

I stuck with what was comfortable – to evaluate the practical. 'Destiny, what time do you normally go home? Is it straight after school?'

'I don't have a home.'

I heard something in her voice I hadn't heard before, an adult quality, hard. Destiny, I realised, was no child. But then this should not be a surprise. What was clear was that I barely knew her. Doing the register and a quick hello at the start of the day was the extent of our relationship.

'Where do you live?'

'I have to go straight back to the children's home as soon as I finish school.'

'You have to? You have no choice?'

'No choice.'

'What time is that? Be precise.'

'It doesn't matter because I was supposed to be at the dentist today.'

'Were you?'

'I was supposed to meet one of the care team at the dentist's in town at ten to three. It was the only appointment they could get.'

I thought this through. She hadn't turned up so it was a question of how long they'd wait. I decided they would have to wait about fifteen minutes to be sure there was a problem, but by then school would be finished anyway. Even if they rang the school office to see if she left, because the school would've been closed by then, the concern would lie with the children's home. At this point, perhaps people would think she'd simply bunked off the dentist's.

Unless a neighbour had seen Destiny being bundled into my car and had felt concerned enough to call the police, it was likely that her absence from the dentist's was the point where Destiny would be missed.

I considered how bad it might've looked when Destiny got in my car. I remembered my crazy backwards driving, and how Destiny had simply stood frozen to the spot so I had had to steer her into the car. I glanced at my reflection in the rear-view – I looked like a mum. The white van, in comparison to my car, wouldn't look like the place Destiny should be. So even if someone had seen and was concerned by my initial driving, the fact I'm a forty-year-old woman driving a compact city car who then sedately drove away, wouldn't cause too much concern. Probably no one had been worried about Destiny until now.

Once it was clear that Destiny was missing from the school and her children's home, I wondered what would happen next.

'Destiny, what happens when someone from your home goes missing?'

Her voice was small but sharp. 'I told you: it's *not* my home.'

I ignored her. The next logical step was that both social services and the police would be alerted as soon as they realised that a vulnerable minor was missing. Then what next? I guessed an alert to all patrol cars would be made to look out for her. They would be given a description. I glanced at Destiny, still in her school uniform.

They were probably not thinking about me but would be looking for Destiny. Maybe that was a good thing. After all, what was I fighting here? The police weren't the bad guys, perhaps they would even take her to her aunt's. Surely no one would think going back to the care home when she was being so vigorously pursued would be the right thing for her? Clearly her situation needed revaluating. 'Destiny – just a thought. Why don't we get the police to take you to your aunt's. I'm sure if you—'

'No!'

'Why not? Think about it – it's different now. I can give a statement about the van chasing us and I'm sure they can corroborate it with CCTV evidence. It'll be quite clear to them that they'll need to take proper—'

'I don't want you to do that!'

Her breathing was harsh and I was worried she was crying again. I gave her a minute to calm down. 'I won't make you do anything you don't want to. Just hear me out.' I paused and she didn't say anything to interrupt me, so I pushed on. 'I think that—'

'Miss!' Destiny said. 'You don't understand! They'll make everything worse. Please take me to Hull. *Please.*'

I breathed out. The truth was, as much as I believed in what I was doing, the police would complicate it. Perhaps it would be simpler for me to take Destiny myself. Although I hadn't done anything wrong – in fact it could only be right to keep a vulnerable child safe – I realised my employment contract might say differently and perhaps I could kiss my teaching career goodbye. I'd have risked it if it was what Destiny wanted, but since it wasn't, it seemed easier for us to go on. After all, we'd be there in a couple of hours – it could take longer than that to give a statement.

Although it seemed better to keep things simple, I realised that if I definitely wasn't handing her over to the police, then I couldn't be spotted with her either. If I was keeping it simple, then simple it needed to stay.

They would be making assumptions that she'd be on foot, either locally around the town or on public transport. That would keep us safe on the roads for now.

Then I realised I had a potential problem: I'd forgotten my earlier police report. Perhaps when it was reported to the police that she was missing, my earlier report would be flagged. They had suggested that they wanted to speak with me again – but I would be missing too. I gripped the wheel.

Did I have time to drop her off and get back before anyone noticed I had gone? Realistically, it was a round trip of eight hours or so – so very probably I wouldn't be back home until early in the morning. If anyone tried me before tomorrow, I'd say I'd been in bed unwell. The question was, would the police wait until tomorrow before wanting to speak with me? This I couldn't know. Maybe there would be a million variables for this, even coming down to how busy they were. But some of those variables might have to do with Destiny. 'Have you gone missing before?'

Pause. Then, 'Yes.'

'OK.' This could change it. If she'd run away before they might assume that's what this was. *No, this* is *what this was*, I corrected myself. I haven't taken Destiny: this was what she asked me to do. She asked me to help her. She told me she was leaving anyway – I was making it safer. I was only a proxy.

I cut a glance at her. She was looking out of the window: I couldn't see her face.

I lifted my chin. I wasn't sure about happy – I couldn't feel it and know that was 'happy', but this felt like something. My stomach felt warm and I knew Destiny was depending on me. Just because I couldn't work people out didn't mean I couldn't work the right thing out for people – perhaps doing this was proving that I was changing. Perhaps I was getting better. I nodded: this felt logical.

A thought occurred and some sort of feeling with it. As usual, I wasn't sure what it meant, but I drove, thinking about it. I decided it might be a good one, because I was being helpful to Destiny. The thought was that perhaps I wasn't just rescuing Destiny; perhaps I was also rescuing myself.

Perhaps I could imagine a future where I wasn't stuck watching other people from the outside – perhaps, one day soon, I too could be on the inside.

Friday
16:32

Jenni

I did not want to think any more about what might be in the future. I can't make the ideas come like some people, and trying makes me feel more empty. It was only what was happening now that mattered. Instead, I decided to take action; I was good at taking action.

Thinking about the alert that would very likely be making its way to the police now, I started looking for road services.

There I would be able to change Destiny's appearance. I looked at her; she'd held herself like a foetus, knees up, head down. It was her uniform that would need to change and her hair. I had already noted where the next services were when I realised Destiny *would* be looked for there. The police might assume that the van had taken her, in which case they would be searching the roads, as well as public transport. We were only minutes from Tunbridge Wells. We would stop there. 'Destiny, we are going to pull off at the nearest town.'

'Why?'

'How would you feel about changing your appearance? Like your uniform?'

She looked down, her hands smoothing down her skirt. 'You think that the police are looking for me, don't you?'

'We need to buy you a complete change of clothes. Maybe . . . and only if you're comfortable, we could buy some hair dye and—'

Destiny made a strange sound.

I couldn't quite see her face. 'Is that a good thing?'

She shook her head vigorously.

'Hey, don't worry, it was only an idea. I thought you might like the change. Forget that, but we'll get you some jeans and a hat so we're a bit safer when we're out and about.'

'I could wear a baseball cap.'

'Great.' I adjusted the sat-nav. 'What's your favourite clothes shop?'

She told me and I asked her to check to see that the town had one. Like every teenager, she spent a lot of time flicking around on her phone. It was good for her to be distracted – I needed to think. Practical matters dealt with, I wondered if I should get to know her. The idea that I didn't care kept niggling at me, like a fly trapped in a car. I did care and I wanted her to know it.

My dad always told me that most people are born with a radar in them but mine is broken. Some people might not like that said about them, but the thing about having a broken radar meant that I didn't mind. It made me neither happy nor sad. I don't really know what those things are, not like other people know. I rubbed my short thumbnail back and forth against the flesh of my finger: maybe she could tell my radar was broken. Maybe everyone could.

Like a needle pricking my skin, I wondered if George knew I was broken. I thought of him saying: 'I don't know why you're not getting it', and wondered . . . *no* . . . I decided, he didn't know I'd been in hospital. Neither teacher training nor the school had required any health info and I'd not volunteered my past.

You're not getting it.

But perhaps I wanted to. Perhaps that's what George meant, perhaps 'getting it' was a euphemism for caring about the right thing.

I could care about the right thing. 'Destiny, why did you run away before?'

Destiny said nothing; instead she continued to play with her phone. She'd undone her long plaits and her hair swung like a privacy curtain around her. I couldn't see what she was doing or what her expression was. Had she simply not heard me in that way I was used to from the kids at school? Or was there more to it?

'Destiny,' I persisted, 'I'd really like to know why you felt you had to run away in the past.'

'I don't want to talk about it.'

'I think you should.'

'There's no point.'

'You're going to your aunt now, why not your mum? Is she dead?'

Destiny laughed, 'I wish!'

'You want your mother dead?'

'The joke of it is, last year, I used to run away to sleep on her floor. But then she . . .'

'Then?'

Destiny ignored me. Being alone with a teenager felt like being lost in unfamiliar countryside at night, with no map, torch or phone. I gave up for a few minutes and just drove. Rear-view check. Lane change. Sat-nav check. But I still wanted to know – I still wanted her to think I cared.

I had an idea. 'I realise it might be too personal or painful to tell me. So why don't I tell you about myself? We might not be so different.'

She darted a look at me.

Good, she was interested. I might not know much about teenagers, but I did know that if you could get a kid interested, then you stood half a chance of being heard. I took a breath. 'I didn't grow up with my mum either.' Pause. I'd never had this conversation with anyone. But then, I'd never needed to before. 'She died when I was little.'

Nothing, then, 'How little?'

'When I was three.'

'How did she die?' Destiny uncurled like a snake and stretched out as if seeking heat from the sun. She waited, watching me with eyes filled with deep expression that I didn't understand.

I heard the engine; the sound of the wheels on the tarmac; the sound of my breathing. But what could it matter to me, after all this time? 'My mother killed herself,' I said. My words sounded hollow, and in that moment I could hear it as clear as a rifle shot, I could hear the difference between me and other people. Normally I can't, but then, as if through Destiny (*the best teachers are the ones who care*) I heard the lack of emotion in my voice.

It was like a deadness. The sound of the car on the road; a functioning machine. Robotic. No, worse: I sounded like one of those creepy AI computers in a dystopian film, with carefully modulated tones hiding a deadly intention. I could be deadly – but I wanted to also be a teacher who cared. But how could I be, when I didn't even know how to care?

'That's terrible,' she muttered. She folded her hands on her lap; it was a careful gesture of a much older person. Although I watched the road, I could tell – for the first time – that she was now looking at me properly. 'Do you mind talking about it?'

'No.' Of course I had to say this – the whole point of my bringing this up was to get Destiny to do the same herself – but I wanted to mind, I wanted to care.

She seemed to consider this for a moment. 'What happened?'

'She hanged herself.'

'Oh, Miss!'

I glanced at her, surprised by the rush of emotion in her voice.

'I suppose she was depressed,' I added. Then, into her silence I added helplessly, 'I don't know.'

'Why not?'

I blinked. I wasn't prepared for this question because I'd never had to answer it. I'd never discussed her death because I had nothing to say about it and nobody to tell it to. I found it hard to make friends as a child, so nobody came home to my house and found me motherless. As an adult, there had never been a time when I'd needed to tell anyone. In the army, it's easier not to talk about home; when you're together, you become each other's family.

All I knew was that my mother had hanged herself. But I don't even know how I knew it. It was merely something I had always known.

Other than that, I knew shockingly little. She wasn't ever discussed in our home and if there were any photos of her around before she died, they must have been taken down after, because there was nothing of her in the house, nothing that ever suggested that she'd ever even lived there. But she must have lived there because I do know that she'd hanged herself in her bedroom using a yellow silk tassel belt strung from the light fitting in front of the bay window. I blinked again. I didn't even know that I knew that.

– she's left a crease –

I shook my head, confused. What did I know?

I breathed deeply. I knew that all she left behind was a crease breaking the smoothness of the soft counterpane, where she must have stood making final adjustments around her neck before she stepped her last step away from her life at 43 Teddingham Terrace.

I walked past that door several times a day when I still lived at home. It was always shut, maybe locked, but I don't know because I never tried the handle. The room could've been stripped bare, or perhaps it was freeze-framed in time, a perfect capsule of life before. But I don't know and I don't want to – not even one little bit. My dad quietly boarded the loft and built stairs and we were the first in the street to convert the loft into a room, and that became his bedroom. But we continued to live in the house and the door remained shut.

That was all I remember, that and she called me her 'Flower', and if I was good she'd rub my hands with her hand cream that smelt of lily of the valley.

I thought of her then, my hands suddenly slippery on the steering wheel. I had a brief scent of her, a wisp of something half-remembered. *Flower, sit right there and don't—*

Then it was gone.

I glanced at Destiny again, and saw her watching me. I didn't know how to tell her these things. These things were small enough to be nothing and yet . . . I was overwhelmed. It occurred to me that perhaps my story was worse than her own and she was curious now about me.

'But why haven't you asked what happened?' she said.

I debated turning on the radio. I didn't know what to do. Eventually, I said, 'There wasn't anyone to ask.'

'What about your dad?'

I almost laughed at the thought. 'I couldn't ask my dad, Destiny.'

'Why not?'

I changed lanes to give me something to do. I needed to do something that allowed me a moment to think about her question. I didn't know why not; I never thought about why not. A blue BMW came up on the inside and beeped its horn at me. Unsettled, realising I'd been travelling too slow in the middle lane, I pulled back into the inside one.

'Why not?' she persisted.

'I don't know.' I thought of my dad, his heavy work boots, the set of his mouth, the way he carried himself as if his spine itself was fashioned from Sheffield steel. He had always been good to me: food on the table; clean clothes for school; trips to the dentist. He did his best but we never talked about the past. He was a man of the present.

I realised Destiny was waiting for my answer. I wasn't used to her being – what was this? – *challenging*, I decided. Was she trying to be? Was this testing me or was this curiosity? Or was it something else, something deeper, like trying to understand the world or draw parallels between us? I wasn't sure, but I did know I wanted to think the best of her – had to, given what I'd done – and part of that was taking her questions at face value. 'I've never asked my father because I don't think he wanted to talk about it, I suppose. I didn't want to upset him.'

'But he must have talked to you about it at some point, otherwise how would you know?'

'He never told me. Or maybe he did. Or maybe I was so young, I heard bits and put them together. Some things you just know, like osmosis. You know that word?'

Destiny nodded. 'I'm in the top set for science.'

'You're in the top set for everything, aren't you?'

She bit at her fingernail. 'Did you always want to be a teacher?'

'I always wanted to be a soldier.'

'Why weren't you then?'

'I was for many years.'

'Did you have a gun?'

'All soldiers have a gun.'

She nodded slowly. ' I remember that assembly you did about that race you do every year and win. That was a cool assembly.'

'I wanted you to know about grit and resilience.'

Destiny looked out of the window. 'I already know about grit and resilience. You don't have to teach me about that.' Her voice sounded like mortar shots.

I didn't know what to say, not wanting to return to any of the subjects we had been talking about. But as I flapped, she made the decision for me.

'Why aren't you in the army any more?'

I could tolerate questions about my dead mother, but I couldn't answer this one. I couldn't talk about Billy. I had done nothing but think of Billy recently; this was supposed to help me forget and now we were here, talking about the army and I wasn't forgetting at all.

I wiped each hand in turn on my trousers, before tightening them against the steering wheel. Perhaps it was the look on my face, the set of my jaw or the hunch of my shoulders, but she realised that, although I could sometimes be pushed, this was a no-go area.

Destiny lapsed into silence. After a moment, she rooted around in her bag, eventually finding a packet of sweets. 'Miss, do you want a Starburst?'

I stiffened. I didn't eat sweets – fitness was my world. 'Sure,' I said, keeping my voice casual, 'if you can unwrap it for me. And I think you should call me Jenni, now, don't you?'

She handed me a sticky red square. I sniffed it and popped it in my mouth. 'This is an Opal Fruit.'

'Starburst,' Destiny corrected me.

I laughed, glad to get rid of the tension between my shoulders.

We sat in silence for a while, her unwrapping, and me accepting sweet after sweet. The fruit flavours coated my tongue, far too sweet for me, but it felt strangely comforting to chew the tastes of my childhood.

We'd fallen into such a companionable silence, that when the sat-nav announced the turn-off for Tunbridge Wells, I was unprepared. I glanced at the clock. We had time to get to the shops, but it would be tight.

As I left the motorway, I realised that as soon as we got out of the privacy of my car, we could be seen by CCTV, the police, even the men from the van, but I pressed my foot against the accelerator, still wanting to get there as soon as possible. After all, it would be easier than dodging questions I couldn't answer about my past.

Friday
16:53

Jenni

We had parked the car without event in a multi-storey car park, and had opened the map facility on her phone so we could walk as directly as possible to the shop she wanted to visit.

As we walked, I was reminded again of being on patrol in Iraq. Tunbridge Wells' beautiful town centre couldn't have been more different to the dry, arid landscape of Basra, but the feeling of being watched was the same. There were unseen eyes watching from windows, behind doors or through the children gathered on street corners. Again I was part of a moving convoy, in charge of my section, working as a team to stay safe. Again I knew the feeling of having to make a journey but knowing that journey could end badly. Tunbridge Wells might have pavement slabs and brick where Basra had dust, but the sudden heavy rain had emptied the streets just as our convoy would empty the streets of Iraq. Just as we didn't know the difference between insurgents and civilians, I had no idea who was in the gang and who was a passing stranger. I had seen one of them; I knew there was at least one other because I saw him in the front of the van. But who else lurked inside of it? There could be two or ten, and each man who passed us could be one of them.

My senses were heightened. I had a mission: to get Destiny into the shop and out with a disguise as quickly as possible. I thought about the town CCTV around us; I thought of using my bank cards or withdrawing cash and I thought of the car park that would have read my number-plate. There would be no denying that I had been here with Destiny.

When I had left, I had thought it would be a round trip of two hours, broken with a quick get out of the car, a doorbell ring, a joyous reunion, and my being away after a cup of tea and back at my desk before anyone had seen me gone. Although the school would be empty of kids, there would be plenty of staff around that I planned on speaking to, to cover my tracks. I'd even imagined how I'd feel like a hero at keeping her safe. How naive I'd been.

We walked quickly past shop after shop, all of which would be closing soon.

Inside, the clothes racks were broken up by large mirrors, mannequins and huge photos of thin, beautiful young women. Pop music played. There were still a few shoppers, all women and girls, watched by a uniformed security guard. I would've felt more sure of myself in combat, but I held my chin up and touched the clothes like the other shoppers, wanting to blend in.

I trailed after Destiny, who went quickly from rack to rack. She selected a pair of black skinny jeans with rips at the knees and black trainers. Satisfied, she moved on to the clothes racks at the back of the store. She pulled a shocking-pink hooded jumper off a hanger and held it up against her, looking at her reflection in the mirror. Then she grabbed a T-shirt emblazoned with the slogan: Sleep, Eat, Game, Repeat. I realised that my life came down to Sleep, Eat, Teach, Run, Repeat. Would it always be like that? I wondered if I had grown tired of it without noticing.

'Get another T-shirt if you need . . . pants and socks too, if you want.'

'Really?'

She smiled and I knew that meant that she was happy. It felt strangely powerful to give something to someone else and change them. Dad didn't want for much, so apart from chucking in a couple of quid for staff leaving presents, I didn't have anyone to buy anything for. 'Get a couple of jumpers as well – you'll need them.'

We went to the till and as I paid, the strange sense of warmth increased. I couldn't figure out what it was and then I saw a mother laughing at the till with her daughter. We are almost like them, I thought, puzzled, yet strangely receptive to the moment of make-believe. 'My daughter,' I said, 'she wants to wear these now. Can she go into the changing room and get changed?'

'Sure!' said the bright young thing behind the till as she flashed me a smile.

Flattered that she seemed to accept that I was Destiny's mother, I passed the bag of clothes to Destiny and she broke into a huge grin.

I realised that I'd never seen her happy in school.

I waited outside the changing room. When she came out, she'd tied her hair into a bun and had put in a pair of huge hoop earrings I hadn't seen before. Dressed in her new clothes, she still looked petite, but older, streetwise and more capable than before.

'You look great!' I told her as she stood there. Like a good parent I took the bags now containing the school uniform and we both left the store. The security guard didn't even look our way.

As we walked back through the town towards the car park, Destiny slid an arm through mine and for that moment our disguise was complete.

Friday
17:27

Aleksander

I watched them both leave the clothes shop, arm in arm, as if they were like everybody else. They didn't see me. I held my paper up even higher, waited until they'd passed my bench, then watched as they headed towards the car park.

I let go of the paper that was full of boring stories written for boring people who live boring lives, and watched it flap into the wind, tumbling separating sheets. The old dear next to me on the bench watched it, then glanced at me, questions in her eyes. I gave her my special smile and enjoyed the way her eyes widened in reaction, before she got up and, with her hand on her stick, moved fast for someone her age. Granny Olympics – how fast can they run?

I lit a fag as Destiny and her teacher disappeared out of sight. The teacher carried Topshop bags – if I knew Destiny, then she would've rinsed that stupid bitch for all her cash.

About now, they'd be getting back to that sporty little Peugeot parked on the second floor of the multi-storey. They could fuck off, but I wasn't worried. I could catch them anytime I wanted. And I will. And when I do, I'll make that bitch go out screaming in pain.

No one runs from me.

I sat and smoked, planning, thinking. I finished my fag, flicking it to the ground. A seagull swooped down and pecked at it, dropping it when it burned. Anything else and I would've laughed, but I like seagulls – they're survivors, like me. I found some peanuts in my pocket, I tore open the silver foil and tipped out a few for the gull. Then, after tipping the rest in my mouth, I got up and followed Destiny. I'll get you, I thought, thinking about my hand on her neck, pressing against her windpipe so gently that . . . I smirked, letting the thought go, already aroused.

I couldn't wait to see her.

Oh yes, Candydoll, Papa's coming to get you.

Friday
17:39

Aleksander

In the multi-storey, I walked up to the fourth floor. I touched the sleek silver of my new Merc; I love to touch it, feel the smooth paint under my fingertips. It's sexy, classy and it's mine. With it, I can remember that I've made it. I didn't even have to think about whether I should part with the cash, business is good. It's a high-risk business and I'm not stupid, if I get caught, I'm looking at fifteen to twenty. But it's worth it – every time I leave the country, I add a bit more to my hidden stash in Poland. One day, I might go back or I might stay here: either way, I'll live like a king.

I got in the passenger seat. I don't pay to drive my own car, unless for fun. And until we get Destiny, there's no fun for anyone. 'So?'

'They've left. They're on the road.'

'I know. *Stupid.*' I turned to look at Gary, his annoying face, the deformed ear on his left side, the creases around his eyes from working too long in the sun. When I found him, he'd been working for a family of travellers. I set him free and now he works for me. 'I meant, where are Jay and Ollie?'

Gary looked at his hands, turning them as if he could read the answer in his palms. 'Sorry. They're in the van. They're still in the layby waiting for your orders.'

'Good. Let's get going. We need to follow Destiny.'

I loved the way the car purred into action. Despite Gary being a *chuj*, he has his uses and behind the wheel, he earns his keep. Back on the motorway, I checked on Destiny's progress. 'She's still on the same road – she's still going north.'

'To Hull? She's definitely going back home?' asked Gary, wonder in his voice.

'Just like a pigeon.' Easy – we could pick her up there. I smiled, imagining her hair in my fists.

I messaged the boys so they knew which way to head, then turned the radio on. Despite wanting to kick back and relax, I kept flipping through channels looking for something I couldn't find. I couldn't settle. It was not having her close, I knew that. I hated losing and right now I felt like I was losing.

I checked my phone again, catching Gary's glance at me. 'Fuck off,' I told him. Gary's place was keeping his eyes on the road, not on me. The small circle that tracked Destiny was drawing closer to us. We were getting closer. 'We need to cut our speed,' I told him.

Ever obedient, Gary eased off the accelerator.

I sat back into the leather seat. I had to get her back, but I needed to be patient. I couldn't risk a scene. Up until now, we'd never had a sniff of Old Bill involvement and I wanted us to stay clean.

I watched the cars on the outside lane overtake us. Something about that had always irritated me. I liked to be the fastest on the road, liked to feel the control, be in charge. And I had achieved that: I was the big man. I thought, oddly, of my dad and what he would say. He would be pleased. Impressed, even. I had money, I had the fear of my contemporaries. When I spoke, people listened. How many people could say that? I thought on this and realised it was better than this: when I spoke, people didn't listen, they fucking *did*. What. I. Fucking. Asked.

But I still didn't have Destiny.

I hadn't solved that one. And that silly bitch had surprised me, I hadn't expected her to do anything, to put Destiny in a car and drive her halfway across the country. I remembered the look she'd given me when I'd shown her my gun. The way she'd met my eye with a look I'd only seen in the psychopathic gun-and-drug-running gang leaders. That unshakable arrogance. That *fuck you* look. It was the look of the fearless. She'd raised her chin, and given me a *fuck you* stare despite the gun.

It occurred to me then that that teacher had something I had never seen outside of my work: she had the look of the insane.

Friday
18:00

George

George knew he was finished. He'd seen Jenni erratically change lanes, before losing her for good. He'd followed on, but he'd now accepted that she was gone – they both were. Now he had no choice but to return home. And what then? Phone Steve and admit the whole sorry truth? Or just slink off home to Sal and confess the extent of his failure and have her look at him with a pity that killed him only slightly less than Steve Wichard's distain?

Either way, something was going to come of his ineptitude.

He glanced at the clock. He had a long drive home; he had time to think it over, before he could finally collapse into his bed.

He released his foot against the accelarator. He dropped below sixty. He wouldn't even mind getting nicked for driving slowly – anything rather than arrive before he'd had a chance to do some serious thinking.

Whether he liked it or not, his life had changed today, forever. And if he wanted out of this situation with a modicum of self-respect, he had to think very carefully about what was the best thing to do from here on.

Friday
18:18

Jenni

I checked the clock and realised we'd been driving for three hours. In an hour, we would be there and I realised that it was unlikely that I would ever see Destiny again.

I had pulled into a layby to check my work emails and realised that no one had tried to contact me. Now it was Friday evening, no one would. Destiny had been missing from her children's home for several hours and although the police must have been called, I wasn't on their radar. How could I be so sure? Because two marked police cars and several grey, sporty saloon cars favoured by undercover traffic cops had passed me, and no one had pulled me over. Destiny's disappearance either didn't rank very highly or wasn't being linked to me at all.

When I had googled children in care going missing, I read a social work article that suggested it was considered normal for them to go AWOL. A social worker had made it sound as if running away was an expected outcome for these children. Clearly, whatever action was needed to stop this problem wasn't being taken. I glanced at Destiny curled into a ball and knew that her disappearance didn't count as much as if she was a 'regular' kid, living in a regular semi, with a regular mum and dad. It didn't seem right that vulnerable kids who'd already suffered so much trauma and neglect were almost expected to drift away from the care system, unnoticed. Yes, a call would be made somewhere, a report written and logged, but there would be no fuss in the press, no anguished parents making tearful requests for help and information, no public outrage or concern. Destiny would be allowed to break away from her path and disappear into the unknown.

And that was what she was doing now. But at least she wasn't alone. At least she had me to keep her safe as she changed the path of her life. And after me, she would have her aunt. I hoped her aunt would be able to give her the safety and support that Destiny deserved. I thought of the clothes I'd bought – it was the closest I'd come to feeling something real. And I liked it. I decided to leave my number with her aunt. I would contribute towards Destiny's financial needs. I had no one else to support; I would support her.

Decision made, I wanted to reach out and pat her, to somehow transfer my concern and support with the briefest of contacts, but it was important to do that and keep a professional boundary.

I realised that Destiny was fiddling with her phone. 'Are you texting someone?'

'I texted my aunt, but she hasn't answered yet.'

'But she is expecting you?'

'Yes. She wants me to come – it was her idea.'

'Then don't worry,' I said automatically. 'It'll be fine.' But now I wondered – what if her aunt wasn't there? I'd been expecting a drop and run. I expected to be at home tonight, waking up to my usual Saturday of silence, running, lunch, then weights, before an evening swim.

I decided not to consider alternatives at the moment: Destiny needed me to be positive. I searched for something cheery to say, but found nothing.

Instead, I decided to try again to find out more about her. It seemed the time to ask the question I was desperate to know. 'You said you've run away before. When was that?'

Destiny stopped flicking through her phone. 'I've run away lots of times.'

'Why?'

She looked back at her phone. For a moment, she didn't say anything. Then, 'I always run.'

'Always?'

'I used to stay with foster families when I couldn't stay with my mum. But . . . it changed.'

'How?'

'I was only allowed to stay in children's homes. I hate them.'

'Are the staff . . .' I didn't know how to ask. 'Are they . . . unkind?'

'You sound like you're trying to ask if they fiddle with me.'

Pause. 'Do they?'

Destiny sighed and looked out of the window. The rain slashed against the windscreen. It was a question she wasn't going to answer. We both listened to the *slish slish* of the beating wipers, both locked in our own thoughts.

I tried another question. 'When was the last time you ran away?'

'I don't come from round here. I shouldn't even be here. Is that running away?'

'Where are you from?'

'Where we are going.'

'Why did you move?'

She turned to look at me with those big eyes full of . . . something. 'I didn't want to move. They made me.'

'The men from the van?'

She shook her head. 'Social services.'

'But why? I don't understand.'

'They told me they'd run out of suitable placements.'

'Run out? Sorry, Destiny, I don't understand, but I want to. Do you mind talking about it?'

She gave a small shrug. 'I've been to lots of foster families and it always goes wrong. I know that sometimes it's my fault. I can't ever believe that it's going to go right. It never has, so . . .' She shrugged again. When she next spoke, her voice sounded different, with a bayonet's edge to it, that I'd not heard before. 'But most of all, it's the foster parents' fault. Some of them are so,' she made a noise like an attack. I kept my eyes on the road, not wanting to give away my surprise.

'So, when no one else would take me, they put me into the local children's home. The last time it went wrong, they said I set fire to another girl's duvet.'

'Did you?'

'It's complicated. But after that, it was someone's bright idea to think about a managed move. They thought I should be out of the area. So some boy who lives down your way, now lives in my hometown, and I get to live in Hastings. I don't even *like* Hastings.'

I thought of the crumbling Victorian properties that lined the promenade. The fish and chip shops and arcades. The smell of frying doughnuts. The relentless beat of the steel-grey Atlantic waves. I couldn't imagine living anywhere else.

'They take my life and treat me like a budget cost,' she said, her voice sounding bitter.

'I don't understand.'

'Swaps are arranged so no one loses out in their budget. I cost the council money.'

I wasn't sure what to say about it – because I believed her take on it. 'Maybe this is an obvious question, but are you saying you don't like anything about where you are? What about our school?'

'I want to go home. That's why I run. Wouldn't you do the same?'

She looked at me with huge blue eyes, and I stared too long trying to understand what she was feeling so that a car beeped me as I nearly edged out of the lane. I yanked on the wheel.

'Don't worry, Miss, I'll get away from you too.' She laughed a high, tinny sound, a thin attempt at humour to lighten the difficult mood.

I didn't judge her for her jab at me. I was more surprised to hear her laugh – I'd never heard her laugh before. There was a lot that I had never heard Destiny do that I heard the other kids do all the time: I'd never heard her swear, gossip, laugh, answer back, jump, run, yell, push, shout or joke. She would shrink silently into any space with a stillness that belied her age. It was as if she was constantly working to make herself invisible. I'm ashamed to admit it but if she hadn't been so unusual – her IQ and being in care – then I probably would never have even noticed her.

'I don't understand, Destiny. Are you running from or running to?'

'No one has ever asked me that.' She ran a careful finger across her forehead to clear her heavy fringe from her eyes. 'I run from.'

'Because they never manage to find you anywhere that's been any good?' I picked my words with care. I didn't want to cause her any pain but I wanted to know. I was potentially sabotaging my life: I deserved to know why.

She shrugged a small movement. 'There was a nice family once. I lived with them when I was six until I was nine. It was good. The best bit was they had another girl; she was called Charlotte. I had a sister.' She said it again, but this time she whispered it: '*I had a sister.*' When she spoke again, her voice was hard and firm. 'I used to miss them a lot.'

'Used to?'

'I don't miss anyone now.'

I felt so bad for Destiny. It must be awful to hurt for someone who was never coming back. 'What happened to them?'

'Dad – I mean Ed – got a job at an IT firm in California. They wanted to adopt me, take me with them, but it wasn't allowed.'

'Why not?'

'My real mother wouldn't *allow* it.'

Quiet, meek Destiny hissed like a provoked snake. I nearly tried to frame this as a positive thing: *Isn't that a good thing that she didn't want to lose you?* But with venom like that, I didn't try. 'But you wanted to?'

'Badly.'

'So they left?'

'They didn't want to. They would've stayed. It wasn't easy for them. Ed had been made redundant and the job he'd been offered was great. To stay would mean that they didn't have any money. But I know they would've for me. I know it.' She bit at her nails. 'One night I came downstairs and found Mum crying. By then I knew what was going on, as I'd had to have meetings with my social worker. They had asked me what I wanted, and then they asked Simone. Simone is my biological mother. It went to court. I couldn't sleep the day after the trial and came downstairs and found Kay and Ed in bits again. I think they were fighting, but . . . well, not with each other, more in that way that safe married couples fight with the other as a way of fighting with themselves, outing that struggle that they feel inside, you know?'

In her pause, I tried to absorb the idea. How could this young girl, only fifteen, be able to make observations about grown-up relationships when I was forty and couldn't make them myself? I shifted in my seat, discomforted by my blindness.

'Simone told the court that she didn't want me to be with them any more. She thought we were getting too close. Even though I was told that I had to leave them, it wasn't until I saw Kay crying that I realised – she was the best mum I ever had. When I left their house, I think I died a bit inside.

'Oh, Destiny. I don't know what to say.'

She shook her head, and I could see, even in my peripheral vision, that she was unable to speak.

Destiny and I were the same: we had both lost our mothers.

Then I realised: no we were not the same. Destiny had lost two.

Friday
18:29

George

George allowed himself to cry. It felt good. Big heaving sobs not fitting for the proper Yorkshire man he was, but he didn't care. It wasn't the knowledge that at some point, he was going to have to give up and head home, that was causing the tears. The joke of it was that the only person who had caused any alarm, was him. Steve Wichard would've rung his mobile when he was established as properly late and had found it off. He would've rung the school, who would've have confirmed him as having left the premises, his signature in the signing-out book. And maybe they would've rung Sal.

He didn't know much about Jenni because she made sure she avoided getting into any personal conversation with anyone, but he knew she lived alone. From what he'd learned from social services, Destiny disappeared every weekend anyway, so perhaps their concern was minimal.

All the time that he followed them he had so many questions. Where were they going and why? Was he doing the right thing? What would he say to Jenni when he saw her?

He had tried to do the right thing, he had. He'd tried to make the call to the police without pulling over – because surely it was all right to make a call when you were driving if it was an emergency and how could he risk losing them? – but the phone had instantly died. Then the agony of realising that he only had a standard charger with him – after all, he had thought that he was going to be sitting in Steve's office where that would've been fine. He didn't like mobile phones enough to have an in-car charger. Besides, when did he need to charge his phone in the car? He never went anywhere. No one ever called him. He never needed to call anyone. Until now.

The low buzz of concern that he hadn't called the police eventually became a deafening chorus. He'd searched the lay-bys for call boxes but he hadn't seen any. Now he would have to do that when he got home. Normally, he loved the weekend. The opportunity to dress in garden clothes and to spend the time with a trowel in his hand, the smell of soil in his nostrils. Saturday morning was a visit to the garden centre; Sunday lunch was either with one of the children and grandchildren, or lunch out at a National Trust property. But that wouldn't be happening this weekend. He'd have to give a police statement, he knew that. He'd also have to answer questions to the board.

But that wasn't why he was crying. He was crying because he knew he was never coming back from this. He'd had the think he knew he needed, and whether he liked it or not, he'd had to accept that all arrows pointed to his career now being over.

All he had to do now was to turn off at the first services and be seen to take action. He would call the police. He would give as much information as he could over the phone. Then he'd call his wife, who by now would be worried about where he was. His stomach burned when he thought about what she might have been thinking. Recently, he'd been close to the edge and he knew that her imagination might have taken her to places she hadn't needed to go. But he was a solid man, a Dales man. He could weather storms if he needed to. He knew what he valued, and he loved his wife and family.

And he'd decided he'd put his resignation in on Monday. A pre-emptive strike.

He didn't have much left, but he could save his dignity. The next services he'd come to, he would make the calls. Perhaps he'd even call Steve Wichard and resign on the spot.

Another cold tear tracked down his face.

Jenni

'Can I have something to eat?' asked Destiny, twisting in her car seat to face me.

My hand flew to my mouth. 'Destiny! I'm so sorry, I didn't even think. Have you been suffering in silence?'

'Only for a bit,' she admitted.

'Anything, *anything* you need, Destiny, you must ask. I'm not used to looking after people – outside of school hours, anyway.' I checked the sat-nav. 'There's a major services coming up in a minute.' I felt relief – how could I forget? But then the next thought chased it – what was *I* going to eat? Damn it. I thought of the tuna steak in my fridge. My diet was strict – no one could compete and win the Ironman competitions without supreme discipline, including over their diet. Tension needled into my shoulders. There would be fast food only, or sandwiches. I started to calculate how many carbs I could eat. I was so distracted by the thought of needing to eat, because now I was suddenly starving, yet not wanting to consume anything rubbish, that I nearly missed the turn-off.

I turned off into the services, and saw all the usual signs of Wimpy, McDonald's and Starbucks. I wondered if I should confess to Destiny that I was on a strict diet, despite my need to model a healthy balanced lifestyle to a vulnerable girl now in my care. Guilt versus need meant I didn't hear Destiny's question.

She repeated it. 'I said, can I have a McDonald's?'

I parked and gave what I hoped was a relaxed-sounding yes.

Before we got out, I checked Destiny's appearance. Now she was dressed in her new jeans and hoodie, she looked different to the description that might have been put out about her. But her hair was the same and I realised we'd forgotten to get her a hat. 'Destiny, what can we do about your lovely hair?'

'I don't want to cut it!' Her eyes rounded with fear.

I put my hands up in what I hoped was a calming measure. 'At the shop you had your hair in a bun. Could you please do that again?'

She twisted her long hair into a ponytail and then into a knot.

'Thank you. Better. Would you possibly consider wearing my reading glasses? The lenses are incredibly weak and you'd only have to wear them for a bit. And if they hurt your eyes at all, then take them off.' I reached in the glove box, trying not to notice the way Destiny shrank away from me as if she thought I might hurt her. I handed them to her. 'If you don't feel comfortable, it's not a problem, it's only an idea. I don't want you to be picked up on the CCTV, because I bet service stations are past all the reports of missing people and we don't want the police on our tail, do we?'

In answer, Destiny took the black-rimmed glasses and put them on. She flipped down the sun visor and looked at her image in the small mirror. She then looked at me. I was surprised how much her hair twisted out of the way and the slightly too-large frames, made a difference to her face. She looked androgynous; younger, more fragile. I nodded, satisfied. *We are going to be safe.* 'Let's go and get you as many burgers as you can eat!'

Friday
18:44

Jenni

The McDonald's area was in the far corner of the dining area; it was the busiest, but there were still plenty of empty tables. Destiny trailed behind me. Again, I felt like there were a hundred eyes on me. But of course there were, I reminded myself, CCTV was everywhere. I controlled my breathing; we were fine, I told myself. Destiny looked completely different and if they were looking for her, they were probably expecting her to be with a group of men.

Besides, she had to eat.

I looked at the menu and knew I couldn't eat any of it. I felt sick. But looking after Destiny had made me feel something and I wanted that again. It would be lovely to sit and eat with Destiny, to share a meal with her at her choice of restaurant with her choice of food.

We were next in the queue. 'What do you want?' I asked her, already pulling my card from my wallet. I paused, then put it back, swapping it for a twenty-pound note. Cash was my friend right now. I knew I was traceable but I didn't have to make it easy.

'What can I have?'

'Anything you like.'

'I'll have a cheeseburger then, fries, a strawberry milkshake and an apple pie. What will you have?'

'I don't really eat at McDonald's,' I said, looking at the menu and seeing only carbs, sugar, salt and saturated fat. Poison, poison, and more poison. I could feel the drum of my heart.

'You've got to eat something, you're driving such a long way.'

I continued to study the menu, desperately searching for the right option. The wraps and salads could be a possible. Perhaps it wasn't as bad as I feared. 'I tend to eat a very strict diet because of my training.'

'I don't want to eat on my own.'

The server smiled a practised beam at me and Destiny looked at me with something like hope. I stared at the menu, looking for something. Tension stabbed my shoulders; I felt my cheeks burn. I had never ordered fast food before. 'The filet of fish please?' a fish portion could be very nice. I almost asked her to hold the bun, then had a rethink – I could do that myself. 'Make that two, please?'

'That's cooked to order so we'll bring that to your table. Would you like fries with that?'

'No, thanks. I'll take the milk to drink, please.'

'That only comes as a children's size.'

I wanted to check its fat content, but I clenched my jaw against the question. 'Give me two. And a black coffee.'

'Anything else?'

'The fruit in a bag. What's that like?'

'Apple slices, grapes.'

'Pre-cut?'

'Yes.' A shadow crossed Destiny's face and she stepped away from me. I tried to think of that rather than what it would've been washed in. But it was a struggle – my body was a highly functioning machine; as a gun needed to be oiled and cleaned, my body needed to be kept free of irritants like chlorine. I breathed, focusing on Destiny. Like a good corporal, I needed to keep her needs in my sights. 'OK, two bags,' I said, doubling my order to emphasise how OK I was with fast food. 'That's it,' I added, wanting this torture to end.

She read back the menu items and I paid.

In the far corner, an older man sat reading a newspaper. There was an overweight man in the other corner, scrolling through his phone. There was a family of five, two young kids squabbling and a toddler in a highchair throwing food on the floor. It looked safe, benign. 'Sit anywhere you like.'

Destiny choose a table in the middle and we sat down.

We'd spent the whole afternoon side-by-side, me busy with the driving, her playing on her phone. Now we were sitting opposite each other, it felt uncomfortable. She bit into her burger and I realised the last time I had eaten a burger was with Billy. I remember him biting into it before passing me a photo of a girl.

We've only been in Iraq two days, when Billy shows me a photo of a young blonde woman with freckles that cover her face. Her eyes are green, her nose is small and turns up a little. 'She's pretty,' I say.

'Her name is Maddie.'

We're sitting in the NAAFI. It's hot and the air is so thick with beer and sweat that you can almost chew it. His pale skin is flushed red. It's noisy too – there's a gang shouting karaoke, arms round each other, yelling to finish each other's words. I look at them, their camaraderie, and feel determined to finally integrate Billy with them. This is the first stage – starting with me. Billy's new to action. Now he's eighteen, he'll be joining us on the tour. As a start, I'm trying to get to know him. It's my job to give him support and leadership and I take that seriously.

Billy's a kid, really, young and very sweaty: the heat has swept a sweat tide mark into his ginger buzz cut. His cheeks pink easily too, and they flush now when he leans across the table, flicks a furtive glance over his shoulder before he says, 'Can I ask you something?'

'Sure.'

'I'm not sure if you're not supposed to ask this kinda thing, but I gotta know, so . . .'

'Ask away.'

'Are you . . . do you feel . . . ?' The hesitation always means the same. Particularly this close to the tour starting.

'Scared?' I finish for him. When he nods, I continue, 'Of course. Your trouble is that you've been waiting too long to see action.'

He nods enthusiastically. 'It's true – two years. I joined on my sixteenth birthday. But now it's here and . . .'

'Why did you sign up so young?'

He shrugged. 'Why not? Good to have a proper job, innit. It's a career.'

'I served in Desert Storm.' He understands this explanation. His eyes widen and he drinks greedily from his pint, my experience a flare to his interest.

'Not in a combat role though, obviously,' I say, gesturing vaguely to my chest area.

His body sags. Like that, I've lost his interest.

'I would've loved to have heard about what Iraq was like then. I bet it was hell.'

He probably thinks I was cooking. 'I saw action, though. I've been a combat medic.'

He's back in, I can tell. I carried a gun and I was on the front. That's the respect in his eyes I was looking for.

'That's a tough one. Did you see a lot of . . . stuff?' He winces at the word, no doubt thinking of limbs missing, guts tumbling from torn bodies, lifeless, staring eyes.

'Yes. Lots and lots of stuff.'

'What did you do? Tell me what was it like.' He bites his lip as if to stop himself from going further.

He is *scared*, I think, proper scared. 'It was tough. But it was my job. The perfect training ground.'

'So now you're combat?'

'Now I'm combat.' I nod. 'Now my gun isn't only to defend.'

I grab our glasses and go to the bar. Elbows out I get through the throng, and hold my height, glad I'm taller than many.

Back at the table I slide Billy's pint towards him.

'So . . . not long now till we go home,' Billy says. Pause. 'Not long now at all.'

We've only just got here and I tell him that. His face sags and I know I've said the wrong thing. I try again. I know what he is talking about. It's what we all talk about. I realise that Billy is a boy of long pauses when he has something on his mind.

'How does your family feel about you going off on tour for the first time?'

His cheeks flush deeper. 'Yeah, my Maddie is not happy but . . .' he shrugs. 'I'll be back before she knows it.'

He looks at me, unwavering, blue eyes locked on mine. In them, I can see emotion, I can tell he's feeling something, but I can't respond, because I can't guess at what I don't know. I don't want to say the wrong thing again. Instead, I clink my glass against his and repeat his words: 'Back before you know it,' I agree.

I blinked, confused. The McDonald's server had brought us the rest of our food on a tray. Destiny accepted the order and put mine in front of me. Then she looked at me as if she was trying to figure something out. Right then, when I thought of Billy, it was more like I was with him than where I actually am. I haven't thought of him since I left the army, but now . . . now my memories are so real, it's as if I'm back there. I blinked again, returning to the present, with Destiny watching me closely. I wonder what Dr Hartley, my psychiatrist at Headley Court would say. Probably PTSD I reckon, but of course, anyone treating soldiers would see so much of that, it's probably the first thing they reach for.

But if it's more than that, then I don't want to know. I'm on my own now. He couldn't help me, the army couldn't help me, but . . . I missed them. I missed being part of something bigger than me.

I opened my milk and reached for something to talk to Destiny about.

We had school in common, but I was sure she had no desire to talk about a place which she hoped she'd left for ever.

What we also shared was the loss of our mothers, but that wasn't dinner chat. I wanted something light-hearted and fun, but light-hearted and fun were not in my skill set.

Destiny spoke first. 'Tell me more about your Ironman competitions.'

I smiled, surprised that she was able to rescue the situation. 'What do you want to know?'

'I remember you showing us photos in assembly; it looks harsh. Is it as hard as it looks?'

'It's very tough. Everyone who competes is at the top of their game when it comes to endurance and strength, but it's great to be able to compete against such amazing athletes.' I removed the fish from the bun and forced myself not to scrape the sauce off it. 'I know this may seem odd, but when you're competing, you have to be very careful about food.'

'Aren't you going to eat that?'

I shake my head. 'But unless you're an athlete, a balanced diet is a good thing.' I felt the responsibility of being a good role model.

'I'll eat it, Miss,' she said, taking a huge bite out of it. 'I'm starving,' she explained through her mouthful.

I was glad I hadn't put her off or seemed too weird to her.

'You look very strong,' she said, munching away. 'You win, don't you?'

I smiled more naturally now. Perhaps this was not going to be the most awkward of social situations. Destiny had her own talents. 'I've won three times.'

'How do you fit it in around teaching?'

'With difficulty. I don't work Wednesdays, which helps me spread the load. But it's still a challenge as many of my competitors compete as their full-time job. And teaching, as you know, well, you probably don't, but it's a massive job, and even on only four days, I still work forty hours a week. But I get up early to do a short run and—'

'What's a short run?'

'About seven miles.'

She sucked on her milkshake nosily. 'That's a long run.'

'I alternate after school with a weights routine or a longer run. On my days off, I really go for it. Swimming, fifteen-mile runs, weights, the lot.' I realised I was showing off, but it was my favourite topic and it felt good to talk in an easy way with her. I finished the fish and opened the next one. I passed her the bun.

'Thanks, Miss.' Destiny watched me. 'Is that the only reason you're funny about food?'

I smiled. 'Well, actually, I think everyone else is funny about food and I'm the normal one.'

'What do you mean?'

Destiny was fifteen; I decided it was OK. 'Take what you're eating, for example. It's full of additives and sugar and probably trans fats and lots of stuff your body doesn't want or need. Yet you eat it anyway.'

Destiny sucked nosily on her straw again. 'It tastes bloody nice.'

I let the swearing go. 'But it's not good for you.'

'But it tastes bloody nice.' She gave me a hint of a smile.

'My body, my fitness, is important to me. It's like a car – how can I expect to get the best speeds and distance from it if I fill it with—'

'Shit?' The hint became a grin. She'd read my mind and knew it.

I decided to shrug off a layer of my usual self. After all, it was a bit late to pretend things were still the same, now I was sitting in a service station halfway up the M1 with a minor in a disguise so the police didn't find us. 'Shit,' I agreed, 'is the right word because it *is* bad for you. Some of it is actually poison to your body.'

Destiny's eyes twinkled. 'But it tastes so—'

'*Good*,' I finished for her, enjoying the joke. 'I know, I know.'

Actually, my fish did taste good. But that was fat and salt for you.

'What's it like winning, Miss?'

'It's not the winning that's important.'

Destiny raised a challenging eyebrow.

'No, really. I used to be in the army, and I missed the training, the structure, so I do it for that. I need something to aim for, the burn, the endurance and I need . . .' I paused, aware of how strong my need was coming across. 'I *like* the challenge.'

Destiny put down her cheeseburger. 'Did you used to fight and . . . you know?'

I had made a decision not to talk about the army in my assembly presentation. George had wanted me to, and he was right, because in many ways I wanted to share what I considered the best job in the world. It had built me, saved me even, and it was an honour to serve Queen and Country. But I still couldn't talk about it. I would've loved to encourage the pupils to consider signing up, to learn a trade and have the opportunity to travel the world, to keep peace where others couldn't . . . but I couldn't because when I thought about it now, all I could remember was my failure. My shame. And I couldn't share that with anybody.

'What's the matter, Miss?'

'Nothing,' I said, attempting to sound light-hearted, but instead I only sounded stiff. 'Nothing,' I tried again, this time successfully softening my voice.

She took another bite of cheeseburger, chewing and looking at me with an expression I didn't understand. 'Did you kill anyone, Miss?' she asked eventually.

I paused. She could be my pupil again one day. I said that to her.

Her expression changed instantly. Mostly people's emotions were lost on me, but it was like watching the sky change from sunny to storm clouds. But still I didn't know what she was feeling – just that it was bad. She mumbled something about how she'd rather die than go back.

'Don't make light of dying,' I told her.

'Who said I was?' she retorted

'Yes,' I said then. It deserved the truth.

She took another bite. More thoughtful chewing. 'Lots of people?'

'Yes.'

'Did you like it?'

'The killing or the army?'

She shrugged. 'Both. Neither.'

'No one enjoys killing, Destiny.'

Her eyes narrowed and she returned to her burger. It was only when it was gone, and I thought the conversation was long behind us, that she added, quietly, as if to herself, 'Some people do.'

Friday
19:03

Jenni

I watched her finish her apple pie before checking my watch. Seeing the time, I felt a thump of disquiet: we still had another hour of driving to do. 'Are you clear where your aunt lives?'

She nodded.

'Good. Have you spoken to her yet?'

'She's messaged me back and says she can't wait to see me.'

I breathed in, relief relaxing my shoulders. As she confirmed she could stay, I was confronted with what many would think was obvious: what would I have done if she hadn't been allowed to?

Everyone has their strengths. Mine is that when I have a mission, I go, go, go. And then I go some more. And then when everyone else is falling by the wayside, I keep going. But I do know that thinking things through can be a weakness.

My focus served me in the army. The only time I lost it, I lost my army career, my self-respect and my only friend.

I vowed I would never lose my focus again.

So when Destiny had wet herself, spoke her strange code name into her phone and I saw the man with the gun, I had all the focus I needed. But that meant that I had been concentrating on one step at a time: get Destiny in the car; throw off the van; change destination; conceal her identity; feed her. Only now I fully considered quite how serious a situation I would've been in if her aunt hadn't been able or willing to take Destiny in. That would be bad. Very bad.

'We need to set off. Do you want the loo?'

Destiny was already up. 'I'll be back in a minute,' she said, calling back over her shoulder. She'd taken me by surprise. I'd wanted to go with her – I didn't like her going off on her own. She was my responsibility and the weight of it felt heavy.

And now she was off and I couldn't see her. I tried to relax, but the earlier feeling of being watched suddenly crackled like electricity. My antennae might not be good at picking up emotions, but it was better than most at picking up danger. I looked around. The family had left, as had the trucker. The man with the paper was also leaving, tipping his rubbish into the bin.

A large group of students had taken over the three tables nearest me, their loud voices disorientating.

I suddenly needed to be out of there. I didn't like Destiny being out of sight.

So I followed her.

Friday
19:11

Jenni

A large influx of people suddenly made the services busier; the current was against me, with everyone flowing towards me. I had to push against them. It felt like they were all conspiring against me getting to Destiny. I put my head down and was bullish in my determination. I knew that if people were unable to make eye contact with me, they were more likely to get out of my way. I bumped into one or two people and had an unfortunate incident with a young child, forcing me to deal with an angry parent, but it only slowed me for a few moments, so I made good time.

I found the loos and went in. Several women milled around the sinks, but there was no queue and several cubicle doors were open. The air was hot and smelt of poo. Several hand dryers were going and a baby in a sling screamed as her flushed mother washed her hands. The noise was disorientating as was the lack of Destiny: I'd expected to see her at the sinks. I felt my heart rate quicken.

'Destiny?' I called out and everyone turned to look. She didn't answer. I pushed against the closed cubicle doors, some giving way. When they didn't, I knocked and called out, 'Destiny, are you in there?' Each time a different woman would answer no. I could see people watching me, concern on their faces.

I bit my lip; I'd never had anyone to lose before, I was unsure how to proceed.

I decided to go back out to McDonald's to see if she'd returned to our table. Perhaps I'd pushed right past her. I trailed slowly, looking about carefully now, trying to spot Destiny browsing magazines in WHSmith or choosing a doughnut. But she wasn't there. In the food hall, I could see clearly that she wasn't back in McDonald's either.

My breathing was controlled. I was focused; I would find Destiny.

I never doubted it.

Others would be disorientated by fear, immobilised. Instead, this was me at my best.

I made a quick assessment of the situation. If she wasn't here, then the gang must have found her. There was no time to enlist the help of the management and put her name over a tannoy or wait for the police. If she wasn't in here, then she was already outside. I had perhaps seconds before she was in the van and away. I would only be able to guess at their direction after that.

Therefore I understood: as soon as she was in the car park, I would lose her for good.

I began to run – not jog – full pelt, towards the entrance. Someone fell to the floor as I pushed them out of the way.

Then I saw her.

A man had her by the hand and was leading her towards the entrance, dragging her away from me.

Friday
19:12

George

George yanked his handbrake with the determination of a man who had decided upon his last actions and had the conviction of them being right. He locked his car, pocketed his key and walked across the car park towards the services.

His stomach rumbled. He'd have a McDonald's after making the call. Perhaps he could even enjoy it a little – it would be a true treat because since his emergency surgery, Sal would never allow him to eat a burger and fries. The thought of it being his last meal almost brought – and it would have if it hadn't felt so bloody accurate – a sad smile to his face. The moment passed but he did wonder whether if he kept the burger in mind, it would help him get through what were about to be some very difficult conversations.

Inside the services, the crowds were thick. A group of Japanese tourists headed towards him, manners making him stand aside. It hurt him to wait. The anxiety of knowing he had to call the police felt like a pressing burden. He wanted it done. Never more had he resented himself for not doing something and he needed to right that wrong.

Several miles back, he'd decided the moment when he had gone wrong was when Jenni had driven past him by the railway crossing. There, right on the corner, was a telephone box. If he'd turned off his car engine – precisely like the signs requested that waiting cars at the crossing did – he could've reached for his mobile phone right then and tried to call the police. He would've found the battery dead. But then he could've got out, run to the telephone box and made the call. He could've described the car and given her name and let the police do the rest. He would've done the right thing. He could've even made his meeting with Steve Wichard.

He was waiting patiently as a mother pushing a pram with three other children passed him when he looked up and saw her – a girl who looked just like Destiny. *No wait* – it was Destiny.

Destiny walked right by him, led by a man.

He was a shortish, thickset man with a shaved head. Destiny was trailing after him, pulled by her hand.

What was Destiny doing here?

Who was he?

And where on earth was Jenni?

Friday
19:19

Jenni

I fixed my sights on her and cut through the crowds. I was a woman on a mission. I felt the tension in my thighs like I feel at the start of a new Ironman race.

Adrenalin coursed through my body. My mind was focused. I was locked on goal. I will win. This time I would save Bil— *Destiny* . . . I would save *Destiny*.

They stepped out of the automatic doors and out into the evening daylight.

I stepped out and was upon them in seconds.

I grabbed Destiny's hand, the one held by the man's, yanking it from his grasp. He turned. I saw surprise in his blue eyes. It was the man with the gun. I couldn't pause – I could only act. I punched him once, twice, hard, straight in the face. All my weight, thrown through my shoulder, through my fist. Bang. Bang.

I felt a crack – heard the crack on the second time. I saw his eyes flash first in shock, then with pain. I had been planning on a third, but when I felt the grind of splintering cartilage finding new, unnatural places against each other, my work was done.

In the pause where he fell back, hands flying to his face, I moved fast. Without even looking at Destiny, I surged forward, still holding her hand. As if her hand were a grenade and my job was to remove it from the crowded area, I clenched it to my chest and powered forward.

I must've hurt her as I yanked her. But I was a hero again, back in another war situation. I ran her out of danger. As she faltered in the centre of the car park, I helped her by placing my hand behind her back, only then glancing back when I was certain I could.

Blood poured through the man's fingers, a crowd stopping to look at him, look at me. No one attempted to follow us. In my pause, Destiny's shock had rooted her to the floor. I pushed against her, realising we had only seconds. I helped her to run towards the car. Her steps became easier once she saw it.

No one tried to stop us. I realised how it would look, a woman hitting a man and then taking the girl. Perhaps they thought I was Destiny's mother; perhaps they thought he was her father or boyfriend. Either way, I again had the advantage of trust. With a steady hand, I found my keys and used the remote to open the car. I opened the passenger door and helped Destiny in.

She was crying with the shock of being snatched. I heard her say through gasping breaths: *you saved me; you saved me; you saved me.* Her reaction reminded me of how young she was; how frightening this must all be to her. For some reason, I remembered Jordan taking the piss, saying I was like a Dalek. Well,

I might be, I thought, but sometimes ruthlessness and determination are what's needed to get the job done.

And I had got the job done.

I turned the key, knocked the gear into reverse and flattened my foot to the floor.

Forget Jordan.

Right now, the only thing that mattered was to get out of here fast – they would be after us, and now they wouldn't only want Destiny, I knew that now they would want me too.

Friday
19:22

Aleksander

The blood from my nose ran down my throat. It was all over my shirt. Ralph *fucking* Lauren. The rage of that ruined shirt alone would've been enough, but I knew that bitch had broken my nose. And she had taken Destiny. I had been so close – she had nearly been mine.

Rage and pain overwhelmed me as I whirled around. Everywhere people. Old people, young people, kids. All staring at me.

I couldn't believe that the teacher – that *woman* – had done this. I clamped my hand over the mess of my nose. Gary stared at me, slack-jawed. Dumb cunt. Even he thought I looked stupid.

I couldn't breathe. I saw a man hefting his way towards me. He was a normal guy, grey hair, longer on the sides, balding on top, boring, old. He walked towards me, sweaty, red-faced, staring at me with his brown puppy eyes. I expected him to stop, to ask me if I was all right.

Instead he grabbed my arm. 'Where were you taking Destiny?' he demanded.

Destiny? How did he know her? We were miles from anywhere where someone might know her.

'Who the fuck are you?' I yelled at him, shaking myself free, the pain in my face infecting my brain with hot, white anger. I could barely see.

'You are not taking her.'

He said it quietly. I could hear the bang of my heart in my ears. This man from the crowd, who was he? He was a nobody. I shook him free.

He grabbed my arm again. 'You are *not* taking her,' he repeated.

I could only stare at him for a long moment. I was amazed that such an old guy, so clearly unfit, would dare to challenge me. Me!

The blood from my nose pulsed through my fingers. I've broken my nose before, but it wasn't like this. That bitch had smashed it good and now she had gone. I could feel my heartbeat in my face and it hurt like hell. I took another step. I became fixated on the old guy in front of me – I didn't like the way he looked at me too closely – it was almost as if he saw the old me, the helpless me.

A woman in the crowd stared at me, her eyes suddenly rounding with understanding. She pulled on the man's shirt. She murmured something, perhaps, *come away*.

I felt the heavy gold of my father's ring and remembered the smell of back home: the smell of the forest that drifted in every morning, warmer now in the spring. My dad did the same; I grew up watching him turn the ring, once, twice, then the punch, always at my mother. I never saw my father raise his fist to anyone outside of the family. Perhaps he did; people always paid their bills on time. I grew up to be like Pavlov's dogs: he would turn the ring, once, twice, and then I would run to her in a childish attempt to protect her.

Until the chain. I don't know why I think of that now, but I do. It is my soft underbelly, my shame. It bothers me still: when the chain came out, I ran in the other direction. I hid in the yard, my face turned to the woods so the birdsong would cover the muffled screaming.

My fist clenched. 'I'm going to fucking kill you.' My rage flashed with supernova heat, burning it from white to ash.

Gary stepped forward, touched my right shoulder. I came back to the smell of the exhaust, heavier in the still of the summer evening. He said my name. It was the worst thing he could have done. I hated that he'd identified me there. I hated that. I swung a punch round at Gary. It was a slow, easy punch, weighted not from my shoulder, but from my fist. It landed with an easy plant; he reeled, even though it wasn't the real thing. It was the kind of punch you'd give a child – enough to hurt them, enough to get them to shut the fuck up, but not enough to do any real damage. His hands came up in defence. He took a step back out of the way. If Ollie and Jay were here, they'd haul me off, but they would be able to do that, Gary couldn't.

Then I looked at the fucker in front of me. Projected the pure beam of my hate at him. I liked the way he stepped in front of me, held his ground. He must know Destiny, I realised. He must've have been with them; perhaps he was another teacher. He said, 'She is only a child.'

'You motherfucker.' I spat at him, blood splattered against his grey shirt. Credit to the dude, he didn't even look down. 'You can't tell me what to do.'

He stepped sideways so that he blocked my path.

Somewhere, someone in the crowd, gasped. A woman with two young boys grabbed them firmly by the hands and led them away, the oldest one protesting, wanting to watch because he scented blood. A young man next to the old man, said to him quietly, 'Mate, come away – for your own good.'

The old man shook his head, never once taking his eyes off me. 'She's a child,' he said again, more to me than to the crowd. He knew it then, that it was too late for him, but he said it anyway.

I admired him.

Then I turned my father's ring, once, twice.

Friday
19:25

Aleksander

My first punch hit him in the eye. He reacted badly; he didn't think about defending himself, he only thought about the pain. Big mistake.

My knee connected with his balls. As he doubled over, I cut him with a left upper hook. *Bang.* I felt his nose shatter. *Good, you fucking scum, feel my pain, feel it with me, let's be in this together.* I gave him a right hook – that was the stinger, that was my full power. I hit him square in the ear and the impact was huge. He went down. Like his fall was a stone dropped in water, the crowds rippled away.

It was now us, us and us alone.

He lay on the ground. I kicked him with full force in the face. His face exploded; I'm sure he lost teeth somewhere in that blood. His head flew back. I went again, two fucking hard kicks to the stomach.

He was coughing into the ground. I smelt sick. I was going to fucking kill him; I felt it now, like a calm peace. I came down, both hands together, hitting his head against the paving slabs, but not full force, I wanted to make it last. He made a gurgling sound, his throat thick with blood.

'Boss,' Gary said, his voice low but clear.

I understood I didn't have much time.

I kicked the old man in the jaw. It was bad. He curled into a ball. I heard the cry of the crowd. This was me at my worst. I knew that I would keep going.

Perhaps he didn't deserve death. I didn't care. Most people don't deserve the shit they get, but they get it anyway. *Take it like a man*, that's how I grew up. I could smell the forest of home again, it was so close.

My father didn't take it like a man.

He cried when he knew I was going to kill him.

He only stopped when I did.

Crouching down, I hauled the old man up from the pavement. The crowd spilled into the car park, but I barely noticed them. He was bleeding heavily from his damaged mouth, his swollen ear, and a cut from under his eye. He was moaning and covering his face. I held him close; we were tied together in our pain. I could hear the laboured sound of his breathing. I held him steady. I was caught between the concrete of my present and the forests of my past. Underneath the constant hum of traffic on the motorway, somehow I could hear the *knock, knock* of a woodpecker. In my confusion, I even told him: *take it like a man*. It's always better to say it rather than hear it.

I dislike that I look like my father. I look in the mirror and I see him in me. But I am different. I wear his ring to remind me that I am different. I have never hit a woman. If I rage, it is only for business. He loved alcohol and I never drink it. He was the bottom of the pile, a pleb fixing tractors in his shed. I am richer now at twenty-nine than he ever was – than he could've ever dreamt he could be. I am like the rising phoenix tattooed on my back.

When a son kills his own father with his bare hands, he gives himself his freedom.

I am free.

Take it like a man, I told the old guy again. I held him by his shirt collar and then brought my head forward. My forehead connected with what was left of the bridge of his nose. His eyes rolled back, and he made a grunt, but it wasn't much. He had nearly rolled into the black. And I wanted this. I dropped him to the ground again and took a step back, regarding his crumpled body. *Go into the black, meet me there; I am waiting. We will be together.*

The crowds around us rippled, ebbing between fear of being too close, yet too shit-scared to stay away. 'Stop!' shouted one loudmouth. Another one glanced at his friend, feeling braver for his shout. 'Security are coming!' that one shouted. Then: 'And we've called the police!'

Bang, I punched that fucker in the face. Call the police on *that*. I saw his hands fly up in reaction, the other guy now hesitated – he was about to say something else, but his courage caught in his throat like a fish hook. I stepped up close to him and he stepped back, but couldn't even manage a full step because of the people behind him. I grabbed him by his Nike jumper, a full scruff, and because he was taller than me, I did a little jump to get the right angle, before bringing my forehead hard, down, against his nose too. Fuck you all. My nose was broken, now yours is too.

Both of them sunk away into the crowd. Cowards.

Somewhere, someone screamed again. For a moment I thought it was my mother, the high-edge panic, the shrill note catching in the same way hers used to.

I punched the man again. My father's ring cut his face.

I thought of the dog collar my father made my mother wear at the end. Thick brown leather that used to belong to Juno our wolfhound.

I thought of that last time. Coming home after two weeks away and finding her tethered by it to a pole in the yard. It was cold and the rain had turned her long hair to rats' tails. But worse was the beaten look in her eyes. Her lips were swollen and the dark under her eyes showed like the thinness in her face. Dried blood caked in the corner of her mouth and she had a cut under one eye. I was like my mother; I never gave up. But I saw then she had given up. It was nearly winter. I don't know how long she'd been there. Even when I stood before her, she didn't raise her face. Her eyes stayed looking in the dirt. I lifted her chin and still she looked at the dirt.

I untied her, led her to my pickup. I ran the engine, so the heater would warm her. My hands shook as I scrambled through the glove compartment, my holdall, looking for food and water. I left her under my winter jacket with a packet of peanuts I'd found in the foot well and a half empty bottle of water.

I let the porch door drop behind me. I knew where I would find him. He was in his favourite chair in front of the fire. I stood where I had stood all my life. Once I had looked up at this man mountain. Now I was looking down.

He had a can in his hand, his eyes were closed. I waited. I let the rage rush over me, redden my cheeks. The heat of the fire baked into my skin, reminding me of how cold it was outside. Did he bring her in at night? How long had she been there? It hurt me. The thought of my mother, baker, giver of cuddles, funny with the faces she could pull and her talent for mimicking voices, ground down into someone who couldn't even raise her gaze.

Perhaps at that thought, I sighed. Perhaps I hit the back of his chair. I don't know. I do remember that he suddenly knew I was there. It would've been a surprise. I no longer lived at home, and had already started to spend a lot of time out of the country. I was already shipping goods and travelling a lot. If I was close by I'd visit home – I was their only surviving child – to pay my respects to my father and to spend time with my mother as often as I could. But sometimes I would be away for a month. This time I'd cut my trip short; my father wouldn't have been expecting to see me. But I'd met a woman I wanted to marry and I wanted to see my mother to discuss it with her. Destiny was still only fourteen and I wanted to ask my mother what she thought I should do. So I had gone home.

My father looked up. We had the same narrow grey eyes. We had the same Slavic cheekbones. Like me, his shoulders were wide and his hands were big. He was a strong man. He was taller than my five foot ten, but his sleepy drunkenness was no match for my fury.

'Get up,' I told him.

He looked at me, steady, unblinking for a long time. His hand still held the beer can, his feet stayed on the footstool. He didn't move.

'Get up,' I repeated.

'What you want, Aleksander? Didn't you leave me for something better? Isn't Jakub a better father to you than me?'

'Get up.'

'You think my own brother is a better father to you than I was?'

I didn't know if he was genuinely hurting or if he was taunting me. I did know he was envious of his younger brother. Part of me wanted to twist the knife, to tell him that Jakub was a better worker, that Jakub had shown me ways to improve my own life; that through Jakub, I had met the woman of my dreams. Perhaps I did with my stare, because my father finally looked away. 'Forget it, I understand. Jakub has made you too good for us now.'

'Get up.'

His hand brushed me away like a horsefly. 'OK, I can see you are upset. Tell her to come in; tell your mother I forgive her, if that makes you feel better. Get yourself a beer and we can sit together and you can tell me how you've been making all your money with my brother. You can tell me how you have both become so rich.'

I tried to haul him up out of the dirty, old chair. The chair he sat in as I used to climb onto his lap when only a child.

He was heavy and he didn't want to move. We struggled, my hands around his dirty jumper, trying to pull on it. He sat like a boar determined not to go to slaughter. He held on to the chair arm with one hand, and kept pushing me back with the other. If he had stood, he could've held me away from him, but he stayed sitting, a stubborn pig in his chair. He didn't realise how strong his son had grown.

I could only think how much I hated him. The fear I had for him was incinerated by anger – he was no longer the big man. Now he was just the man who was killing my mother bit by bit each day.

He hadn't moved. I punched him in the shoulder. 'You understand now, pig?'

He stared at me with hatred in his eyes. He wouldn't get up.

I pulled at him again. Stepped back, frustrated. Then punched him in the other shoulder.

'Aleksander! Go back to your new life. This is not your fight.'

My mother *was* my fight. I punched him in the face. His head bounced back, hitting the back of the chair. When he opened his eyes, his grey eyes were first shocked, then narrowed. He'd been stunned; even through his booze-addled brain, the punch had shown him that his son was bigger now, had become a man. This surprised him because he'd barely noticed me all my life, and when I started going away on business he'd noticed me even less. He hated that I didn't want to learn his trade and be a mechanic, like him. When I was fifteen, we had terrible fights about it. Once or twice I had tried to point out that he hadn't learnt his own father's farming trade. He hated any kind of smarts and would dish out the punishment. But now everything was different – now *I* was in control.

The rage overpowered me. I reached for the fire poker and hit him across the face and head. I don't properly remember. I've heard men talk about the red mist, but it wasn't like that with me. I saw the disgust on his face when he looked at me and thought of the way he must have looked at her when he tied her up. There was no mist. There was nothing but seeing the poker, feeling the release of my anger, and then his collarbone was broken through his skin and he was crying but half conscious.

Whatever went on afterwards, I am not sure he would've come back from that even if I had driven him to the nearest hospital. Not that I would – I didn't want to save him, I only wanted him gone. So I hit him again.

When he finally slumped, I was able to drag him out of the house. He was a big man and normally it would've been hard, slow work. But my anger meant that I dragged him easily. I pulled him through the mud of our garden, careful only to check that my mother couldn't see.

He was bleeding and mumbling, but was nearly gone; I couldn't hear what he was saying through the blood bubbles – I didn't want to.

The stake was still driven in the ground and the chain and dog collar still attached.

I pulled him closer to the pole and attached the collar to his neck and then I kicked him in the face and I knew then that I wanted to destroy him and then it was easy because—

'Someone do *something*!'

I heard cars, but I wasn't thinking. I smelt exhaust, but I was still so, so angry.

I punched the old man again. I felt something give underneath my fist, more teeth perhaps or—

'Please!'

I had to kill him. If I didn't, he would've killed her. I had to save her. I held his neck and he looked up at me, still fogged with surprise. I hated him for what he did. I punched—

But this man was not my father.

I stopped, stood back, rolled the tension out of my shoulders.

Someone near me was screaming again. I couldn't see who it was, but I wanted it to stop. I looked around, wiping the sweat and the blood from my face. It was in my eyes, and stinging.

Gary pulled on my sleeve. I popped him one. He flinched in time and it only cuffed him on the side of his stupid face. It didn't stop him. 'Aleksander, we have to go – *you* have to go.'

I stopped and looked down. My own blood was down my face, my shirt.

The older man on the floor was not moving. People from the crowd had gathered around, but their faces were more turned to me than to him.

Gary was still saying my name.

'Shut the fuck up,' I told him, already thinking about witness reports. I glanced around, but couldn't see any police. The CCTV would've caught it all.

Instead, I placed my boot on the man's head.

Friday
19:33

George

I could feel the tread of his boot against my face.

I felt calm. My face was a mess of blood, of saliva. I lay waiting as the pressure increased. I thought of Sal, squeezing my hand in childbirth. Caitlin had been first; her delivery slow. Sal had gripped my fingers, telling me that the pain was killing her, telling me that I didn't understand.

I understood now.

But where her pain had been the beginning, I knew that mine was the end. That I would die here. But there was no panic, no anything.

I hurt, so bad, but even that had started to blur.

I think of Sal, smiling at me through the window of the house. I am in the garden. In one hand I hold secateurs, in the other, cut roses. I lift them up to show my beautiful wife what I have picked for her. Even from here, I can see the pleasure flush in her face. I drop the secateurs and raise my gloved hand to her, she raises hers in response. I don't understand if I'm greeting her or if I'm saying goodbye. It doesn't matter.

My beloved children.

I think of them aged eight and six. They are arguing over a bucket on the beach. I don't understand why this has come to me so vividly now, but it does: we are in Cornwall. The sun is strong, but not strong enough to make me sweat. I have a camera. I take photos of them, amused by their tussle, before it becomes so heated that I'm forced to intervene. I tell them they must share. Their mother is swimming, so I am free to produce a packet of jammy dodgers and Caitlin throws her arms around my neck, kissing me all over my face. *I love you, Daddy, I love you forever. You are the best daddy.* James is laughing, pretending to make sick noises. He grabs the bucket while I am distracted and throws it at her; it glances off her forehead and she starts to cry. But we are happy. We love Cornwall. We love each other.

The pressure on my face increased. I didn't mind. I had finally done the right thing.

I felt the tread of his boot.

I understood.

Friday
19:37

Aleksander

The man moved; he was still alive. I nearly pressed, nearly snapped his neck.

But I took my boot away.

He would live.

I ran, glancing back at the crowd behind me. A couple of them were pointing at me, while talking to a man wearing a grey polo shirt and grey trousers – staff from the services, perhaps.

I was close enough to see his face. He was looking at me as if considering challenging me. He wouldn't.

I ducked into some nearby shrubs. Gary had told me that he would get the car and meet me by the petrol station. The petrol station was ahead. I took off my shirt. Underneath was a black T-shirt. The blood didn't show. I nearly threw my shirt into the undergrowth but, fearing DNA profiling, balled it in my hand: I would burn it later.

Busting out the other side of the undergrowth, I'd meet Gary and then we would get on the road.

Then I'd get to Destiny and that teacher bitch.

When I found them, there would be more blood, I promised myself.

Friday
19:40

Aleksander

Gary didn't speak, waiting for me to say something. I flicked through the radio stations; I wanted to think about something other than the pounding in my face. I kept hearing that woman scream. I kept thinking about my mother.

I gave up and went back to Radio 1. I could see her in a few days; I'll be back in Poland then. I could make the journey, do that bit on my own. Maybe I should. I thought about the cash I could give her; I had seen her a month ago, but I worried about her not having enough, she is still so thin. I worried if she was happy. She wanted me to come home. I told her that I would, perhaps in a couple of years, perhaps a little longer. She wasn't yet fifty. I worried that she would never meet anyone else. I worried that she would.

We never talked about what happened with my father. After I killed him, I drove her to the next town and left her with her sister. Her sister screamed at the sight of her, she hadn't been allowed to see her in three months, she told me. She cried about how thin my mother had become, touching her injuries with a touch used for nervous horses. I left her there, drove back to the piece of land that had once been my grandfather's farm, prosperous then, but now overgrown and silent. The cold rain lashed, and I was glad for it. Our nearest neighbour was Maja Nowak, but she was an old lady now and a thirty-minute walk. She would never risk the wolves and be out at dusk; that and the rain would keep others away.

I dug a ditch in a dark patch of land on the north side and pulled and rolled my father's body to it and dropped him in with the water and the mud.

I stared at him, lying in the pooling rain water. And then I pissed on him.

He was scum. I am from scum and have become scum. But my children will be something else – I swore it then. I swore it over my father's dead body. I swore that the next generation I raised would be different.

I buried him, then forked the manure from our one pony over the top. He would rest under shit for the rest of his life.

My mother hasn't been back. I bought her a house in the same village as her sister.

I sold the horse. The house stands empty. It'll stand empty until I'm in my grave too.

'Boss?' Gary's voice drifted to me. 'You . . . OK?'

'Shut the fuck up.' I didn't want Gary to know that I felt unsettled, had remembered my father's death more than I had in a long time. For a moment, it felt like I was there again, punching him, feeling the release.

'We're still tracking Destiny?' I asked.

'Boss,' Gary nodded.

'Good. I'll be on CCTV now, won't I?

'We'll get you a hat, boss.' Pause. 'If you want that?'

I thought about it for a split second. 'It's a good idea.'

I listened to the thrum of the road. 'And the car, you've pulled the fake plate?' Although I already know the answer because Gary only pulled over a couple of minutes ago and I'd asked him then. 'I mean, without being seen?'

It wasn't just DNA profiling we lived in fear of, we also feared long-range CCTV. We were always planning against it.

'I put another one on. I thought we would ditch them both nearer Hull.'

Gary is pretty dumb, but everyone is guaranteed at least one good idea once a year. I nod in approval. It's the biggest bone I'm prepared to chuck him. 'So I should be pretty safe.'

'Safe as houses,' Gary agreed.

My thoughts turned back to Destiny. I watched her tracker on my phone. She was one mile up the road. I liked to see the black dot on the map. I watched it for a few minutes. Then, when I felt like it hadn't all fallen apart, I thought about tonight. 'Have you heard from Ollie and Jay?'

'I gave them a call when I was waiting for you. They're cool.'

'The van,' I realised is what he is talking about. 'It got through the MOT OK? No issues?'

'Jay had it done by his mate. He stayed in the garage the whole time.'

'They definitely didn't find the modifications? You're sure?'

'Sure. He said to tell you that he did exactly what you said – he didn't even take a wazz. He watched the guy like his life depended on it. He said to say it exactly like that. That's why I'm saying it exactly like that. I did good. I remembered it right.'

I still didn't feel reassured. One look at the modifications and we'd be rumbled. But I had to take Jay at his word. He's no fool and it was his face fronting it. But the van's in my name and it would be me doing time on it.

'And the passports?'

Gary's face flashed with panic. 'I dunno about no passports! You never said anything about no passports!'

I knew I hadn't, but I still felt irritated. The truth was, the passports were too important to leave to Gary. I had the passports in my bag, but I still felt a flash of irritation that he didn't know. With Destiny only a black dot on the map instead of her being right where I wanted her, I was irritated with Gary, though there was no reason why I should have been. I was tempted to smack him but he was driving.

Instead, I said nothing and watched the black dot on the map.

Friday
19:47

Jenni

Destiny was beside me, bent over and shaking. She was making a grating sound, a bit like she was clearing her throat; I might've thought she was crying but I wasn't sure. It was strange and I wasn't sure what I should do. At some point I was sure I heard her calling for her mum, but it couldn't be, because she had told me that she didn't miss her mum. And if she did, did she mean Kay or Simone? I was puzzled. When it had gone on a bit, I decided to pull over.

Her hair was loose and she was rocking, making noise still. I stared at her, unsure. Finally, I decided that I'd do what I'd seen people do in films or TV dramas – there was nothing from my life that I could draw on – and I touched her shoulder, lightly, professionally, and said, 'Destiny, I will never, *ever* let anyone hurt you.' I'd hoped my words would soothe her, even calm or bolster her, but it didn't and in the end, I decided that the best thing to do was to get as far away from that man as possible. Perhaps she simply needed to feel the distance between him and her.

The sat-nav said we were only a little over thirty minutes from our destination. I couldn't make up my mind whether to pull off the motorway and find some quieter back roads or stay where I was. This was the most direct route and it had the added advantage of lots of people and CCTV around in case he found us. Not that I wanted to be found, but I recognised that there might now be a point where being caught by the police would no longer be a concern – perhaps it would even be desirable. But the back roads might increase our safety – surely he'd be looking for us right now.

Destiny's crying was making it hard to think. I thought of the woman in the service station toilets – how did people with babies cope?

I wanted someone to tell me what to do. My entire career – except for the last two years – had been about being told what to do. In fact, success often depended on not thinking for oneself. Even teaching was highly structured. But this? I cut a glance at her. She was now rocking and crying and saying she wanted to get out. I imagined her running and running and ending up a homeless teenager; my imagination took me to ugly scenarios.

It wasn't supposed to be like this. This had all gone badly wrong. I considered calling the police. Maybe I had stuffed up. Yes, they were going to take her but perhaps the police should get involved. Perhaps, I should've trusted them; perhaps if I hadn't got involved, she would've been safer. I had imagined that this would be a simple drop-off. But then she had lied to me to get me to start this journey and starting this on a lie, had perhaps meant this was never going to work. I looked at her rocking and crying, begging to leave and run, to take her chances on foot, and didn't blame her for any of it. Not for asking me in the first place; not for lying to me about where she wanted to go; not for wanting to change her plan again and now run. It wasn't her fault that this man was after her, prepared to snatch her in broad daylight.

But not blaming her didn't mean I knew what to do now. Some people would, but that wasn't me.

I shouldn't have allowed myself to get involved with other people. I should've learnt my lesson. I let people down when it mattered. I didn't save them. I thought of Billy. Of the distance between us. Of his outstretched hand, reaching, reaching . . .

I thought of that same hand earlier twisting on my sleeve.

'You just check in, like this is a normal airport?' Billy asks me, holding his bags, flush rising again under his freckled cheeks.

Sure, I tell him. But this isn't a normal airport; this is Air Force Brize Norton.

But I know what he means: everyone sits around waiting to be called, and yes, we do have to check our bags, and then we'll leave, but at this airport there are only troops in fatigues. There's a couple more in front of us at the airport, then it will be us.

The queue shortens, then is gone. We step forward to the check-in desk. It seems to trigger Billy's nerves again and beyond the usual nail-biting and feet tapping, there's a nervous twitch he does with his mouth. He pulls it sometimes when he's under pressure and he's doing it again. He pulls his mouth down at the side, in a stroke-type grimace. It doesn't look good – it makes him look like he can't cope.

I've seen it before: lads who find it difficult to cope become weaker instead of stronger. Then the others pick up on it, smell the weakness, then they fear the weak. In another job, weaknesses in a team is not a problem. In the army it can kill you or those around you. Is it better that those who can't hack it, go?

Maybe.

'Stop pulling that face,' I tell him in a whisper. 'It's not going to help.' I was half-expecting him to ask *what face?* But he doesn't, so he knows he does it.

The woman behind the counter checks us in; her name badge says Corporal Louise Kingshott. She asks us each if we have packed our bags. Billy needs another prompt.

She raises an eyebrow. 'Please confirm that you have packed your bags.'

'Yes. Yes I have.' Face pull.

For the briefest of moments, Kingshott catches my eye. But she continues to type information into her computer. She asks Billy the usual questions about his bags, but when she asks if he has his body armour and helmet, he pauses again. 'Yes, Billy?' I prompt him. 'Yes,' he tells her. We are dismissed and the queue moves on.

We have to wait in departures. This is the thirteenth time I've been through Brize Norton. I've only flown out of Gatwick once. I'd never been on holiday with my dad and I guess he didn't fancy going to France or anywhere else he called fancy-pants, but then he didn't even take me to Butlin's. Not feeling like I'd missed out on anything, but wondering if I should do, I booked myself a trip to the Med when I was twenty-two. I never went again.

Now I'm going to Iraq. I look out of the window and see our plane on the runway. Freedom.

I glance over at Billy. He too is watching the plane.

Eventually we are called. We file out. We walk across the runway and then take the steps up to the plane. This is my favourite bit, when it's all still ahead of us.

Our feet are heavy on the metal. The tang of metal against boot reminds me: we are the best in the world.

We take our seats. I like who I become when I'm on tour: ordered, controlled, part of a unit. I miss it when I'm not with the lads; now I can't wait to be back with my section. They are the only people I need.

Everyone else is sitting in groups. Some chatting, some reading, some sitting. Phones are gone.

We sit in silence for a while, which works for me. That's the thing about growing up as an only child with a single taciturn parent: you get used to your own company. It's a good thing. You become more self-reliant and you're less needy of other people's approval. Billy's one of five. He's told me this like the details he's always sharing with me. He's the second oldest and he had to take care of his younger siblings. He's desperate to get married and have kids as soon as he can — he didn't tell me this bit, I've worked it out for myself. But it's understandable if you live in a noisy house, perhaps you can't wait to get out. When I was a kid, there were times when I sat in the silence of my house and knew even then that it was the only way I wanted to live. I've never met that someone special and I wonder if part of it is because the idea of living with someone else's noise and mess is the reason. Possibly. Although I've had no offers so it's difficult to say.

'Maddie begged me not to go.'

Billy has been sitting with his head in his hands, not saying anything. I've been happy with that because I like to look out of the huge windows at the airfield. I like to watch them fuel the planes; I find it relaxing to watch the ordered activity. But now he's looking at me and I can tell by his fixed look that he's panicked.

'When was that?'

'Last week. She told me that she'd had a dream that I was going to die.' A beat, then, 'Do you think I'm going to die? Yes but,' he adds, as if I've argued with him when really I haven't had a chance to say a word, 'the casualty rate is high, really high, isn't it? I mean, it's not good, is it?'

I'm not going to answer that. Instead, I steer him back to more positive thoughts. 'Tell me about Maddie's family.'

His eyes flash with happiness. He's easy to distract. 'She's got two sisters and they've both got babies. I'm already Uncle Billy. You should see my nieces – both girls. Maddie says we are going to break the run of girls in her family – she says she's counting on me for boys!'

'So, remind me again, when's the big day?'

He mouth pulls with nerves again and I know I've said the wrong thing. 'She said last week she can't marry a dead man.' He stares at the stretcher beds on one side of the airplane. 'She says it's her or the army.'

'You'll get home to her for the wedding – I promise.' I say as we click our seat belts into place.

Billy falls silent. He's still looking at the stretchers.

He stays quiet all the way to Iraq. The journey is uneventful but when the plane goes into blackout so we can land without being mortared, Billy's hand twists against my sleeve like he's a nervous child too afraid to voice his fears.

I blinked, surprised to be in the car. How much time had I lost? My stomach felt cold that I have been driving and yet so absent.

I don't know why, then, I reached out to Destiny. I think I thought I should try and be like most people. Or perhaps I needed to feel someone real, someone still alive. I tried to touch Destiny and she actually screamed.

I gave up. She went back to rocking and her strange grating sound saying: *they nearly got me, they nearly got me, they nearly got me.*

What *had* they done to her?

And then, I thought, checking the sat-nav and seeing we would be at our destination in twenty minutes, would she even be safe with her aunt?

But of course, it was too late to try and save her any other way.

Friday
20:20

Jenni

'You have reached your destination.'

I stopped the car. We had arrived in a long, wide street, lined with scruffy terraced houses. Cars were jammed nose to bumper on both sides of the road. Number 16 had a dirty green door and nets the colour of cigarette smoke covered the window. An old fridge had been dumped on the pavement.

I turned off the engine and looked at Destiny.

She had calmed down a little while ago, becoming silent. Since we'd driven into the neighbourhood Destiny had sat up, looking around. She'd pulled her bag on her lap and put her coat back on.

'I'm going to come in with you.'

'No.' She darted a look at me and I saw tears had tracked mascara trails down her cheeks.

'Destiny, I can't just leave you on a street corner, miles from your home.'

'That place was *not* my home.'

'OK, OK.' I unclicked my seat belt. 'I'm still coming with you. Let's go and meet your aunt.'

Destiny paused. 'You don't have to, Miss. You've done enough. Thank you for being kind.'

She blinked at me under her fine eyelashes and I realised that I'd been important to her in my own small way. She'd asked me for help and I'd given it to her. Perhaps that wasn't something that had happened enough for her in her life. I felt better. That gave me confidence: 'You're still a minor, Destiny, it wouldn't be right to leave you on a doorstep.'

I waited on the pavement for Destiny to get out. She looked pale; this was a big moment for her. Was it because she was simply exhausted or was it more than that? I hoped she hadn't overstated her aunt's enthusiasm for taking in a teenager. Perhaps as someone who'd been bounced around the care system, she understandably feared last-minute rejection. And if she was rejected? I'd have to call the local social services. I could hardly play mum myself.

She seemed reluctant to climb out of my car. I wondered if she was sorry to be leaving me; after all, she'd trusted me enough to tell me about her problems and had come to me instead of anyone else for help. I'd saved her twice from that man, a man she was so scared of that she'd been reduced to a shaking, hysterical mess.

As she slammed the car door, her shoulders were slumped and her hair hung over her face. If it went well, we'd never see each other again. I felt an unfamiliar sensation tug inside my chest – I wasn't sure what it was. I spoke quickly to cover up my confusion. 'Hey, Destiny, I'll give you my number and email – you'll let me know how you're going, won't you?'

She nodded slowly and came and stood next to me on the doorstep. We stood in front of the door, dirty with exhaust and cobwebs. The road was silent now; perhaps it was a cut-through during rush hour or perhaps it had never been cleaned in twenty years.

We looked at each other. 'This one, definitely?'

Destiny nodded.

'Want to knock?'

She shook her head. 'You do it, Miss.'

'Jenni,' I reminded her, then I knocked on the door.

Friday
20:23

Jenni

We stood on the pavement waiting for Destiny's aunt to come to the front door.

Nobody came.

I knocked again. 'Did you say her name was Kath?'

Destiny nodded.

We stood, neither of us saying anything until I knocked a third time. 'She's out, I think. Does she work?'

'I think so, in Tesco.'

I checked my watch; it might not be closed until late – maybe really late.

'Do you have her work number?'

Destiny shook her head.

Hull was a big place; it would have a lot of Tescos. 'Do you know where it is?'

She shrugged. 'No.'

Some people would judge me for not already considering the possibility of a missing aunt and thinking this through. But this was me: a doer not a planner.

As I tried to peer into the front room, failing to see anything because of the dirty glass and the nicotine nets, I regretted my lack of foresight. It was impossible to see into the front room, but I stayed peering under my cupped hand for longer than I should, hoping for any movement, because if there was, it would save me from floundering as to what I was going to do with Destiny. Because now I was stuck in a city I didn't know, with a child who was clearly vulnerable, one I shouldn't be with, with every possibility that at least one nasty thug, if not a gang of them, were after us. The options felt slight.

'Don't feel you have to stay, Miss. I used to live round here. There's loads of people I can bunk with until she comes back.' She paused. 'We've not really talked about it, but it'd be better for you if you weren't seen with me. So maybe . . .'

I sighed. 'Don't you understand that I couldn't possibly leave you? I'd never forgive myself.'

'Come on, Miss, you worry too much. Let me go and find some old mates.' She gave me a weak smile. 'I'm not a baby – next month I can legally live where I want.'

I smiled back. 'I'm not leaving you, Destiny. Now, come on, you must have a number for your aunt.'

Wordlessly, Destiny found her mobile. She turned away from me to make the call. After a moment, she dialled again. Again she turned away from me, and when she spoke into the answer machine, I could hear the held-back tears strain her voice. 'Hi, auntie Kath it's me, Destiny. Please call me back as soon as you get this. It's important – really important. Please. Thank you.'

When she turned back, I could see the threatened tears were now in her eyes. She looked at me, blinking. 'What are we going to do now, Miss?'

Friday
20:27

Jenni

After another peer through the dirty, netted window, I suggested booking two rooms in a Travelodge. I'm sure I sounded confident. Being in the army had taught me to be confident in action and being a teacher had taught me to be confident in voice. That confidence could and should be faked when necessary. Now was necessary.

As soon as I made my suggestion, I realised how someone like Destiny might hear it. She looked at me with big eyes. I felt a brush of apprehension: was she thinking I was a paedophile looking for the opportunity to prey upon her? Was she scared of being alone in a hotel with me because I was her teacher and neither of us thought it would come to this?

I checked my watch and knew that at this moment, in an alternative life where I never agreed to help Destiny, I should be jogging down John Street or, if I was making good time, even have made it as far as Edgeware Avenue. I shut my eyes against the overwhelming desire to be alone, to feel my feet pounding against the pavement, my Fitbit measuring my performance, listening to nothing but the sound of my ordered breathing.

But instead I was here. Stuck in a situation that constantly threatened to lurch further out of control. For me, in a world that was only about routine, discipline and control, it felt ungovernable.

But I made sure I sounded confident, for her sake.

I told her that I would book *two* bedrooms, and that 'we will get up early to have breakfast and we will try to find your aunt's Tesco, but I bet your aunt will have rung you back before then'. I had tried contacting the main Tesco, but had only got an answer-machine. I'd nearly left a message, but hesitated about whether I wanted to be so traceably involved. Of course I already was, and if the police went looking to make a case against me, there was plenty for them to find. I'd also found the numbers for two small convenience Tescos, but neither had heard of Kath.

I glanced at Destiny, whose face was, yet again, turned away from me, an island herself again. We watched more streets slide by on our way towards yet another destination.

Friday
20:45

Jenni

My heart sank when I saw how full the car park was at the Travelodge. It didn't bode well, but I didn't say that to Destiny. As difficult as two hotel bedrooms might have felt, the prospect of driving around looking for somewhere else to stay – or even worse, sleeping in the car – plunged this difficult situation into darker depths.

Once we found a space and parked, I realised the lack of suitcases might look suspicious. I grabbed the carrier bags containing Destiny's uniform and spare new clothes. 'You're my daughter, remember,' I said, feeling strange when she smiled back at me.

The Travelodge was a long red-brick building with a low hanging roof. Inside, I waited in line behind an elderly couple checking in, while Destiny sat on a chair in the far corner of reception. The couple asked endless questions and the receptionist, a woman in her late twenties with an oversized but very neat bun balanced improbably on top of her head, answered each one with a big smile.

Becoming increasing irritated, I toyed with the idea of coughing or tapping my watch, but abandoned it, knowing that it was better that I remained as unmemorable as possible.

Eventually, the couple left and I stepped up to the reception. 'Good evening,' said the receptionist. 'Are you checking in?'

'I haven't got a room booked, but I'm hoping you have two free.'

Her frown creased her smooth skin and I felt my anxiety deepen. 'Oh, I'll double check but I don't think we have, I'm sorry.' The pause as she checked her computer felt long and anxious. 'Oh, wait, what do you know? We've had a cancellation, so we do have one room available for tonight, a double, but with single beds. Would you like that?'

I glanced over at Destiny, sitting hunched over her phone yet again. I might've taken it personally if I wasn't so used to teenagers.

'You've got nothing else? One room isn't enough.'

'I'm sorry.' She glanced over at Destiny. 'Perhaps your daughter will understand?'

I gave her my card to distract her. The less she saw of Destiny, the better. 'My daughter,' I said trying the words again in my mouth, 'won't mind.'

The receptionist smiled, clicking on her computer. The fact I've been forced to use my bank card, feels like stepping over a line that I've been so careful to keep. But what choice do I have? She then handed me a form to complete and I filled it out, continuing the lie.

Destiny and I walked down the long corridor together. I still hadn't told her that I'd failed to get her a room of her own. I thought of newspaper headlines, screaming innuendo that wasn't true.

In one hand I held our pitiful carrier bags, in the other, the key cards. I'd had to ask for two, at first the receptionist tried to decline my request, saying they preferred minors not to have them as they should be with a parent at all times in the hotel. But I leant across the desk, and said: '*Please*. She'll be sixteen in two weeks.' We both looked at her, slumped in the chair, headphones in. We could see that she didn't want to be there, 'She needs a bit of . . . space, sometimes. But she's very responsible.'

The receptionist had given me a sympathetic smile and a second card.

I found room 29. I swiped a card through the receiver and a small green light appeared. I stepped in, not even daring to glance at Destiny.

Inside, wardrobes were to the right and on the left, was the bathroom. The space then opened up into what was a large room, with two neat single beds, a TV and two reading chairs.

Destiny squealed and rushed past me, before jumping onto the bed. 'This is great! I've never stayed in a hotel before.' She stretched out, knocking scatter cushions to the floor. 'It's lovely! So posh! Is this my room or your room?'

I turned to face her, feeling like a fraud. 'I'm sleeping in the car,' I said without thinking about it, instantly pleased with the resolution. 'They only had this room, but you'll be safe in here and I'll be comfortable in the car.'

She had re-plaited her hair into a long single braid that fell over one shoulder and now she twirled the end round her finger, her eyes narrowed, 'Really?' She watched me for a moment. 'You'd do that?'

'Of course. It wouldn't be . . . appropriate if I stayed in here with you. We'd both feel a bit uncomfortable. But you can stay in here and I'll nip out in a bit, and no one will know. All I ask is, if a staff member realises you're on your own, tell them we had a big row and that I am sleeping in the car. It would make it seem believable.'

'I could say that you'd gone crazy.'

Something about the way she looked at me with those big blue eyes and the silly tone of her voice, confused me. I had risked my job, my reputation and now I had suggested sleeping in my car while she had the hotel room that I'd paid for – without thanks.

Then the strange look was gone. Even if I hadn't imagined it, Destiny was still a child and one who had lived in challenging circumstances her whole life. If she wasn't straightforward or well mannered, well, it should surprise no one.

'I'm going to clean my teeth.' I remembered that I had no toothbrush but I went to the bathroom anyway, taking care to lock the door. I sat on the loo before I washed my hands and my face. I never wore make-up so there was none to remove, but the cold water made me feel better, so I scrubbed at my face with the body wash provided. I stared at myself in the mirror. I had dark shadows under my eyes – I looked tired. I *was* tired.

The last few years had been terrible. Leaving the army, then nothing for a long, long time, then a year of teacher training, then the first year into my job. You had to do it to understand how hard it was. Trying to get into teaching, because I needed the routine, the stability and because I liked the idea of working with kids more than adults. Then trying hard to like it. And not just coping with the present, but trying to accept my past.

Trying to accept what I didn't do.

As I stared at myself, I remembered Destiny's words: remembering felt like pressing on a splinter.

Was I crazy? Many would say I was after my behaviour today. But I wasn't – and I knew I wasn't.

I saw Billy's eyes again, wide and beseeching: *Help me. Save me, Jenni.* I stood there, staring at the need I saw there, in the eyes of my friend. Eighteen, but sometimes seeming younger. Rubbish at poker but the best singer I'd ever met. Sweet Billy. So kind. He provoked something in me, something almost like a real feeling. It wasn't romantic, I knew that, but something else, something important. I liked it as well – I liked what it was.

Protective. The word came to me. I felt the need to keep him safe. Me, who never felt anything really, but I had felt something for him.

There are two Land Rovers; four men in each, out on a simple detail.

One minute we're moving across the desert, the next we hear the *crack crack* of a sniper. Billy's vehicle is leading mine and it suddenly swerves. The land around us is near flat, but the Land Rover finds the only hillock, small really, but it hits it at such a speed and angle that it loses control, and rolls. I can see the driver, who is called Karl, but is nicknamed Frank for some reason long forgotten, lying clear of the vehicle, his neck angled like a baby bird's dropped from a nest, and I know Frank is dead.

'Get down! Get down! Ambush!' I shout. The bullets whistle past him. Some find the side of the Land Rover, making dull metallic thuds. We stop moving. 'Go! Go!'

No one answers.

Crack ... thump. Crack ... thump. There is not much time between the sounds; this means the sniper is close.

'Riddle?'

Crack, crack ... thump, thump.

'Riddle!' He is sitting in the driver's seat next to me. I angle my head, careful to keep it low. Riddle is gone. It would've been instant.

'Josh? Tom?'

No answer. I push my body forward so I'm hanging in the footwell, but it means that I can look back over my shoulder. They've both gone the same way as Riddle.

I reach for the radio and radio command. The signal's dodgy, but I request urgent back-up and I know they'll be here in ten minutes.

Billy. I need to get to him. I can't wait for back-up. I might not be able to save Riddle, Frank, Josh and Tom, but Billy and Dan and Alfie might still be alive.

I have to try.

The sniper is on my right, somewhere between my one and six o'clock, which works for me, as I'm on the left, up front next to poor old Riddle. I slowly open my door and drop down onto the dusty ground, the Land Rover giving me cover. I know this is a risk as they may see me in the gap under the vehicle, but I roll and land in the ditch to the side of the road.

I commando-crawl along the ditch, my breath short and sharp, like my movements.

In places there's very little between me and the road, but I am focused and I take my chances. I guess I'm right because all this time the sniper isn't shooting, so he can't see me. He's waiting for someone to break cover . . . and I don't intend on doing that.

I make it to the rolled Land Rover. There's a couple of metres of open ground between me and it. I'm able to raise my head a little above the rut I'm lying in, trying to get a sense of where the sniper might be holed up. There are scrub bushes on the other side of the road and behind them, there's what looks like a building for animals. It's about a hundred feet away and little more than a single-storey whitewashed mud shack, but it's got an arrow slit window. That's the mark.

Using the large wheels as cover, I enter the rolled vehicle at an angle, so the arrow slit window can't see me.

I find Dan first. He's moaning in pain but when he sees me, he calls out in a hushed voice. His face is blanched with agony.

'My legs are broken,' he whispers. 'I can't push myself out.' I grab him and pull. At first he doesn't give, but then he moves something around him and he almost – not quite because he's so heavy – pops out like a cork.

With a final yank, he's free and next to me in the ditch.

His legs aren't just broken but he's also got a flesh wound in the right thigh – it's bad, deep and has been bleeding out, but I grab the first-aid kit from under the seat and tourniquet the wound.

Next, I reach for Alfie who has been watching me silently – mute either from shock because of the bullet wound in his forearm or from fear of giving our position away to the sniper. He allows me to cut him free as his seat-belt release can't be reached. I guide him out and leave him to stem his bleeding. Our eyes lock for a moment: that's all the communication we need.

Next I try to get Billy. Billy's in the back, still belted in. Because the vehicle is on its left side and he's back right, he's suspended above me, the belt holding him in. He's got his hand clamped over his neck. Blood is seeping through his fingers: his hand is tight shut, but the blood is still leaking out.

At first I think it's an injury from the crash, but as I move up a little to get a better look, I see what I don't want to: his blood is all down his neck and shoulder. A bullet has nipped his neck.

I give him a grin and a wink. I want the back-up now, but I don't show him how bad I want it.

I quickly assess his situation. The animal hut is at five o'clock and Billy's hanging in front of the Land Rover window, giving the sniper a direct line of sight to his position. And the sniper's close. I can see from my crouched position that Billy's exposed. If he moves, he'll give away he's alive and then he's a sitting duck.

I rack my brains trying to figure it out. He's staring down at me, wide blue eyes locked on me. He needs me to rescue him and the way he's bleeding out, he's not got much time. I promised him he was getting home for his wedding.

Promised.

I stretch out my crouch, trying to get closer. My knife is out: if only I can get near enough to cut him free, he might fall before the sniper can get him. It means exposing my position while I cut him down, but I don't care, I'm already up and next to him, his face so close to mine I can feel his panting breath.

'Billy – look at me.' But he is, his eyes are nowhere but on me. 'I'm going to get you out.'

'Maddie said I would die.'

I start to cut. 'You'll make your wedding. And I want a place at the top table.'

'She told me. She dreamt it.'

Crack . . .

And the *thump* is into me. I feel it in my shoulder. It punches me down, and I struggle to breathe for a moment. Then I look up at Billy. He's staring at me with blue, blue eyes. 'She dreamt it.'

I need to stand to cut him down, but if I do I'll be shot again, for sure. I stare at the seat belt holding him. It's got a crease in it, where I started to cut . . .

. . . the *crease* . . .

I can't take it, I can't breathe, he's bleeding out, but all I can do is stare at that mark. I smell Lily of the Valley and I think of my mother and remember her – *stay put, flower, don't move* – and feel like it's already over, that I've already lost . . .

I'm pausing and I mustn't pause, I must stand up and cut . . .

. . . *the crease . . . stay put, flower . . .*

. . . cut Billy free.

But I haven't moved before the bullets come again; it is only seconds but our luck has timed out. We are looking at each other and it's instant. I see the light from his eyes go. It's as clear as if he is here—

—and then he is gone.

Switch flicked.

A bullet glances off my helmet cuffing me with *you took too many chances, dumb fuck.* Dazed, I fall further back, but still stare back up at him. His hand drops from his neck as instantly as if a puppet master has cut his strings and his fingers stretch down towards me, swinging slightly, as if trying to reach me. *You promised.*

I never take my eyes off his, even when the blood from his neck falls on my face.

Not even when the back-up comes and mortars the sniper, not even when they pull me free, because Billy's eyes are burnt in deep in my mind and his hand still reaches for me, still wanting me to keep my promise . . . but I didn't.

This was why I was mad with grief – but not crazy.

Not crazy.

'I am fine,' I told my image in the bathroom face. But when I didn't sound clear enough, I said it again: 'I am *fine*.'

I washed my face again before leaving the bathroom. Destiny was sitting on the bed fiddling with her phone. 'What are you doing?' I asked, attempting conversation.

'Candy Crush,' she said, without looking up.

'Night, then,' I said.

Then she looked up. 'Thanks, Miss. I know you wanted to save me. No one's ever tried to save me before.'

I smiled back. 'I promised, didn't I?' I said, before I pulled the door behind me and stepped out into the hallway.

I walked down the corridor and felt better. Saving Destiny had helped to fill the hole within me. No matter how difficult it had been or how difficult it would be, it had been the right decision.

I had saved her.

I had.

Friday
21:22

Destiny

As soon as Miss had shut the door, I counted to a hundred to be sure that the crazy cow had gone, before I messaged Aleksander – *Save me now.*

A message back: *Can you talk?*

Yes.

The phone rang. It was him. I cried with relief at the sound of his voice. He let me cry it out. I was surprised at how long it took.

'Are you sure you're OK?' he asked, finally.

When I still couldn't speak for the tears, he told me how he's going to rip her tongue out before making her suffocate on his shit.

'Don't hurt her!' He was as surprised as me that I said this. I had been plotting with him on Messenger, how I would help him hurt her. Towards the end of the journey, I felt like *I* was going crazy, not her.

But I changed my mind. She only wanted to help me, I knew that. I could see how much I meant to her in her face, when I cheeked her about being crazy.

But, I also realised, as nuts as she was, she really cared about me. I had thought that only Gary and Aleksander cared for me, so it surprised me and I found I wasn't now as pissed off as I had been. Besides, she had driven me home to Hull. She had tried hard – she was a nice teacher. Crazy but nice.

'I'll come and get you,' he told me.

'I'll leave the hotel and come and stand by the front door. She's in her car but the car park is at the back.'

He paused. 'You've got a room?'

I heard the change in his voice; I knew that change. 'I want to get out of here, Aleksander.'

'But you have a room?'

I sighed. I knew he would continue until I said yes. I looked around the room. It had bold Rothko rip-offs on the walls, the blues matching the cushions and the piece of material on the bed that I didn't know the name of, but looked nice. Aleksander would like this room. 'Meet me out the front.'

'But you have a room!'

I said nothing. I was thinking about Miss who paid for it. She got it for me because she thought I needed protecting from Aleksander. She was wrong – he's the best thing that has ever happened to me. I knew he loved me. Together, we're getting rich. But although I loved him, I didn't want him in here. Besides, she might come back.

'What room number are you?'

I told him, then added, 'You won't get in. You need a card.'

'Tell me what you can see from your window.'

I went to the window. 'I can see a road and in the distance there is a roundabout and a B&Q sign and a sofa shop.'

'Are you on the ground floor or the one above?'

'Second floor.'

'Then I will stand beneath your window and you will drop your door card down to me.'

'I will be Juliet.'

'You what?'

'Like in *Romeo and Juliet*. You'll be Romeo under my window. What light through yonder window breaks?'

'I'll break you if you don't quit being so soft. You will be Destiny. And I will be five minutes.'

He was outside my window in just under ten. It was black outside and since he was wearing dark jeans and had his black leather jacket over a black hoodie, he was almost invisible. But then he tilted his face up towards me and I saw the pale round of his face against the night: he was everything I wanted. He would guide me through the dark.

I dropped my card down to him.

I waited for him on the bed.

Friday
21:37

Destiny

The door clicked: Aleksander was in. He shut the door and leant against it. I wasn't sure if he was keeping me in or other people out.

I looked at his face but didn't say anything. Most people would – he was a mess. But I knew better. His nose was at a strange angle and looked swollen. There was bruising across his face. She must've hit him hard.

As much as I loved Aleksander, I felt even less pissed off with Miss for taking me when she showed she cared enough to hit someone for me. I remember how she'd grabbed my hand and dragged me away. How I didn't dare yell out for anyone to help me, first because I was too surprised, then because I thought someone might've called the filth and I would've ended up back at that children's prison that I had to tolerate even though I've never done anything wrong. Anywhere – even being alone with a teacher who's living in a parallel universe – was better than there. In the end, I could see it was just a lift back home – with a crazy lady – but a lift home anyways.

I stood up and picked up my bags, trying to make my point, even though I knew it was useless. 'I want to get out of here.'

His voice was low, and his smile had that twist, like men do when they want to have sex. 'What, and waste this room?'

'Please, Aleksander.'

But he was already next to me, his hands in my hair, tugging my plait loose. He rubbed his hands over my tits, too hard. 'I have missed you, Candydoll.' He pushed me against the wall. Destiny, I nearly told him. *Call me by my name*, but if I was near to asking, I was silenced as he kissed me. For a moment I felt surprised, as if I had forgotten his thick lips, the feel of his tongue.

He must have sensed this, because he broke away. 'What is the matter?' He pushed my hair from my face. 'Have you not missed me?'

'I don't want her to come in. Something might happen.'

'The only thing that is going to happen, is this,' he said, and took my hand and pressed it against his hard dick. I wanted to take it away, but it would annoy him.

He pulled at my clothes and I was soon naked. He hadn't even taken his coat off. He forced two fingers inside of me. 'What's the matter with you?' he said, as he pulled them out so quick it made me gasp. He spat on his fingers and pushed them back harder.

'What if she comes in?' I whispered.

He pulled his gun out from his waistband. Then he passed me a condom as he gave me a wink I didn't like. He held his gun with one hand and pointed it at the door, as I put the condom on, and then he took his dick in the other and pushed it inside me.

He held on to his gun the whole time.

It did not stay pointed at the door.

Friday
22:01

Destiny

I let go of Aleksander's hand as we walked past the reception desk. The receptionist did a double take and I knew I was rumbled. I didn't want her to call the room to speak to who she thought was my mum, because of course, she'd get no one and that would be worse. Instead, I headed directly to the desk. 'Excuse me, is there a 24-hour pharmacist near here please?'

She gave me directions, which I made a point of asking her to write down, like I really needed them. 'My mum has a really bad headache. She gets migraines sometimes, and the noise and lights cause her a lot of pain.'

She nodded and I could tell from her face that she believed me. Then she glanced at Aleksander and noticed his nose – it was like a neon flashing sign saying: *I'm trouble – want some?*

I spoke fast. 'My cousin is going to drive me – which is pretty brave considering he's just been in a car accident.' This time, her expression didn't shift, but I took the directions and left. In my experience, if you give people enough to doubt themselves, they won't do whatever it is that they think they should do. Most people don't like to swim against the tide. As I left, I knew she wouldn't make that call to the room for the fear of disturbing my 'mother' with her migraine. She'd think about it, not liking the look of Aleksander, or that I've left with him, and she might even go to pick up the phone, doubting that he is my cousin, maybe doubting his injury is a result of a car accident. Her hand may even hover as she thinks about it, but the doubt I've created will make her hand drop away and she'll tell herself that it would be better not to disturb an ill woman because her daughter has got her cousin to give her a lift to the pharmacist to buy medicine, and maybe he's a decent man despite the scowls, the stocky heavily muscled body and the tattoos on his neck – maybe he's put himself out to get in a car to drive his cousin. Maybe it would be wrong to be judgemental.

I had to be careful that my smile didn't turn into a smirk. But then we were away and my hand was back in Aleksander's. It was late and in the cold of the night, his hand felt warm and strong. Finally I was safe.

He led me to the car park. The van wasn't there, but his gorgeous Mercedes was. Gary sat in the front and his darling face broke into a grin. 'Destiny!' he held up his palm and I high-fived him.

I worried about Gary. He was even more challenged than Jamie Drew in my English class and that is saying something. Jamie has to have a TA in every lesson. I only had English with him, as they mixed us up and didn't set us for English. Even with his TA, he complained all the time that he didn't understand anything. Once we studied *Macbeth* and a whole term later, after doing weeks and weeks of contemporary poetry, the teacher asked him who he thought the speaker was in one of the poems. He said, 'Macbeth?' Everyone laughed at him for not realising we had finished *Macbeth* two months previously, with the obvious clue that we hadn't taken out our *Macbeth* texts in all that time, but I didn't laugh. Instead I though of Gary and how things are for him, and then I thought how hard Jamie's life is going to be, and I felt sad for him.

I got in the back of the car with Aleksander; he was happy and kept his hand on my leg.

'You're not going to hurt my teacher?' I asked suddenly, aware that she was asleep in her car around the back of the hotel. Aleksander wouldn't just hurt her for screwing up his face – it would be bad. No matter how she had terrified me, she'd done it for me.

'I am going to fuck her up,' he replied, 'but not tonight. We've got work to do.' He kissed my forehead. 'And for that, I need you, my queen.'

Friday
22:15

Destiny

It was good to be back in the town I had been in only last weekend. Gary drove us through familiar streets towards what we all called 'the office'. I felt a small burn of glee – this time I wouldn't be going back to the children's home on Monday. Every weekend I got away, I'd have to face more meetings on my return – more telling offs, more threatening me with a secure unit. Before I felt that they wouldn't do it, because I put my head down at school and stopped giving the care staff grief. But after coming back with my black eye last weekend, I really think they might now.

Well, they wouldn't get the chance. Now I wouldn't go back. *Fuck them, they couldn't hold me.*

I'd stay with Aleksander.

Aleksander was building us a life. He was right: people like us never did well in the straight world – who would give us decent jobs? But we didn't need their crap jobs, not when he was making a fortune for us. He even put money in a bank account for me, just for me, my own account. He said he believed in feminism and that meant I had to have my own money. He'd done proper finance research, both of us going through what our banking options were. That's what I loved about Aleksander, I thought as I squeezed his hand in the back of the car, Aleksander did proper research on everything. He'd found me a high-interest account, although he was careful to explain that there were no real high-interest accounts any more. He reckoned it was because no one had any savings to put into bank accounts. Well, the legits anyway. Those people like my teachers, who did their degrees, worked hard, and earned shit all. I'm going to do my degree – maybe even a doctorate – but only because I can, not because I want to get a poxy normal job. I don't need that kind of job, not when my bank account is growing. I already have twelve thousand pounds. I've never met a kid my age who has twelve thousand pounds. I reckon those ones on *Made In Chelsea* will have had real money at my age and I know that when I'm older, I will be like them – driving a Porsche and wearing designer clothes and taking holidays in the sun, even in winter.

Especially in winter.

Aleksander said that if we keep growing the business like we are, by the time I am eighteen, I'll have a hundred kay. I'd be able to buy my own flat by the time I'm twenty-one. He said I'd need at least a million to buy one of those flashy places in London, so I'm going to wait until I have a million. I want to live in Canary Wharf and write about my life so people know what it's like to be a kid in care. I'm going to tell everyone about all the shit things that have happened to me. I'm going to blow the whole secret system wide open. I'm going to lobby the government so all those people who are cruel to children get proper justice: *real* justice.

Then I'm going to adopt three kids. Maybe more. And at Christmas, I'm going to shower them with gifts. It won't be for them, like it is for me. No one but the state to buy me a present; just a job on an employee's list of jobs, bought because there's a council budget for it that seems to get smaller every year – I'm going to buy my children gifts with lots of money and give them lots of love. But first I'm going to get my own home.

I dream of it.

I work for it.

I do what I have to, like everyone else. But I refuse to stay down like people expect. No one has expectations for me, but *I* have expectations for me and if that means that I have to be tough like Aleksander, I'll be tough. I *am* tough. I have been tough and I will continue to do things that might be . . . not very nice, but I will do whatever it takes.

Aleksander doesn't laugh at me for any of it. He helps me. When he found out that I liked buying interior decorating magazines, he got me a subscription for them. When the first one came in the post it felt amazing, as I had never had anything addressed to me in the post before, but the staff ruined even that. They nicked it first and read it with their coffee; they didn't mean to be cunty but they creased the pages, so the pictures were no longer any good for cutting out.

I like to make what are called 'mood boards', putting ideas together for what works well. Like a stone feature wall from one picture and a polished concrete wall from another. Then adding side lamps and cutting out pictures of sofas that I think will go. Turquoise; acid yellow; ink black. Or aqua and rose pink and washed-out silks. The other kids in the home proper take the piss out of me for it, but they don't know I am going to have an amazing place. Aleksander loves my creativity and showed me Pinterest. He says I'm going to be an amazing designer when I'm older. Now, every month he hands me all the architecture and garden design magazines so I can keep them nice. He even bought me a proper file to store them in. 'You're amazing, Destiny,' he told me and he looks at all my work. No one else encourages me. Maybe some of the teachers at school. But Aleksander loves me too.

He will marry me, he says when I'm a proper adult, which he says is twenty-one. He says he won't marry me before, because although he says I'm a real woman in body and attitude, he says I need to be a real woman in spirit too. And that's why social services are wrong about him. They might look at his charge sheet, they might tell me that he's a violent crim with a history of robbery and assault, but they don't know him like I do. We are the same. And he's the only person that's ever treated me like my opinion counts.

That means a lot.

That means everything.

I leant across to give him a long slow kiss like I knew he liked. I am his queen. And together we will change our world.

Friday
22:22

Destiny

We arrived at our latest squat. We found it last month, Jay changed the lock and then made sure we weren't here too much so none of the neighbours noticed. Aleksander found his key and opened the dirty green door.

'I was here only a couple of hours ago,' I said, as I looked up, almost expecting to see Miss drive up the road. 'I came here with her. She even tried to look in the window. But no one was here.'

'Of course not, we were behind you. Why did you come here with her?'

'I didn't know where else to go. She wanted an actual address – where else could I give her? Besides, I knew I wanted to get here and I knew if you were in, you'd have sorted her.' I shrugged. 'If you weren't here, I was hoping she was going to let me go.'

We stepped inside the hallway. The outside of the house was scruffy, but it's a squat and it wasn't the worst I'd ever seen. We never tarted them up from the outside because we don't want the neighbours to know that the house has become occupied. We keep them only for one party, two at most, and then let them go and nobody, except those who come to the parties, are ever the wiser that we had been there.

We line them up in advance, always working two jobs ahead of time. We've got one in Grimsby that we've not done up yet and we've got another in Scarborough that's ready to go next weekend.

Inside, the house was a bit better. We were here last month and rollered the walls cream. It was a rough job, trim rollered over too, nothing fancy – nothing modern, nothing like I would choose for myself. Just enough to make it decent enough to make drunk people want to stay. I'd added pictures, cushions and sofas I'd bought in a charity shop. It was all for less than a ton. We always do the same: the week before the party we scout round and find some bits and take the time to put them in the place. We always leave it all behind.

We found that when we didn't tart places up, people didn't stay. Yes, some scumbags will party anywhere, but they tended to be the hardened druggies and they weren't our target audience. Our more tender young things needed a place they could feel comfortable, a place they could relax. They needed a sofa they could sit on and a fresh wall and a picture to feel safe. They needed the bullshit. Sure, it takes a weekend to slap on a bit of paint and to put a nail in a wall, but it could be kinda fun, and of course, the rewards made it well worth the effort.

But this one, I noticed, still stank of dog urine – I hoped nothing worse – so I made a mental note to buy some incense for next time. In fact, I decided I'd always buy it in future, as incense would be a good addition at any party as it would make people feel chilled, like they're around good hippy folk. People who buy organic rye bread and fruit in paper bags.

I pulled out the first-aid stuff I'd bought and tidied Aleksander's nose. It looked nasty. I cleaned it and dressed it, and Aleksander agreed that tomorrow, after our work was done, he'd go to a hospital.

But it would have to wait: tonight was party night. Tonight our hard work would pay off.

'We *are* still going ahead, aren't we?' I asked Aleksander, suddenly unsure. I checked my watch. It was late and we should've, if I hadn't been taken by Miss, started about an hour ago.

We went through to the kitchen. Gary had cleaned it before we left last week, but there was no food in the cupboards because we only ever ate take-out. I opened the fridge and pulled a face. 'There's no wine.'

'Don't whine.'

Aleksander loved homophones. 'Well done,' I told him, always keen to help him improve, although his English was already perfect. I knew it was important to him to be better.

He went to a cupboard under the stairs and brought out a stack of four huge boxes of wine and put the two white in the fridge. 'See? We are ready. That bitch is *not* stopping tonight. Ollie and Jay are already in the pubs, putting the word out.'

Jay's the best at that. He's good-looking and he always gets loads of girls. Ollie does all right as well because he makes the most out of his posh accent and that seems to get people to want to come to his parties. Jay and Ollie showed me a picture of their parents' house – it's amazing. I once asked them why they don't use their private school educations and get jobs in the city. Jay laughed and said that they were too lazy. They knew Aleksander because he used to hit them up; then they wanted to deal themselves, coke and weed to their posh friends, so Aleksander supplied them. Then Aleksander's uncle wanted to bring him in on the big game and we needed more help and so now we're a gang. It's been working OK-ish. Ollie doesn't like me, because I'm cleverer than him and I suspect he's a raving misogynist, but I don't care because I hate him more, so we stay away from each other. When I complained to Aleksander about him, he said that Ollie's coldness was his strength. I think it's his only one.

'I reckon by midnight, we'll be started,' said Aleksander. He touched his nose and tried not to wince. Aleksander was very brave; it looked terrible, even worse than an hour ago. I wondered how I could encourage him to let me put some make-up on it – the last thing we needed was him scaring a rabbit.

Destiny

I changed my mind and wanted beer, so Gary was sent off to find a late-night offy. When he came back, he passed the bottles and the change back to Aleksander, and Aleksander checked the receipt against the coins – Gary's not allowed money and Aleksander is always paranoid that he's siphoning off coins here, there and everywhere, trying to build up an escape fund.

Aleksander gives me a beer before rolling himself a joint. As he burns the gear, Gary looks at the beers with that expectant wide-eyed look like a dog that can see a bone on the kitchen counter, but isn't allowed it; I could almost hear him salivating, so ignoring Aleksander's dark look, I took one and passed it to him.

'Thanks, Destiny,' he said, his voice pitiful with gratitude.

Aleksander glared at Gary but he didn't say anything. He never liked me being kind to Gary, but I'd always have the row later for Gary: Gary was my friend. Gary gave me a little smile – it's a secret one and a big risk for him to give it, but I loved it, it was cheeky and just for me. I smiled back only with my eyes. I didn't want to make his life any harder than it was.

Gary's sweet and pure and he never wanted anything from me and I'd never had anyone else be like that in my entire life. Most people could never understand the power of that – most people have people love them with no expectation and have had that from the moment they were born. I know I will never meet my dad because my mum doesn't know who he was. I've never had grandparents. I never had a brother or sister. No aunt, no cousin, no nothing— that's a double negative: I wish I could double negative family into a positive, into existence.

Even my beloved foster family still needed me to be my best self and all the time I was with them, the self-control I needed to stay perfect was like holding my breath. *When you come from shit, you are shit.* I remember my mother screaming that at me when I was about four. I remember squeezing my eyes tight, my arms around myself, while her alcohol breath flecked spittle on my face, the smacks on my head, my shoulders, my arms, landing to punctuate every word and thinking, *no, no, no, I'm not like you.*

But she was right. I am.

But Gary doesn't criticise and he doesn't want anything from me. He will risk a severe beating to give me a smile of thanks. And for that I don't need to do anything in return. I don't have to be sexy for Gary, I don't need to be smart or sweet, I don't need to be anything. And for that, I wouldn't just give him a beer, I'd give him anything.

Aleksander was looking at his phone, perhaps choosing to ignore our exchange.

'It's out on Facebook and we seem to have got a few possibles. We need to do it tonight because the connection won't like a delay. He's been chasing me for the last hour, and I've been putting him off.' Aleksander checked his watch, a huge gold Rolex.

It's fair that he's got that because it's his contacts we're using, and he'd been in this sort of game for a while before he met me – but just a bit of dealing and touting the homeless. He'd take their beggings and give them protection in return. But he didn't do haulage, as I like to call it, that was my idea – and it started with a homeless woman. I saw her when making Aleksander's round with him; she'd come in from some other country and she slept on dirty cardboard and her life was shit, and I thought it was a shame she couldn't try again somewhere else, and then a little light went off in my head: *bing!* Aleksander made some enquiries back in Poland and found someone who'd pay amazing cash to take females and move them on and that's how it started.

We watched the Facebook account.

And we waited.

Friday
22:50

Destiny

We drank the beer and Aleksander smoked while we waited. People wouldn't leave the pub until nearer midnight, so we had time to kill between now and then.

The waiting was hard. I couldn't drink too much because I needed to be top of my game. But nerves made me want to drink – I always worried I couldn't become the person I needed to be for the business.

Sometimes becoming the person I needed to be was hard. Sometimes it came easy – then I might just punch them because I could. When I could be like that, it actually made me feel better – it made me feel that my mum was right. She used to tell me that I had the word *bitch* running through me like *Brighton* ran through a stick of rock. When I was really young, I used to look at my body and think it was real, that I really did have the word *bitch* inside of me. I imagined it as long, black letters stretching up each finger, up each arm and all the way down through my body to my toes. I remember the tears on her face when I cut my finger look-ing for it – at first I thought she was crying. I remember holding up my bleeding finger, the blood running down it scaring me, and her shoulders were heaving. But I realised she was howling with laughter, complaining her sides were going to split, before telling me, 'It's not *really* there, you bloody doughnut.'

Doughnut. Stick of rock.

Bitch. Cunt.

But sometimes I'm not the bitch she said I was. Sometimes I feel like candyfloss. Then I don't want to do it. I only said that once and Aleksander put me right. 'Remember why we are doing this,' he told me. 'I can't do it without you.'

And he can't, because girls feel safe with other girls. They trust us because they only deal with me.

I allowed myself to down my first beer, then had a second straight away. Now I was safe, among friends, my hands began to shake. The last few hours had been shit and I allowed myself to realise exactly how scared I had been at times.

It had been so weird seeing Miss like that – convinced I'd asked her for help, when I hadn't. At first, when she grabbed me and kept going on and on about my 'aunt', I thought she was on drugs or had confused me for someone else. I tried telling her: *I don't have an aunt*, but she ignored me like I hadn't even spoken.

Once when I was ten, I had tried to kill myself and I spent a week in a psychiatric ward for teenagers. It stopped me from ever trying to kill myself again. If I do decide to do it in the future, I'll just jump off the tallest cliff I can find and then I'll be so smashed up there'll be no saving me, no locking me in a place like that ever again.

When I was on the ward, there was a girl of about seventeen who used to hear people talking to her, telling her to do bad things. Proper mental, the same as Miss. Miss thought I'd told her to help me, but I never. The only good bit was when I decided to play along and told her to take me to Hull. Aleksander says that's a sign of being clever, getting what you can out of a situation. I saw a sign once in a shop: if you have lemons, make lemonade, or something equally shit, but if you've had a life like mine, you don't make lemonade, but you do learn to adapt.

You learn to survive.

Maybe some people would say I used her and that I wasn't really scared. Sometimes I wasn't; sometimes it felt like she was normal. And then sometimes she would not be there, even though she was there, and sometimes she would talk about conversations we had but we never had them. Then I would get scared. But mostly I'm good round nutters, I've been round nutters all my life. Most nutters have never even see the inside of a psychiatric ward. Most nutters walk the streets or sit on sofas with a needle in their arm.

As I lifted the bottle to my mouth, Aleksander, who never missed anything, saw the tremor in my hand. 'Why are you shaking?'

'Because I've just been abducted,' I snapped, pissed off that he'd caught me being nervous. I liked to show him my stronger side. Last week I had shown him how strong I could be. I think we were both surprised. Even when the rabbit fought back, even when I got a black eye, I didn't stop.

'Dee, you were always safe. I used that app to track your phone – you never go anywhere without me knowing about it. I know where you are all the time – you know that.'

I smiled, but felt a prickle of discomfort. I knew he was tracking me, of course I did, he'd been doing it for over a year. The app had saved me, but it occurred to me then, that being taken and being followed may not be so different.

'You understand, Destiny, that we couldn't grab you just because you wanted us to? We could hardly drive her off the road without risking your life or getting the filth involved.' He paused. 'Maybe you shouldn't have told her that you needed to go to your aunt's.'

I felt peeved – how could he criticise me after what I'd been through? Hadn't I explained all this, back at the hotel? 'I think I played it pretty cool.'

'Girl,' he said, his voice cold, 'you were *not* cool.'

I remembered the panicked messages I sent him and I cast my face downwards. I felt ashamed – I'd behaved like a baby. Although Miss was crazy, I should've known that she would never hurt me. She was simply confused. I just didn't know it before, because I couldn't tell when she was teaching. I already know there is often a big difference between how people seem and how they really are. Behind closed doors people change. Some little kids are scared of monsters – but I never was. I learnt early on that real monsters look like normal people, act, talk, even laugh like them, but there's a big difference to what they're really like deep down. Most people are rotten inside. They just pretend not to be.

I let myself think about it for a bit and reminded myself that this wasn't the worst thing that'd happened to me. Yes, at times I had been really scared when Miss was rambling about some bollocks and I knew then that she was living in a different world, but I still, when it came to it, knew she wasn't going to hurt me. No matter what, I trusted her. I had got out of her car and it had ultimately not been any more than a lift back to Hull. It wasn't the worst thing that had happened to me.

Then I started to think about the worst things that had happened to me.

It had only been a few minutes, but it was enough. I packed up my thoughts like putting things in a suitcase like someone once, I don't know who, had taught me to do. Maybe I had taught myself that, I don't know. I take hold of each memory and call it something like jumper; socks; shoes. I say it, this man, what he did to me is *shoes*. I think what type of shoes then. *That man, that time, he is trainers with pink laces.* I focus on the details of the pink laces, I imagine my thumb running along their rough texture, I rub the plastic ends between my thumb and forefinger. Then I imagine picking up the trainers and putting them in a suitcase. Then I take the next memory, and the next, and pack them all away. Sometimes it can take a couple of hours. Sometimes I can do it in ten minutes. When I'm at my worst, it can take all night. But no matter how long it takes, I always get to the point of when I can pull shut the lid. I then zip it up. Then I tie chains around it and drop it into the ocean. Many a time, I've put some horrible experience into that case, zipped it up, put the iron padlock on, wrapped it in chains that are as thick as my arm, and pushed it off the side of the boat, so it drops deep into the deepest part of the ocean, so dark that there's no light down there, only the occasional fish that is so scary-looking, no one's going to open my Pandora's box.

Then I go and do something else. I don't, won't – *can't* – think about what has happened to me.

Because I was going to the dentist, because I don't like ... interference with my mouth, I had spent ages packing the night before. That's why I had overslept. That's why I had been late and pissy by the time I got to school. That's why I had been cranky and looking for an argument in tutor time.

That's why I took Aleksander's call.

It was only later, much later, that I realised that Miss thought I'd wet myself. I'd seen her take other staff to one side about me, but at the time, all I could think about was getting to Aleksander. I wasn't expecting him until later. But him being outside my school meant that he wanted to leave for Hull early. And leaving for Hull early meant that I wouldn't be going to the dentist.

I hadn't wet myself. Miss had sat heavily on the table and knocked over her water bottle. She jumped back up and hadn't seen that she'd simply knocked her lidless bottle over. Then she'd left the room and I'd tidied up. There was nothing more on me than a few splashes. I never realised until she'd said that she had thought I'd wet myself.

I got up, grabbed a third beer and found my make-up case. Tonight was work. I had bruises to cover and so did Aleksander. I looked closely at his face. 'I'm not sure I can cover all this.' His nose was swollen and still plugged with bog roll. Both eyes were also swollen.

He took my mirror, turned his head so he could seen the damage from different angles. 'I can't work tonight.' He looked at me. 'Can you do it without me? With only Ollie and Jay?'

Gary never does the work. He always stays out of the way until later. 'Yes, sure. I'll work the front of house and Jay and Ollie can do the usual.'

'OK,' said Aleksander, still looking at his face. 'I'll stay in the basement with Gary.'

I had to get ready. The bruise under my eye would have to go – it made me look dangerous or damaged when I needed to look fun – normal.

I finished my make-up and felt pleased – my bruise was covered, the bruise that had started all of this. How ironic Miss looked at my bruised eye and assumed *I* was the victim.

I felt a jab of self-doubt: perhaps all this was my fault. If I hadn't have been involved in all of this, then the rabbit wouldn't have punched me. If I hadn't got up late, I would've had time to cover the bruise with concealer. If I hadn't taken the phone call from Aleksander in front of Miss, she wouldn't have known about him; I could've just nipped off to the loos before my lesson started. I didn't have to balls it out in front of her.

I checked my make-up again. I checked my phone. There were likes on Facebook and Jay had messaged me to say they were bringing back some girls they'd found in a bar. 'We're on,' I told them.

Gary gave an excited chuckle and clapped his hands. Aleksander nodded as if he never doubted it. 'If I had grabbed you,' he said, as he leant against the counter, 'then it could've got nasty and public. Much better to watch you and wait for the right time.' He touched his nose again.

Why couldn't he let it go? 'You're right, it was.'

His eyes narrowed. 'Of course I'm right.' His hand hovered above the other, his fingertips dancing on the ring he wore.

I took a step back. 'If you grabbed me, she could've kicked off. It would've been a nightmare.'

'Why? Do you think I couldn't handle her kicking off?' The fingertips danced, light nervous butterflies as if they wanted to settle.

'You can handle anything.' I wanted this conversation over. 'You outsmarted her for sure.' I stared at my beer bottle.

Gary, stupid or brave, broke the silence. 'She sounds mental. Poor you, Destiny.'

Aleksander cuffed him on the ear with his palm. 'This is a private conversation, dickhead.'

Gary's head rocked with the connecting slap, but he didn't touch his reddened ear.

Aleksander got me a glass of wine and I knew the moment had passed. I glanced at Gary, who sat away from us. He flashed me a small smile: I realised then how brave Gary was. He was brave for me.

Destiny

Aleksander skinned up and passed it to me to light. Again I was his queen. After a moment, he said, 'You were all right. I knew you would be. Although I was less than chuffed when you checked into a hotel.' His eyes narrowed, 'She didn't try any lezzy stuff did she?'

Gary giggled. Even he could tell that, although we were still talking about it, the mood had changed, the danger had passed.

'No! She's not like that.' I paused. 'I mean, she might be, but not with me, not with her pupils. She's nice. She wanted to take care of me. Even if she's a nut job.'

'I take care of you.' His hand lazed through my hair, my head rested on his shoulder. I knew we could talk about it now.

'You showed her your gun. If you hadn't done that, it might have been all right. She thought you wanted to fuck with me and she called the police and the social worker.'

'I knew the school would do that – that's why I sent Jay in. He used the fake social work ID we had from the Kennington job. I am always one step ahead.' Aleksander checked his phone. 'He and Ollie are on their way. Gary, put some music on, make it feel like people can party here.'

I was barely listening. Now Aleksander was no longer angry, I felt able to be. 'Fucking social services wouldn't send anyone out for me.'

He drained an energy drink, crunched the empty can in his fingers, then reached for another. Once he'd taken a swig, he threw one to Gary. Gary had put on some garage music on the serious stereo we lugged from party house to party house. We were united again, ready for the job.

'Thanks, guv. Destiny,' Gary said, turning to me, 'We didn't forget you, you know. We followed you the whole way.'

I said, 'Thank you, Gary,' at the same time as Aleksander said, 'She knows that, you pleb.'

Aleksander looked me up and down. 'So, you're all right then? I mean, you were messaging me the whole time, so I wasn't worried.'

I paused. I wanted to say I wasn't worried, but I couldn't. Even to think of it brought back that horrible sick feeling I'd had when I realised that she was imagining whole conversations with me. I remember the screaming fit I'd had, shouting and pleading to be freed. I flexed my hands, remembering how I had hurt them banging them repeatedly against the consol. Then, later, the constant low-level beat of anxiety that she was never going to free me, that perhaps she was going to . . . going to . . .

'*Were* you worried?' Aleksander asked me, curiosity in his voice.

I saw concern etched in his eyes. He always saw me as strong, clever, resilient. I wasn't sure that it suited me for him to see me as anything else – what if he didn't like me any more? Without Aleksander I would be alone. Again. I never wanted to be alone again.

I forced a laugh out. 'It would take a lot more than Miss to make me worried.'

He flashed a smile; he was pleased. Then: 'I don't know how she got you in the car anyway.'

I felt a jab of anger at the easiness of his accusation. 'She got me because she's much stronger and bigger than me. I had no choice.' I remembered being bundled into the car.

But how *was* she there waiting for me?

I pulled on the joint as I tried to figure it out, how she was waiting for me outside the school in school time. It only needed a moment to think it through, it was so simple. I had a note from the children's home staff, to request that I leave early for my dentist appointment. That note would've been put on the computer system. She could've easily looked me up, seen I had permission to leave early and made her own excuses. I walked out of the front doors, down the drive, out of the school gates, completely legitimately, and she was there waiting for me. Her, in her head, believing I had somehow bunked over the school gates, as I was so fearful of my beloved Aleksander, although I was running straight to him.

Gary asked me if I was OK.

'She invented it all,' I told them both, hearing my own incredulity in my voice. 'She imagined I'd asked her for help. But I'd never asked her for help. I didn't even want her help. But the worst time was—' *When she punched you, Aleksander, in the face and led me away.* But I realised that was the wrong thing to say. He'd crossed his arms, his huge muscles bulging under his sleeve tattoos.

I'd never seen anyone beat Aleksander in a fight and, of course, Miss was a woman. Although she wasn't *like* any woman I'd ever met before: she was supercharged. She was strong and tall like a man and she didn't let anyone tell her what to do. Even the toughest boys in school did what Miss told them to do. I'd even see her take apart the headmaster before. Despite her crazy ideas, I realised a small part of me admired her.

'What was the worst time, Destiny?'

I lifted my chin and looked Aleksander directly in the eye. 'Being without you.'

He touched my cheek. 'You're a good girl,' he said with real pride. He then told Gary to fuck off and leave us alone for a moment. Gary got up saying he would get downstairs ready for tonight and went off into the cellar.

Then Aleksander came up close to me and put his arms around me. I could smell his aftershave again; he wears too much but he won't listen. I thought of him putting his dick into me while holding his gun at my head. He'd done it a couple of times before and maybe it was becoming a bit of a habit. 'I'm sorry, Destiny, that I didn't stop her taking you. I fucked up.' He put a gentle finger under my chin and pulled it up so he could look me in the eyes. 'I am sorry.'

I shut my eyes briefly, then kissed him, quick, before he could stick his tongue in. 'I love you, Aleksander.'

'And I love you, Destiny.' He kissed me softly on the tip of my nose and then smiled and I could see his gold tooth. 'And I'm going to fuck up that cunt so she regrets the day she ever saw you.'

I kissed him again. This time I put my tongue in his mouth first and he made a noise like he was pleased. When I broke away, I said to him, 'Good.' And I realised that this time I meant it. Because away from her and the situation, I couldn't see her good points – like she was kind to me and wanted to help me – all I could feel was the fear of her dragging me away in public, pushing me into her car and then, when I thought I was free, punching Aleksander, beating the one person who made me feel safe and taking me away from him again. *She* had decided that she knew what was best for me. And all my life, that's what I've had from social services, taking me away from where I really want to be, and making me live somewhere where there's no safety, only fear. And despite the fact that she meant well, I realised that that counts for nothing, because lots of people mean well, but it doesn't mean that they act well. And whether someone is ruining my life because of a heroin addiction or because of a risk assessment or because they've gone mad, in the end it doesn't mean any different to me because they're still making me feel scared and powerless. And I realised, that if Aleksander wanted to fuck her up, I wasn't going to stand in his way. Sometimes I watched him do stuff and although I wouldn't want to actually watch him with this one, I did mean it.

Good.

Saturday
00:02

Aleksander

I watch Gary draw. Destiny bought him one of those artist's pads and a pack of colouring pens. I swear he's just a big kid. He loves it – everywhere he goes, out comes the sketch pad. All he draws is leaves and flowers but not like I thought he would. They're good, good enough to sell – not that I'd tell him that. They're proper detailed pictures that look real. Curling autumn leaves; pretty daisies. Destiny says its proper too – she says it's botanical art. My lady is super smart.

We dance together, her and me. She has her arms around my neck, but they're not holding me tight. Her arms are straight, resting on my shoulders, like I'm scaffolding holding her up. Or perhaps I'm convenient. Perhaps, if there was somebody else, another man, then she would let them hold her up too.

My hands tighten around her waist. She moves, a flex, to encourage me to loosen my hold. Instead, I tighten again, like the python. She can never get away.

I like that part of her body, where it narrows down to her hips before they flare out. I pull her to me and inhale her smell. It's her deodorant and something else I can smell in her hair, per-haps shampoo. She doesn't wear perfume; no matter how much I buy for her, she won't wear it. She says she will when I com-plain, but she doesn't.

Under her other smells, I can smell her sweat. Her arms are bare and I lift the right one up. Underneath, the flesh is soft, smooth and I nuzzle it before I get the urge to bite. The smell of sweat is stronger there. Despite her faults, I love her so much, sometimes it scares me. I want to consume her, take her into me so that she can be only mine. I bite her there, where it is soft, and feel her body stiffen: that excites me. I want to do it again, but I can see that I've already left my teeth marks red against the pale of her skin. I know that the wanting to makes me like my father.

Of course I am like him, but I mind less now that I have decided that my children will not be. Destiny will be their mother. I will put a baby in her as soon as she is twenty-one. Together we will raise them to be so much better than us. They will be the finest of the fine. Good people will look up to them.

Destiny will be a good mother. She wants the chance to start our own family. She has none of her own who are any good. Her own mother is a drug-soaked slag. I know it because I met her mother first, through Jakob. Her mother, Simone, was get-ting her brown from him, cutting it and passing it on to other people. She had a wicked sense of humour, laughed lots and had a great pair of legs. Shrewd too, she did all right. When Jakob knew I liked Destiny, he asked Simone out for him and Destiny for me.

But Simone let her down. We didn't know that Destiny wasn't supposed to be with her mother, but instead was running away from foster homes to be with her. When Simone was nicked for dealing, the social workers found out and put her into a secure unit. After Destiny was gone, it changed. The magic left for Jakob. Family is important to us and she'd let Destiny down. We didn't know about the beatings, about the men. It was good Simone was nicked – I think it would've been worse for her if we had sorted her.

But for nearly five months, we were a happy four: Jakob and Simone, me and Destiny.

I was disappointed when it finished: I had enjoyed spending time with my uncle, taking the women to fancy restaurants. I was still new to the country then and it wasn't just Destiny I fell in love with. I loved London the most: the buildings, the food, the cars, the nightlife. I loved it all, but most of all I loved the *class*. I loved the feeling of being important, of being stylish. I loved that it made me feel anything was possible.

It was a crazy time; we went everywhere together. Jakob had enough money for us all – anything we wanted. He knew things at home were dead for me, he told me he wanted me to see that there was something else. The four of us saw that something else together. Although Destiny was still fourteen, she was well developed and with make-up she passed for eighteen. We went out every night; we made a strange little family and we used to joke that Destiny was my cousin. It was nice – I had never gone anywhere with my family and now we had a tight little group: a beautiful girl on my arm, Destiny's mother and my uncle.

Together we lived the life: Jakob gave me a taste of what it was like to have money, how money let you fit in. I felt the power of sitting in a Bentley. I will have a Bentley one day and then I will truly feel that I've made it.

Jakob's business is still going well. I'm glad for him – he is a good uncle and I owe him a lot. It's his contacts that set me up. Have everything that is mine, he said, but stay out of my patch. I thought of him sharing a meal at my house when I was a small boy and I thought of us now, sharing expensive wine. Times had changed, we'd moved on, but he was still my uncle, sharing what he had with me, trying to help me.

Our agreement was that I work the north, so he can keep the south. The only issue was when Destiny was moved south. Although the care home has given up fighting her about leaving with me at the weekends, she ain't going back now. We are done pretending. They think I am her cousin anyway. At the time she was taken back into care, her mum was still with Jakob, so it was true. Destiny's mum told them I was her cousin, but why they believed that stoned cow, I don't know. Sometimes people choose to believe something if it suits them. And when they choose, most people pick the easy option.

I think of that now, with Destiny in my arms as we move to the music. I think about what she tells me: that she will love me for ever, that she will have my babies, be my wife. I feel a flicker of doubt. Am I believing her because it suits me? Am I making a choice?

I remember Simone looking at me one night. She was stoned and she looked at me, my arm around Destiny as Destiny cuddled up to me, like something was funny. What's making you laugh, woman? I asked her. Destiny, her mother said. I asked her why. Because she's like me, Simone said. She's a survivor.

I thought of the rats we caught that we drowned in the well when I was a kid. I remember how they would scrabble on their dead brothers and sisters to try and stay afloat. I thought of how me and a boy from the village would watch with our torches, fascinated how they would do anything to survive. Was I just another body for Destiny to scrabble up from, in her desperation to stay alive?

I'm not dancing now; I'm only holding her tight. She's stopped trying to move and lets me stand like this for a while.

She knows I will never let her go.

Saturday
00:06

Destiny

The doorbell went again; my job was to play party girl hostess with the mostess and answer it with a beaming smile. 'Come in!' I told the people standing on the doorstep, raising my voice so they could hear me above the noise of the party. Part of the evening involved weeding the right people out from the wrong, but that came later. To start with, nearly everyone was welcome. Because even if they weren't right, they might have brought someone with them who was.

In they came, loads of them, the invite having been passed round from groups of strangers to groups of strangers – social networking made my job easy. All of them thought they were the lucky ones, getting into a house party, when really, we were the ones who were lucky.

The gig was always the same, no matter what town we were in. This bit was always 'my' part. My patter was that this is my parents' house and they're away for the weekend. It didn't matter that I don't know these people – everyone assumed everyone else was my friend. Everyone assumed this was a normal situation.

The bell sounded again. This time there were six people on the doorstep, two boys, and four girls, all around seventeen. I heard the clink of booze in carrier bags. I gave one of them a high-five and they went into the kitchen. They're all here for one thing: a good time. My job was to create the good time – until that's no longer needed.

I'd barely shut the door before the bell rang again. I opened it and this time it was six girls, definitely too old, but I let them in anyway.

The music was loud enough for a party, but quiet enough not to bother the neighbours too much. We've marked the right volume on the stereo in Tippex. We can never risk the police.

I hung around, twitchy from the coke, twitchy from the adrenalin from the day, twitchy about the evening. Jay and Ollie chatted people up, poured drinks, lined up lines for the lucky girls and gave the boys too-strong joints or machoed them into pulling a cone on a bong. Within a couple of hours, there'd be the usual divide of over-hyped girls and sleeping boys.

But that would come later.

The door had eventually quietened down, so I started a bit of vetting. I was the best at this because I'm a girl and they trusted me – by 'they', I mean the girls trusted me. The lighting was low, and I moved through the shadows like a jaguar. It felt good to be the one doing the hunting. I felt powerful. In my entire life, it was only doing this that ever stopped me feeling like the victim.

I wore skinny jeans – the ones Miss bought me – and a pair of heels and a low-cut top that I'd left upstairs ready, when we were doing up the place. And my short blonde wig. I loved it. It was made of real hair and dead convincing, especially after I lopped six inches off my own hair to make it fit right. Aleksander wouldn't be happy when he'd clocked my cut, but as I twiddled a lock into place, I knew I loved this look and would cut all my hair off and dye it blonde as soon as I could. For now, though, it would remain. With my make-up done, I knew I passed for eighteen. I also knew that someone might try to chat me up, so it was just as well that Aleksander was out of the way. He used to be cool with it, with me being the honeypot, but I'd noticed it had worn too thin for him. He couldn't bear anyone else touching me, which considering how I came to know him, is pretty funny really.

I kept to beer. I opened it myself, I held on to it, drank it quickly and it was fine.

I had a long conversation with two girls who are seventeen. I found out where they live, what their parents do, what their relationship was like with their parents. Stuff like that can really help. I offered them a line upstairs and one accepted. The other hesitated and made an excuse that she had a cold. I shrugged and then turned to the other – a pretty dark-haired girl – and asked, 'Are you coming anyway?'

She said yes, and I thought: *gotcha*. It's crucial to know if she would leave her friend behind and she would. We went upstairs and I looked down over the banister and her friend seemed relaxed, leaning against the wall drinking from her glass. It's a glass from Ollie; I know this because we are careful to use certain glasses for certain things – that way the wrong person doesn't get drugged.

The bathroom was occupied so I took her into 'my room'. I got a kick from kitting this room out – I chose posters of bands I don't listen to, and got a duvet set, mattress and a second-hand wardrobe, which if anyone looked inside they would find empty. It all cost less than thirty quid from the same place as the sofa.

I blew the top of the chest of drawers to make sure it was clean, then tipped out some coke from my wrap. It's great shit, but then it should be, because Aleksander bought it in directly from the importer. There were still crystals in it, so I used my bank card to flatten them before I cut it even finer. I then made two generous lines. I've got my eye on her, so I'm happy to blast her socks off.

I found a note and rolled it into a tube. Since Aleksander, I've always had a real wedge folded in my pocket. Someone at my last children's home, not far from here, before they moved me all the way down south, must've noticed, because a social worker came to talk to me about it. They thought I was turning tricks. I felt like shouting at them: do you think I'm stupid? Do you think I'm my *mother*? But I didn't. I looked out of the window and tried to be as bland and non-committal as possible. Looking back, I suspect it went against me. I bet they talked about my cash flow in my review. We're allowed to know what is discussed, but I refused to be patronised by their condescension and filtered information, so I haven't asked, but it may have contributed to my move out of the area.

I put the end of the tube in my nose and inhaled.

For a moment, everything went sexy marshmallow and I thought nothing about anything except how I felt in that moment. Electric ooze. Vibrant power.

I passed the rolled note to her and watched: she looked confused. Good. Another tick on the ol' checklist. And there was an actual checklist that the four of us – not Gary – devised together.

'Block one nostril with your finger, like this,' I said, as I pressed my fingertip against my right nostril. 'Most people have a favourite side, where they can inhale more strongly. Why not try?'

The girl practised with one side and then the other. 'I think my right side is strongest,' she said tentatively.

I gave her an impressed face. 'That's supposed to be a sign of genius,' I told her. It was meant to be a joke, but she looked pleased. This girl could give Gary a run for his money. That's another tick. The blue-eyed, reasonably pretty girl started to look like the rabbit and if she was, I realised, we could get to bed before two. Right then, that idea was amazing. 'What's your name?'

'Macey.'

'Well, Macey, who's very possibly a genius, take a blast.'

She bent over and inhaled, following down the line. She was too far away, so her hoovering was poor.

'Closer!'

She obliged and did better. When she sat up, I thought her eyes were going to pop out.

'Good, hey?'

She couldn't speak. She couldn't even look at me. But I thought she was happy.

I took another pop and offered her another. Although she'd clearly had enough and she should say no, she agreed. Another tick.

'So,' I asked her after she came back to earth after her line. 'Macey, I think you said you're at college?'

She nodded, expression tranquil. 'Catering,' she said, then added, 'but only part-time, which is just as well because it's super boring. We have to do all the stuff with numbers and I didn't think it would be like that but what's even worse is customer service which I thought I would . . .'

I let her waffle on. If she's this bad on coke, I thought, I'd hate to see her on speed. When she'd finished, I asked the crucial question. 'Why part-time?' But I'd already guessed. And then it was as I suspected.

'I've got a kid. Want to see her picture? She's too cute. She's round my mum's tonight.' This was not a tick – this was a big, fat cross. She started to get her phone out, but I'd already stood up. Macey could be a ten, instead of the seven that she was, and I would've still walked away. It's the rules. It's my rules.

'Are you going?' she asked.

I knew this was subtext for *are you taking the coke away from me?*

I answered both questions with one word. 'Yes.'

Saturday
00:24

Destiny

Downstairs, I became restless. I felt exhausted. Now I hoped that Jay or Ollie had someone lined up or else I could see me going to bed sometime never.

Macey had drifted down behind me, but I blanked her. I went into the kitchen to get another drink, but she followed me anyway. Ollie saw me across the small but crowded room and raised his eyebrow in a question. I shook my head, and formed a zero with my thumb and forefinger. He did the same back to me – tonight was not going well. We ususally had at least one by now.

Macey leant next to me against the counter, chatting to me like I was her new best friend. I ignored her and looked around the room. Through the crowd, I spotted three dark-haired girls who weren't there before I went upstairs, one of which was a definite nine out of ten. Neither Jay or Ollie was with them so I made a beeline for them. Maybe, I thought, it should be called a waspline.

I stood near them and sparked a joint, wondering if it would help me start a conversation with them. Amazingly, Macey did my work for me. She greeted them, obviously knowing the nine and one of the other girls. I only had to pass Macey the joint and she introduced me, telling them it was my house. Then it was easy. We got talking, one thing led to another, then the nine said she was in care, and I heard sirens and saw fireworks. She asked me my name; I told her I was called Shay.

I moved over to the window, and she followed a little, so she was no longer near her friends. I told her about my own life in care – a version that suits me, but wasn't too far from the truth. It's a life that bonds people in care together, as no one else can relate to what it's like. It's a tragic little club and one I exploited. Maybe there should be honour among thieves, but my life has taught me that there is no honour. There are only those who thieve and those who thieve harder. And the winners are those who thieve the hardest.

Her name was Ella and she was sixteen, which was a tick because I won't touch anyone younger. She had long dark hair, similar to mine and blue eyes, and although her nose was too big, it gave her a Roman look, especially as her cheekbones were good. She was cool enough to wear old-school trainers. She also had a tight dress that showed off a killer figure. She was perfect and I gave her a big smile, which she thought was me being friendly, but really it was me thinking about how much Aleksander was going to love her.

As I grinned, I remembered a children's book I must've read a long time ago, about an enormous crocodile that tries to trick the little children into the river so he can eat them. I realised I was the enormous crocodile. I widened my grin at her, and as she smiled back at me, I thought, *I'm going to eat you all up.*

'If you're in care, is this your foster parents' house?' Ella asked.

I nodded, suddenly flustered. I was getting my story muddled up; the drink and drugs and the nightmare of the day were getting to me. I needed to be careful. I told her I was going to get some drinks and to keep her in the right place, I handed her my coke wrap and I told her to help herself, adding, 'I'll be back.'

She giggled. 'Are you the Terminator?'

'Yes,' I told her. And I meant it.

Saturday
01:14

Destiny

Ollie was in the front room lounged out on the sofa, his arm around some girl who looked like she'd been short-changed. That's the usual reaction. Ollie's sort of odd looking, with his too large nose and wide-space eyes. Maybe that's why he always drones on about his degree in philosophy from Cambridge to anyone who'll listen. Bet he didn't say it was third class. The fact was, he's a privileged bastard coasting until he inherits his parents' pile. But being rich hasn't set him free, it's only made him bitter. He can't ever achieve what his father has, so he can't bring himself to try and fail.

He was slow to get up when I indicated with a nod of my head to come over. That was because he didn't like doing anything I suggested. And my suggestions were always better than his. He might've been smarter than Jay, and he might've been eight years older than me, but he knew that I was smarter than him. And that bothered him because he was a chauvinist pig. If he had his way, things would've been very different in our business.

'I've got one. You?'

'Nope. Jay is insisting he's got one, but I think no.'

'Why?'

'See for yourself,' he shrugged and pointed outside. I went to take a look.

The back of the house was a small paved yard. In it stood Jay and a woman smoking a joint. One look at her and I could see how old she was – too old. Ollie was right.

'OK, Ollie,' I said on my return, 'I'll go and tell Aleksander we're done, and you wrap this up. First, I need a mickey finn.'

He took a small plastic bag out of his pocket and handed me a capsule. I don't thank him for it – it's not for me.

In the kitchen, I poured two drinks, broke the capsule into one, mixed it carefully and carried it back to her. 'This is for you,' I told her. I clocked that Ella had lined up a big line – just one. I saw guilt in her blue eyes that she'd been caught, and thought: *naughty, greedy girl.*

She felt bad, but I was happy – she'd jumped into my snare and I was only too happy to tighten the wire.

I downed my drink and then covered the line with my hand. 'It's mine if you can't down your drink in one, like me.' My tone made it sound like a joke – but the message was clear. Like a good girl, she downed it in one.

Gotcha.

Saturday
01:20

Destiny

I let the ketamine hit her system before I took her upstairs. I left her on the bed, knowing she wouldn't be moving anywhere until morning. Not out of choice, anyway.

Then I moved around the party, telling people my parents were coming home early and they would call the police. Most people left immediately. It was late, they were carrying drugs or didn't want the grief of being stuck in someone else's bust.

Although it was a dramatic end to a party, I figured that it was still in keeping with what they were expecting to see. It's all about the optics. If something presents in a way that make sense to them, they don't look very closely, because they don't have to. Don't give anyone a reason to question what they're seeing and they won't see anything wrong.

In our little venture, optics were everything. We knew that the police could put some heavy manpower on our tails. Because of that, we were careful to move our operation after each party. We knew that if we were discovered, they'd be all over any partygoers as witnesses. Therefore, we need them to not notice any details and to do that, we have to make sure that there is nothing *to* notice. By the time anyone real-ised something was badly wrong, we were always long gone, transactions made, leaving just the scorch marks of another party where people drank too much, did too many drugs, and couldn't quite remember what they had seen in the poorly lit house way after midnight.

After a couple of minutes, I had an afterthought and ran back upstairs. I pulled a sheet across Ella's body, her face. I didn't want to risk anyone coming up and seeing her lying on the mattress, and them then telling the police if there was a fuss: *yes, I saw Ella. She'd fallen asleep at the party. Yes, she was definitely there. And yes, she was definitely alive.*

Saturday
01:50

Destiny

'I have to sleep,' I told the group. We were sitting in the basement. It stank of mould and woodlice and something rotting. I hated it. But I also knew that we would be out of there tomorrow evening and we would never be back.

Gary rubbed his face in agreement. 'Destiny, you've had the toughest day ever,' he said, with sympathy.

Aleksander tightened his arm around me. 'Of course, baby, you're so strong you always keep going, but you must rest. We all need to sleep.'

We all looked at sleeping beauty. Now she was asleep and I would never speak to her again, I worked hard to forget she even had a name, which was as it should be. Her right hand and right leg were each handcuffed to a hundred-pound kettlebell. When they weren't holding a girl, Aleksander and Gary used them for weightlifting; I couldn't even lift one.

Aleksander looked at Gary. 'You're on guard, so sleep down here. If she stirs, give her another benzee, but for goodness' sake, don't do what you did last time.'

Gary looked at the floor. Even under his stubble, he blushed with shame. Last month, he decided to give a girl another one 'just to make sure', and we had her in a coma. We ended up dumping her and we lost twenty grand. The thing that pissed us off was that she was a ten, so the money was all but in the bank. That was the thing with Gary: although Aleksander didn't have to pay him and, as Aleksander said, 'scared muscle is the most loyal muscle', he couldn't actually be left with even the simplest of tasks.

'Right,' says Ollie standing up, Jay following, then us, 'I reckon that's it. Tomorrow we ship her out, but for now, I'm crashing.'

We all shuffled off upstairs, into sleeping bags, ready for the export tomorrow.

I wanted us to sleep; to be ready for our work. But even in the dark, I could see that as soon as Aleksander came into the room, he had that look in his eye. He moved towards me like I was a deer that might bolt. The lights were off, the glow from the streetlights outside, pooling orange into the room. Like prey, I shut my eyes and didn't move and hoped for the best.

For the briefest of moments, I thought of Miss. I thought that she might come here to this house tomorrow to look for me. But if she did, I would be already gone. I felt a shard of disappointment and as Aleksander crawled in next to me, I didn't know if it was because she wouldn't be able to take me somewhere else, or rescue me from the person I was turning into.

Saturday
04:02

Jenni

I woke in the car with a pain in my back and a stiff neck. In the army, I was used to crashing in uncomfortable places, grabbing sleep where I could. Normally it wouldn't have been a problem to me, as I would've gone back to sleep, but I thought: *Destiny*.

Then I was properly awake.

I debated if I should check on her or let her have her privacy. I could tell that towards the end, she'd started to feel a bit crowded by me, which was understandable because she was under massive stress and probably, sadly, not used to people showing her much concern.

But I really needed a wee.

I wasn't averse to weeing outside, but I would sleep so much better if I knew she was OK.

I deliberated. If I snuck in her room, perhaps I could use the bathroom without waking her. I looked in my glove compartment and found a torch – that decided it for me. I could get in, check she was OK and use the bathroom without turning on the light and the fan, and get out again before waking her. Another of the benefits of my army training was that I knew how to be quiet.

I got out, shook myself a bit and shut the car door carefully. I crossed the silent car park in moonlight. I tried the reception door. Locked. It took me a second to remember to hold up my key card – a small green light flashed and I was in. I had imagined having to give an explanation to a receptionist, someone who would be suspicious of me wanting to access my room in the middle of the night, but no one was there. Skirting past the lift, I turned the corner and took the stairs.

On the second floor, I moved quietly down the corridor. I came to Destiny's room. Holding the key card up, I got the green light and was in.

I kept my torch low, not trusting her to not have dropped clothes on the floor. I did not need to trip. Conscious of my breathing as I stepped up to the bed, I thought of how I should best calm her if she were to wake up and see me standing over her in the dark – I didn't want her to think I was up to no good. And it was dark: blackout curtains and no streetlights meant that until my eyes adjusted, I couldn't have seen her even if she was standing in front of me. But I didn't want to lurk in the dark, as it made me feel like I was doing something wrong. It was a difficult position to be in: to do the best for Destiny as she was a fifteen-year-old in my care, and yet to do nothing that might cause her to feel upset. She'd probably had enough of people in positions of trust behaving in ways that were creepy. I didn't want to add to that.

As I lifted the beam of the torch from the floor to the bed, I rehearsed my response: *Don't worry, Destiny, I'm just checking on you and will leave right—*

The bed was empty.

The sheets were smooth; the bed unslept in.

I whirled round, the beam of the torch turning with me. I expected to see her standing behind me, a ghostly figure with her hair loose, eyes wide with fright. But there was nobody there.

Perhaps she was in the bathroom. Even as I crossed to it, I knew it was unlikely as I had passed the open door to the bathroom as I came in and the light was off. I wanted to call her name, but was frightened that I'd disturb her in some troubled sleep-walking state. I imagined her facing the corner of the room like a zombie hiding from the light in some second-rate horror film. After I'd glanced in the bathroom, I felt that I could now turn on the light. Before I did, I said 'Destiny?' into the black.

In the silence that echoed back at me, I snapped the light on.

The bathroom fan whirred into action. Although the shower curtain revealed most of the bath, I thrashed it back, hoping.

I turned on the bedroom light as well. This room was also empty.

I checked the bed more carefully – perhaps it had been remade by her. But the sheets were tucked in and it looked like it had been done by a professional. I checked down the far side, almost hoping for the worst – that she'd fallen, hit her head, was passed out on the floor – at least she would be in the room, safe. But she wasn't on the far side of the bed, between the bed and the window. I checked the wardrobes – empty. I checked the bathroom again, looking behind the door – nothing. I realised that I had to accept it, she was gone.

I felt an overwhelming surge of loss. I'd failed her. She was not safe. With that realisation, I felt the disappointment in myself wash over me. I collapsed onto the bed. The bed, the ultimate sign of what I'd tried to achieve, a place of safety, of comfort, was untouched, abandoned. She had stepped away from me into . . .

. . . into what? Where had she gone?

– *you're swinging, stop swinging, stop swinging, Mummy –*

I remembered a slipper falling from a bare foot.

I remembered struggling to put it back on.

Destiny.

Her loss brought me back. I breathed in, sharply. Then I checked my watch; I gasped when I saw the time: 5:01. What had I been *doing*?

Once again I'd failed. Once I'd been so successful in my missions, I could only now accept that anything I had done well before was the result of some happenstance, a bit of luck. The reality was, just as I had let Billy down, I had also let Destiny down – I had failed to save them both.

I put my face in my hands, wanting to feel sadness, wanting to cry. Self-hatred dug needles in my heart, and I embraced the feeling. There were no surprises. My loathing was familiar. It was my friend, my lover, my parent.

It was correct that I should feel that way. I was not a saviour but had only taken her further away from the social services who knew her. Perhaps they'd been on the verge of rescuing her. Since I'd rung them and alerted them that a stranger had impersonated a care worker to give false reassurances about Destiny's safety, perhaps they had decided to remove her from school. I imagined them driving up to the school as I was driving Destiny away to an imagined safety, when really I was only putting her in danger.

I hated myself. I hated my actions. At that point, I came the closest I had ever come to the self-awareness that some people have, that some people seem so effortlessly to evaluate themselves and their lives with, but had always eluded me. I realised that I'd tried to do the right thing, because I had failed so spectacularly with doing the right thing with Billy. As I realised this, my hands clenched into fists. Then I saw what was lying on the floor in front of me.

A condom wrapper.

My breath escaped from me as if I had been punched in the stomach. The square foil packet, ripped along one edge, was bent over almost as if it winked at me.

I sat up in disgust and then I saw it.

Like a flattened slug, the condom lay on the floor, spilling its slimy contents behind it. It had been dropped by some foul man without even doing the courtesy of tying a knot. I thought of the man with the gun and thought: *I know you.*

I stood, embracing my raised heart rate and the coursing adrenalin that shot through my veins. I may not have my army rifle any more, but I still had me. And with me, this guy was going to get a fight.

And then, after I had killed him, I was going to take her back. Make her safe.

I would *not* fail this time.

Saturday
05:25

Jenni

When I was a kid, I thought, as I sat in my car staring at my army knife, you knew you were late home when you heard the electric whine of the milk cart. Now milk came, not in glass bottles topped with bird-pecked foil, but in plastic containers from Tesco. Now milk cost less than water. Now the dairy farmers farmed in debt; the plastic scums our seas and the electric carts rust in silence.

There would be no commute today because it was Saturday. I had no gun, just my emergency knife which I kept in my glove box. It wasn't actually my army knife because I'd had to return it like the rest of my kit, but one I'd bought in an army surplus store, buying from under the counter. It had a serrated edge sharp enough to cut skin at breathing distance, and was 6 inches and therefore over the legal carry limit.

I ran my finger along the blade, watching the blood bead.

I knew there was more than one man, because I'd seen another sitting up front in the van.

I could take two, maybe three, but four would be too much – in another time and place I might have hoped it was possible if

I'd a lucky break, but I no longer believed in lucky breaks. Did I ever? I wondered.

No.

But two men or twenty, I knew I would die trying. Somewhere between the hotel room and this car, I had had an epiphany – I realised that my life was useless. My job made me useful to society, but after seeing that condom on the floor, I was hit with an almost overwhelming understanding that I was pointless. Serving Queen and Country had stopped me from feeling that. But like Destiny now, that life was far away from me. I couldn't get one of them back, but I would die trying to save the other one.

I turned the knife over in my hands, no longer seeing it. I was thinking through my options. The facts were this: I knew where her aunt lived; I knew roughly where her old children's home was, but a quick check on Google told me that I wouldn't be able to get an accurate address from the Internet; I also knew the van that she would've been taken in; I knew the face of one of the people she would be with; I knew it was early on a Saturday morning so most people were asleep – this meant I would have at least two hours of driving every road in the city to look for the van, but I had nothing to lose by starting with her aunt's house first.

I turned the car key. In fact, I thought, I should wake her up because she might know where else we could look.

I pulled out of the car park. If her aunt was caring enough to take Destiny in, then she would be caring enough to help me find her. I wondered what she would say when she answered the door so early and found me standing there.

Saturday
05:27

Jenni

I stood on the doorstep that I had stood on only nine hours ago, but that felt like an age. The green door was black under the light of the moon, its bronze knocker even duller.

I was glad of the six hours' sleep I'd had – my usual. More and I felt muddle-headed. Now I was mentally fighting fit; I imagined waking the aunt – it would take several knocks, and she, perhaps only thirty, would come tussle-headed and dressing-gowned to the door. She would be expecting police, as I was under no illusions that if she was related to Destiny, then she'd be no angel.

I lifted the knocker. The road was silent, with no sign of anyone. I'd parked far down the road, near the junction, keen not to wake the neighbours. I paused, thinking through all the possible variations of the next thing that would happen. Perhaps a man would come to the door instead; perhaps her aunt had a boyfriend or a husband. Perhaps a son.

I hesitated. I knew nothing about this aunt. But what else could I do? Although I knew this was true, it was a terrible time to wake someone, a stranger.

I bent down and pressed open the flap of the letterbox to see if I could see a light on inside. As soon as I pushed against the flap, I got a waft of a familiar smell – cannabis. I shone my light inside. The house looked like a hovel. There were no coats or shoes in the hallway. This wasn't the ordered life of someone who would be much help.

I decided I would wake her but only after I'd exhausted my other options. I glanced at my watch and decided if I hadn't found Destiny by six thirty, I'd come back. And if we hadn't found her by seven o'clock, I'd go to the police and tell them everything.

Perhaps it would be a good move to get a sense of this aunt first. I had nowhere else to look. I decided I'd go round to the rear of the house, perhaps bunk over a wall – it would make sense to do a recce before knocking the door.

Only three houses up, I could see what I'd missed before – there was an arch between two terraces, showing a path that would lead to the rear.

As I stepped under the archway, something scuttled on the gravel ahead of me. I moved the torch and the beam picked out a fox; it glanced back at me, eyes green fire in my torch beam, before it turned and ran silently away.

I followed the path, and turned right. The footpath stretched down the back of the terrace; judging by the distance to the back of the house, the yards were small. I moved slowly down the path, careful to avoid the broken bottles, overgrown weeds and dog poo. I counted down the houses and, within a few short minutes, stood at the back of the aunt's terrace.

The wall between me and the house was six foot of brick. I placed my hands on the top, and pulled myself up a few inches, so I could have a clear sight of the house. Holding on to the wall, only my eyes looked over the top. Motionless, I surveyed the area.

The backyard was little more than broken paving slabs and ambitious weeds inching out homes in broken grout. In one corner, a children's cooker toy lay on one side, clearly long abandoned. There was a single garden chair facing away from the house. Several wine bottles were grouped together by the back door, as if left over from a party. It looked forgotten, not a place where anyone would linger.

I paused. I could either retreat and approach the house openly from the front, or I could jump down and do further surveillance. But I couldn't break the habit of a lifetime.

The truth was, I had driven Destiny to a place that didn't look like the kind of place I wanted for her. I wasn't naive – there would never be a truly happy ever after for a girl like Destiny – but all I wanted was for her to have a chance. But this? My torch beam picked out the scattered fag butts dropped by the back door. Not this.

There was a dim light coming from what looked like a basement window. People didn't tend to leave basement lights on at night – porch or bathroom lights, perhaps, and in children's bedrooms, definitely. But why light a basement?

Perhaps it was better to check it out first.

I bunked over the top and dropped silently to the ground.

Saturday
05:37

Jenni

The basement window was a long narrow oblong window that was only inches from the ground. I'd had to lie on the ground to get a proper look in, but even then, I could only see the top half of the room. The window was stuck shut, probably bolted from within. Not daring to use my torch, I examined the windowframe in the half-light. The paint had all but been chipped away, and the wood itself was damp and rotten. Even better, the putty was missing in places, cracked in others. Even with my finger, I could knock out whole chunks of it. Using my army knife, I eased out the entire top line of the putty and then the sides became free. I was careful to wedge the blade into the gap, so when the pane became loose, I was able to ease it towards me in one piece, only making a soft grating sound as I inched it out. I carefully placed it on the ground next to the window.

With the windowpane missing, I was able to lean right through to get a proper look inside the basement.

My breath caught in my throat.

The basement was about ten foot square, with a staircase on the side wall. The room was dark, lit by a single lantern, like the type used by night fishermen, which sat on the floor. The glow lit a circle of three metres, the rest of the room in shadow. In the gloom, against the far wall, lots of junk, tools, old bikes, were stacked against one side. On the other, also in the gloom, Destiny lay on her side, away from me, one arm and one leg chained to a weightlifting kettlebell. Near to her, in the light, stretched out on a second camping mat, was a middle-aged man. Lying next to him, a knife.

Acid burned in my throat. How dare they? I wanted to tear him apart limb from limb. They – and it would be *they*, because this wasn't the man I'd seen – had taken Destiny from her place of safety, molested her and chained her like an animal in a filthy basement. How she would've tried to fight. Poor girl. If I hadn't come, or if I had knocked on the door, what would've happened to her?

I wouldn't waste a second now. I would save Destiny.

I pushed through the window, using my upper body strength to slowly lever myself down. I did twenty chin-ups a day, and my lats barely felt the pressure of my weight.

Soft feet to the ground, I moved towards my prey.

His mouth was open, and he sounded like he had sinus problems. He had stubble as though he hadn't shaved in days, and his dark hair was starting to recede above a deformed ear. His skin had seen a lot of weather, but his face seemed gentle, even with a silvered trail of saliva leaving his mouth. His clothes looked cheap and had holes, not just at the knees of his jeans, but also at the elbows of his dirty sleeves. He had swallows tattooed on his hands, above each thumb. It used to mean that the tattooed had done time in prison, but perhaps it didn't any more.

What was clear, however, was that he was holding Destiny against her will. I had a flash of huge outrage. Where was the kindness? Where were the morals? How could they live with themselves?

Looking at his knife, I removed my own, its weight familiar in my hand.

I almost faltered. Unless one was sick, taking someone's life was always hard, and hand-to-hand combat was the hardest and most intimate way of killing. Then there was the killing of a sleeping man, well, that was a class in its own. I knew what it was to draw a knife across someone's neck, see his eyes flash open with first shock, then understanding.

But I also knew that it would be impossible to get Destiny free without making a noise. This man probably had the key in his pocket and there would be at least one other man and a gun upstairs.

I knew I would die fighting to save Destiny. And this man, with his broad knuckles and gentle face, would die fighting to keep her.

Even then I paused.

Even then, I thought about the choices I had. I could ring the police, but if I did it here, I would wake him. If I climbed back out and rang the police, he might hear me climbing out and then I would be further away from Destiny. I could tie him up, but it would mean a fight.

The only answer was to kill him now. Get her out, before anyone upstairs realised. Then, with her safe, I could call the police.

I shouldn't hesitate. I had to put her first. Besides, anyone who took a child and then tied them up deserved no compassion.

I took a deep breath and bent down, bringing the knife blade up to his neck.

Saturday
05:47

Jenni

I couldn't do it. It was the realisation that I would have to wake Destiny, then get her to step round the huge puddle of blood he'd be lying in. She was just a child. She had been frightened enough.

I thought again.

I punched him in the face twice. He made a sound, perhaps trying to speak or maybe surprise. Blood spurted from his nose. I was becoming an expert in breaking noses. After punching him twice more, I knelt on his chest and put the knife to his neck. I leant in close to his ear. 'You feel this?' I hissed, pressing harder.

He made a noise like air through water. Bubbles of blood popped.

'Say it. Tell me what I have.'

'A knife.'

'Yes. Put your hands on your head.' He did. 'You are scum,' I told him, still in a whisper. 'And I might kill you. But first you are going to give me the key to those handcuffs. Where is it?'

He made a noise and I repeated the question.

'In my pocket.'

'Good. In your jeans pocket or another pocket?'

'I don't want you to hurt me.'

'I only hurt people who don't do what I say. Tell me exactly where the keys are. You don't want to make a mistake.'

'This ain't nothing to do with me! I'm just their lad. They won't let me go home.'

'Where is the key?'

Big tears rolled from his eyes, falling into the heavy creases etched below. His expression and his speech pattern made me pause: this man evidently had a profound learning disability, I realised. I also realised that he might be telling the truth.

'They're in my jeans.'

'Good choice. When I tell you, and not before, you're going to reach in your jeans' pocket. Tell me what I just said.'

He repeated it back.

'Good, but first, you're going to tell me if you're going to use your left hand or your right hand.'

He was crying openly now, his head turned to one side. His chest under my knees heaved great silent sobs.

'What's your name?' I tried again.

'Gary.'

'Gary, nice to meet you. My name is Jenni. I'm going to promise not to kill you if you can help me. Do you think you can do that, Gary?'

He nodded, his movement jerky and exaggerated. 'I'll help you, Jenni. I promise.'

'Good. Now are you going to use your left hand or your right?'

'I don't know which is which. I'm no good at that school stuff.'

'OK, don't worry. When I say "go", you're going to reach into your pocket with one hand and get your keys, while keeping your other hand on your head. Are you ready to do that?'

Gary nodded miserably.

'OK. Go.'

Gary reached with one shaking hand into his pocket. But instead of taking it out, he looked at me. His eyes were wide, fully of emotion. 'Can you take me with you, please?'

His statement was so clearly meant, I felt confused. 'What?'

'I want to go with you. Please! You're taking her, aren't you?'

The surprise of his request stunned me to silence. He took this as encouragement.

'When you go, take me, please. I promise to be good.'

I didn't know what to say. When you hold a knife to a man's neck, you don't expect him to want to trot off behind you when you leave. 'You get the key and we'll see.'

He spent time digging in his pocket. 'It's not there. Can I look in the other one? I promise not to do nothing.' When I agreed he started to feel around in the other one.

I heard keys before I saw them because he and I kept our eyes locked on each other the whole time.

'I've found them!' He managed to give me a huge smile. 'Now can I go with you?'

As I leant on his chest, him grinning at me like he was trying to sell me a car, I glanced over my shoulder: good, Destiny hadn't moved. I did not want her to see this. 'Maybe, Gary. Let's see how this goes.'

When I think about all that went wrong, it was this moment that I regret most of all. I hate myself that I didn't just say 'Yes.' I evaluate all the possible reasons why I didn't say yes: that my mind was already working at a hundred per cent listening for the man with the gun; I was concerned that Destiny would wake and be distressed; the planning of controlling a man thirty pounds heavier than me; the stress of considering my next move. I couldn't – or wouldn't – take on the commitment of a promise I hadn't planned for. This all makes perfect sense, the logical side of me accepting these reasons as both accurate and rational. But sometimes, when I tire of thinking of Destiny, I think instead of Gary's hopeful blue eyes as he asked me if I would take him with me.

Now I know that what he really meant, if not with his words but with his pleading eyes, was: *save me.*

But I did not save him. I could've just pointed to the window and told him to make a run for it. I know that if it had ended differently, that's exactly what I would've done. But I didn't.

And that regret, that single word, *maybe*, piles up with all the other regrets, like stones in a dry stone wall, each interlocking with the others and gaining permanence over time. And the regret of not saving Gary remains one of the biggest and most permanent of all.

Saturday
05:53

Jenni

I had the key in my hand. 'OK. Now, Gary, you're going to listen to some easy instructions. Very simple to follow. It's going to end well for you. Are you ready for success?'

Gary nodded.

'That's great. When I say "go", you're going to shut your eyes. Then you're going to kneel forwards. What's going to happen if you try to make a grab for me?'

'I don't want to make a grab for you.'

'OK, but what could happen if you did?'

'But I don't want to.'

I took a different tack. 'That's good, because if you did I'd have to kill you.' He winced and despite him guarding Destiny and chaining her up like an animal in a filthy basement, I began to see him differently. There was something . . . innocent about this man. 'You need to get on your knees with your eyes closed and your hands still on your head. Do you think you can do that for me, Gary?'

'Yes.'

'You're going to make a success of that?'

'Yes.'

'Remind me what you're going to do.'

He told me word for word.

'OK, Gary, do it now.' I moved off his chest, the point of my knife still against his neck. He didn't move. Pause. Then: 'Gary?'

'Yes?'

'What are you doing?'

'I'm waiting for you to say "go".'

'I did.'

'You said: "Do it now".'

'Go, Gary. *Go*.'

Gary sat up, eyes shut and hands to his head. He got to his knees and waited. I gently pushed him forward so his forehead was touching the cement floor. 'And stay exactly like that,' I told him.

I'd already realised that I had to leave him, as I had nothing to bind his hands. I could look for something suitable around the basement, or retrieve the cuffs from Destiny, but it amounted to the same thing – trusting him not to rush me. If I stepped away to find bonds, then he could rush me anyway and I needed to be out of there before the game-changer came in the room. The gun. There would be some people in the same situation who would've done things differently. But I made a judgement that Gary would stay put. I gave him a final warning about what would happen if he moved while I took the key to the sleeping Destiny.

Moving quickly, I unlocked her arm first, and then took the shackle to Gary and cuffed both his hands together behind his back. Then I returned and retrieved the leg cuff. But as I went to put it on him, he whined. 'Please, lady, if you do that I can't come with you and I need to.'

'Why?'

'Because I want to go home. I haven't been home in three years.'

'Why not?'

'Cause Aleksander won't let me.'

'Go yourself then. Go tonight.'

'I have no money.'

I laughed. 'A crim with no money.'

'Lady, he takes my giro and I don't get paid, except with food and beer.'

From anyone else I wouldn't have believed it, but something in the way Gary said it, made me hesitate. Perhaps it was the wanting tone of his voice that made me feel back at school, that made me feel responsible for him, so I left the cuffs off his legs. Besides, I was desperate to get to Destiny.

I stepped out of the pool of light cast by the lantern, into the shadows.

She lay huddled in the corner on a roll matt, a dirty blanket pulled over her. It was her shackled arm and leg that made me wince: how quickly they reduced her to nothing. How quickly they objectified her as if she was a thing, non-human. Animal.

I bent down over the top of Destiny and gently squeezed her shoulder. 'Destiny?' I whispered. She didn't move. I tried again, a little louder, a little firmer. Nothing. She should have woken by now. Starting to suspect she might have been drugged, I pulled her onto her back.

And gasped.

Saturday
05:57

Jenni

I put my hand out to steady myself and my fingers felt the cold, slimy wall. I breathed in the dank air. 'This isn't Destiny.'

'Of course not, Miss. Destiny is upstairs with Aleksander.'

Goosebumps flared my skin. I'd bet a month's wages that Destiny would also be chained up like this poor girl. They obviously took one each.

'Well, who is this?'

'Another rabbit.'

I blinked. Then swore at him.

'We get them at parties and then we drive them out of the country.'

'Why?'

'Aleksander gets good money for them.'

I couldn't believe it – trafficking. Destiny was going to be trafficked; this girl was going to be trafficked. I saw it so clearly: the van, the gun, a girl. My instincts were right. An image of George briefly flickered in my mind – for some reason it felt suddenly important to tell him: *I didn't let you down.*

I took another look at her. She was young, not school age young, but not yet twenty either. What had I stumbled on? She moaned but didn't move. 'Is she drugged?'

'You're not allowed to give her any more. If you do she could end up like that other one.'

I put my hand in front of her nose and mouth, and waited. For a moment, when I didn't feel any heat of her breathing against my palm, I thought she might be dead, but then I did and I felt the relief of realising that she was still alive. I opened her eyelid and shone my torch into her eye. Her pupil was dilated. 'What has she had?'

'Something that Ollie has in a bag. They don't give none to me – not since last time.'

I realised that she wouldn't be going anywhere soon. Not unless I put her over my shoulder and carried her out. And that, I realised, was what I was going to have to do. 'Is it just Aleksander and Destiny upstairs, or are there others?'

'There's Ollie and Jay too. Watch out for Ollie – he's mean.' He paused. 'Can we go?'

'No.' I thought about it. 'I'm going to get this girl out and then you're going to help me get Destiny.'

He started crying and moaning, but I blanked out what he was saying. I didn't want to hear about how and why it wasn't possible. Of course it was possible, anything was possible with the right preparation and attitude. But first I needed to get this girl out.

I unlocked Gary and together we carried the girl to the window. I climbed out first, pulling fresh air into my lungs as soon as

I stood back out under the stars. Gary stood her up and she did manage to stand with his help, even mumbling a little and opening her eyes a few times. I hooked my hands under her armpits, and with him lifting her body, it was fairly easy to get her out of the basement. I was tempted to move her further away, in case it went wrong for me. It was likely to go wrong, too – I was one person against four others, if Gary couldn't be trusted, which he probably couldn't. They also had at least one gun, when all I had was my knife. But I'd taken part in similar operations and still come out alive.

Instead, I tried to help her help herself by smacking her face: 'Come on, girl, wake up.'

She murmured something incoherent. I tried the gate, bolted on my side and the bolt slid back easily. I left her out on the pathway in the recovery position. I hoped it would be enough for her if I didn't come out alive.

Then I climbed back into the basement.

Saturday
06:05

Aleksander

The teacher lowered herself back in the basement, while we watched in the shadows. She came back in facing away from us, then turned after she hit the floor. When she did, I stepped forwards.

'Miss Wales.' I was going to say more but the expression in her eyes made me falter. I'm used to hate. I even like it. But this woman had a coldness in her face that I haven't seen in a woman before. I didn't understand her. She was tall and strong like a man – taller and stronger than most men. But it's not her strength that was confusing – what confused me was that she wasn't scared.

I'm used to women being scared. My mother was scared of my father, my grandmother was scared of her husband. My teachers were scared of me. The women that we take are scared of everything. Destiny is bold and I like that in her – but sometimes, in her eyes, I can see that she's afraid of what I might do. I know this is because of her background and not because of me, but I see it anyway. I don't try to change it. She should fear me: I'm her man. But even though this woman was on her own, and Gary, who was helping her, was now crying like I was going to execute him, and I had my gun and Ollie and Jay, she didn't look scared. Instead she lifted her chin and told me that she was going to kill me. And she looked like she meant it.

Who was this woman?

'I've been watching you,' I told her. I use the gun to show where I've left the small wireless CCTV unit.

I've always kept a camera on Gary. I've always suspected he might run. Give him money or drugs to hold and he's as good as gold. Leave him alone with Destiny and she's as safe with him as she would be with me. If I tell him go, he goes; if I tell him stop, he stops.

But would he run? Yes. First moment he'd get. I keep him in check and short of cash and of course he's a retard so he doesn't think right, but even so, I never trusted him. When I saw this small CCTV unit, I bought it. Wherever I leave him, I plug it in and put something over the top of it, usually a baseball cap or something else with a little gap, so I can watch him. He's too stupid to notice. I can't sleep until I know that everyone is doing what they are supposed to be doing. I was watching him on my phone as I smoked a last joint before bed. I saw it all.

The teacher saw the unit and understood.

I held Destiny close. I wanted the teacher to see – to under-stand – that Destiny is with me because she wants to be. She's not like that rabbit outside. Destiny is my girl and this teacher is wrong. I told her this, but the teacher kept her eyes fixed on me like she could hurt me with her gaze.

I turned away from her and instead stepped up close to Gary; he was taller than me too, but he looked at me with frightened eyes. I pistol-whipped him. I enjoyed seeing the pain in his eyes. I did it again across the other cheek and it started to bleed. 'I saw it all, you fucker. I know what you did.'

Gary started blubbing again. He knew how this was going to end. He might be cheap muscle and as stupid as fuck, but unless he could be relied on, he's worth jackshit. And if he was worth jackshit, he knew I wouldn't carry him no more.

Destiny called out my name.

'Baby?' I answered.

She came close and whispered in my ear, 'Please don't hurt Gary.'

'OK, then,' I said, and then I kicked Gary hard in the balls. He bent forward like he was bowing to me and as his face came down, I kneed him in the face. He made a noise like a punch bag and fell to his knees.

'Hey!' said Destiny, like she was pissed off.

'I know, baby, but he's double-crossed all of us. Out there, somewhere in the dark is our twenty grand. In fact,' I turned to the brothers, and told them to go and get the rabbit back. Jay moved first, followed by Ollie and they both disappeared up the stairs.

I sat down on an old sofa chair while we waited. I kept the gun pointed on the teacher. I'd seen her move and I wasn't taking any chances. As we stared at each other, I felt something odd – I couldn't place it straight away. When I did, it surprised me: I felt respect. Apart from my mother, I don't respect no woman as an equal. Not even Destiny.

I felt Destiny glare at me, but I didn't care. I know she is fond of Gary, feels safe with him when she doesn't feel safe with no other man but me, but I can't trust him now. Destiny is young; when she gets older she will become wise. I'll explain later – I have to watch the teacher.

After a few minutes, Jay came back down the cellar steps alone. 'Boss?'

'Yes?'

'She's gone.'

'Look again.'

'I've checked the back alley path and looked in the neighbours' gardens and can't see anything. Ollie's out the front checking the street, but he's texted to say that he is two streets away and he hasn't seen her yet.'

I could tell from his voice that he'd been running or was nervous or both. He should've been both – he knew we'd all be pissed off. We were going to move her in only a couple of hours in the converted van and we'd have her in Europe before lunch. British birds make a lot of money, and now she's flown the coop, we'd get none.

Destiny carries a fake engagement ring, which we keep in case we get stopped and asked why we are going to Poland so early on a Saturday – because we are so excited, we can't wait to share the news with my family, we will tell them. Yes, we make lots of crossings, but that's because I'm close to my family back home.

We've got the perfect set-up. We take a girl on the way out and get to a safe contact. We get decent cash, then drive straight to a different contact, where we swap the cash for smack. We bring the drugs back home, cut it, and then pass it on to dealers. These days, we don't have to bag it or see a single user. In one trip, we can make as much as sixty kay. Sometimes we do one rabbit once a week – sometimes two. My contact can't get rid of enough white through me and my buyer can't buy enough women.

The English did the same with the slaving routes back in the eighteenth century – they did one big triangle, slaves from Africa to the Caribbean for the sugar fields, then Jamaican sugar to England, and then money and goods back out to Africa to trade for more slaves. I love to read history books and when Destiny gave me the idea of moving women, I put two and two together and we got the full operation. We are like those old slaving ships.

I'm an importer the same as those old families who had the stately homes. Destiny and I checked a couple of those out in the National Trust, and I told her: this is what I will buy you. A palace for a queen. We will be the new royalty. In every European country, the rich always did what they wanted and that's how they made their money and their money bought class. They didn't sit around waiting for permission from society, they just did what they had to do. We do the same. And we will make our money and we will rise to the top. A girl with Destiny's brains and beauty should be there. Society won't put her there, she has to grab it for herself. And that's what we do – we grab.

Jay paused. 'What shall I tell Ollie?'

'Keep looking for the rabbit until you've got her – I don't want to let down the contact. It could be bad for business.'

'But what if we can't find her? She could be anywhere.'

'What if she blabs to the filth? Find her! She's got shitloads of drugs in her system and no shoes. She hasn't gone far. Look again – under cars, in the big street bins, unlocked sheds. Don't come back until you find her.' I threw the van keys to Jay. 'Take these, you'll need it to put her in when you find her.'

He left. Destiny, Gary and the teacher all stared at me. I only looked at the teacher. I don't need to look at Gary to know he's still on his knees, his beaten face like a dog that's been slung out for the night.

Gary would stay like that – it was the teacher I needed to deal with.

I realised it made sense to kill her now.

Saturday
06:20

Aleksander

I realised that it would be better to kill her if Destiny wasn't around. 'Destiny, go get the boys. Tell them they've only got twenty minutes. Then we have to get out. If the girl finds the police we need to be gone.'

She nodded and as she turned to leave, she paused, her foot already on the stairs. She came back, leant in close to whisper in my ear. 'Promise you won't hurt Gary.'

I nodded without breaking eye-contact with the teacher. I was surprised, then irritated: if Destiny were to beg for anyone's pardon, I would've thought it would be for her teacher. I'm not sure I like her liking Gary enough to put him first.

Destiny still hesitated. She chewed her lovely bottom lip, wondering about something. I could tell that she didn't quite trust me. She shouldn't: I knew I would pop Gary as soon as I could. He knew everything about the operation and could put me inside for twenty years. Now I couldn't trust him, he had become useless. Destiny knew this, but it annoyed me that my word was not good enough for her.

I'm fucked off that she decided to plead for him *again*: I'm her number one, I'm the only thing that should matter. She should only want what I want.

'Please, baby,' she whispered. 'Don't hurt Gary. He's my only friend.'

I was already pissed when she called me baby as a way to get something for Gary, like I was some kind of fool, but when she added: 'He's my only friend,' she stabbed me in the heart. Who was I then? Just some nonce she hung around with?

He was dead. When she left, I would shoot the teacher and then take out Gary. The brothers would come back and we'd put their bodies in the hidden compartment in the floor of the van and then dump them somewhere.

'Sure, Candydoll,' I said, already knowing that she will learn what is important between us. 'I'll do what you say.'

I could tell, though, even without looking at her, that she wasn't sure that I would. 'Don't come back without the boys,' I told her, about to add: *I need them here.* But I didn't, because I didn't want that teacher bitch – who hadn't moved an inch, but stared at me like a tiger waiting to pounce – to know that, for once, I was nervous.

Saturday
06:23

Jenni

He still had the gun pointed at me when Destiny left – but I could tell she was frightened. I don't know what she said to him when she whispered to him, but he agreed, but still she didn't trust him. She looked back at him as she walked slowly upstairs, her eyes watchful, her right thumb flicking through her fingers one by one, like she always does when she's nervous.

Aleksander stood up, walked over to Gary. I was still waiting for the moment to make my move. Sometimes there's a perfect moment and sometimes there is only the good-enough moment. You can wait for the perfect moment if you've got time. You have to assess each situation against what you have: now I've got time, but I've got no resources, no other back-up, no guns or other weaponry apart from my knife, nothing else I can use, yet what I want is precise: I want Destiny out of here alive.

So I knew there wouldn't be a perfect moment, I would have to take what I can get. I couldn't afford to die. If I die – and I didn't mind too much about that because I always thought I would die in action – Destiny still wouldn't be safe. She'd be shipped out of the country ending up in whatever nightmare these girls find themselves in. There was only me standing between her and freedom.

Gary was moaning on the floor. He was pleading with Aleksander. Aleksander now had his gun pressed against Gary's neck. I could go now, I thought. I'm only nine feet away. I could do that in under a second. But there was no cover for me to break to and Aleksander was expecting me to make a move. He held a semi-automatic, so he could get several shots into me before I made it to him. I had no Kevlar; I'd be an open target. But if I went now, Destiny would not see it. I wanted to protect her. Gary was moaning loudly. I wanted to save him but he was not my purpose. I would not be distracted.

Aleksander was now shouting at him. In case I thought he might have forgotten me, he glanced my way to remind me that he knew I was here, waiting.

He shouted: 'Gary! Put your head down!'

Gary told him no and shook his head wildly. He was begging not to die.

Aleksander shouted it again. '*Put your head down. Die like a man.*'

Gary reached up and tried to take Aleksander's hand. 'So sorry, boss, I'm so sorry,' he kept saying, promising him it wouldn't happen again.

Aleksander shook him off. He pushed Gary's head down to the floor.

Gary was trying to turn his head, still talking, still crying, still pleading.

Aleksander pushed the gun against Gary's neck. 'Because you refuse to die with honour . . .' He moved it to his knee. 'I'm going to punish you first.' He fired a bullet into his leg. Gary screamed. Then he sobbed, 'Please, boss, I'm sorry!'

'Fuck you,' he said stepping over the blood already running onto the floor before moving the gun to Gary's other knee. He fired again.

Gary screamed again, but this time, it was a lower, more guttural sound.

'Now you know what is coming,' he said, moving the gun to Gary's stomach, 'I'm going to make sure you have enough time for you to think about all the ways you've wronged me.' Aleksander stood and watched him with an emotionless face. I started to think that he wasn't going to do it, but when Gary maybe thought the same and said: 'Please, boss, give me another chance. I'll be . . . I'll be . . .'

'In about two minutes all you'll be is . . .' He said and pulled the trigger.

Gary fell forward, a gasp like he'd been punched in the stomach.

'. . . is dead.'

Saturday
06:29

Destiny

I had dithered. I stood by the front door, wondering if I could go back and check on Aleksander, to make sure he wasn't doing anything too bad to Gary, but couldn't make up my mind, because I could tell that Aleksander was becoming pissed off that I didn't trust him.

And then I did make up my mind, decided to and had turned back around. Then I heard the bang from the cellar, followed by Gary's scream and I knew I was too late.

I stood in the hall and for a moment I wanted to cry. To cry for Gary, for myself, for all the poor bastards who live like we do.

Then I heard another bang, another scream and I became angry. All this could've been something real. This was supposed to be my way out; I could've been something different – this was my plan of how I was going to make it. But now it was ruined.

Those girls were nothing to me. But Gary was different. Gary was someone who always tried to do his best, who was always kind, who never treated me like I owed him something. And Aleksander not only took Gary away from me but, in killing him, had also taken himself. How could I love him now?

How could I look up to someone who didn't care about me?

I felt everything I loved about Aleksander – his strength; his street smarts; his tenacity – fracture. He was clever, strong and on my side. Now he hadn't only ruined Gary, he had also ruined us. I had asked him to leave Gary alone and he hadn't. I hadn't even got out of the house yet. It felt like disrespect: it felt like he didn't regard me as his equal. Aleksander was now someone else who didn't listen to me. He was just like every other adult I had ever met. Just like my mother; just like the social workers; just like those men who I won't, *can't*, think about.

He was Just. Like. Them.

I felt the burn of rage in my chest, my neck, my cheeks. And then I was running through the hall, opening the door that led to the cellar and down the steps, about to call out to Aleksander, when I heard the third shot. I saw Gary fall forward and I knew I was too late.

I nearly slipped on the stairs. I grabbed at the rail and steadied myself. Then, before I was even at the bottom, I could smell it: the stink of meat.

Miss was standing in *exactly* the same position and Gary was on the floor, face down, body collapsed forwards with blood on his legs and coming from his stomach. Aleksander looked up at me and I flew at him. I don't know what got him first: my hands, my feet, my teeth, my nails, and I think I said: 'He was my friend' or maybe 'He was so kind' or maybe 'He looked after me', but maybe it was all of those things or maybe it was none of them.

Saturday
06:31

Aleksander

Destiny has gone mental, kicking and punching me. But I don't see her, because I keep my eyes on the teacher. I manage to grab one of Destiny's wrists. 'He had to go,' I tell her again and again.

She won't listen. She rants and screams about him being pure, so I keep repeating it again and again. 'He *had* to go.'

I never stop staring at the teacher, so I don't know how she does it, because one second she still hasn't moved, like she's some kind of crazy statue and the next second – less than a second – she's upon me. I'm still holding Destiny's wrist when I realise that the teacher is bringing up her foot and is aiming it for my head. I recognise the move as some sort of karate kick before the pain connects with my jaw.

I hit the ground hard.

I am no longer holding Destiny. I know I have to move fast, so I put my hands down and twist round. I'm ready for it now. I know I can take her out. I have killed a man with my bare hands; I can kill this woman.

Another kick connects, this time in my face. The world edges grey.

Then I panic as I realise I'm no longer holding my gun. Where is it? I can't even see it. There is only grey.

Another kick. I shut my eyes against the pain.

There's white noise and the hyper feeling like when electiricy in a storm is about to strike really close, like happened in the forest when I was a kid and stayed out late to watch the lightning strikes across the sky. I haven't thought of it in years, but I hear again the crack as the lightning splits the tree and smell burnt pine as it smokes in the heavy rain.

I remember the terror, thinking it was the end of the world.

I'm still smelling the hot wood when I feel the press against my neck. I can't see; I can't see. I can feel it and it's cold and hard and I know that if I don't move now then the teacher will—

Jenni

After I told Destiny that Aleksander was dead, I held her tight. She screamed and cried and raged, turning on me like she'd turned on Aleksander after he'd killed Gary. Then she quietened. Some part of her had to accept that they were both dead and it was all over, before I called the police.

Our culture doesn't really handle death very well. Other places I've travelled, the Far East, for example, live alongside death in a more – to my mind – realistic way than we do here. So I sat away from them and allowed Destiny to spend time with both Aleksander's and Gary's bodies, to say goodbye. It was messy and she was noisy but it was the right thing to do; it would help her in the long run. I knew that once the police arrived, it would rightly become a crime scene and she would never get a chance to touch either of them again.

She cried and cried and threw insults at me, at one point, even started picking up the things around her and randomly throwing them at me. I didn't mind, it even felt like a privilege to help her process her anger. I felt a huge sense of achievement from the moment that man was dead – I knew then that Destiny was safe. In less than a day, I had driven my life into a wall, wrecking it beyond saving, but I would do it again. There has never been a point that I would not have done it again.

To save someone's life is the greatest honour there is.

I could tell when Destiny was ready. She sat back on the floor, away from the bodies. Her face and hands, her clothes even, were smeared with their blood. But her face had become tranquil and she was quiet.

Then the other two men came down the cellar stairs. They were talking quietly as they came, and their mouths dropped open at the sight of their boss and Gary lying dead on the floor, Destiny sitting quietly by and me further away, the gun safely by my side, watching them.

They looked at her, then at me, then back at Destiny. She was sitting like a broken doll and looked at them and started crying again. Big heaving sobs of grief, noisy, unchecked.

They stared at her as if it were a horror movie – I guess to them it was. They were probably small-time thieves or drug dealers, led on by Aleksander's big money and bigger deals than they had been used to. They may never have even seen a dead body before.

I ended it for them. 'The police will be here any moment,' I said. They left. They did not speak; they did not collect anything; they did not look back.

Without question, they would never bother Destiny again.

Now we were ready. First, I took a bottle of water left by the makeshift bed in the corner and held Destiny's hands out. Like a young child, she let me wash the blood from her hands and using her ruined jumper as a flannel, I washed her face. She had struggles ahead and I would not be able to help her with those but I could help her now, not just keeping her safe, but with her dignity.

As I used careful, gentle dabs, the already sticky blood coming away with difficulty in some places, I thought of Billy. I hadn't cleaned his face. Blood had poured downwards, covering him and I had just left it there. I didn't even close his eyes. But that was then and this was now. I had done better, this time. 'There,' I told her, briefly placing my hand against her dry cheek, 'we are ready now.'

I dug my phone out of my rucksack and dialled 999.

'What service do you require?' a female voice asked me.

'Police, please,' I said and listened to her repeat my number as she connected me to them.

Saturday
07:37

Jenni

I didn't mention what had happened on the phone, other than to say that there had been a double murder and we had a gun for disposal. I'd had to stop to ask Destiny the address. She gave it in a dull voice as if I'd answered a question in class that was so easy I'd both bored and insulted her. They asked me to remain at the property. I said, of course – where else would I go?

Destiny jumped when the police started banging on the door, but neither of us bothered to get to our feet. I suppose, looking back, we were both exhausted. Certainly not from the lack of sleep in my case, as I'd actually had several hours and could function on very little. But I later found out that Destiny hadn't slept at all and of course, had not had the benefit of military training.

When they burst in, visors down, shields up, shouting at us to remain on the floor, I almost felt relief. I'd listened to the shouts through the letterbox, then silence while they decided what to do, then they came back with a battering ram. By the time they came in, I had finished cleaning the gun. It was soothing to do while Destiny sat mutely, watching me. It made me feel like

I was back in service and everything was as it should be. I'd left it next to me, but only to stop Destiny from grabbing it. It was clear that she'd decided to hate me for what had happened, and she was a child, in a heightened state, and I wanted to protect her from herself.

I had removed the magazine and placed the two parts next to each other, knowing that when they came in they would see a gun, but they would also see that it was disarmed.

I thought briefly about washing my own hands, but I didn't need to. I was the cleanest I had been for a very long time.

Saturday
07:59

Jenni

Some people don't believe in the Devil. This is understandable if they don't believe in God, or heaven or hell, and live a nine-to-five existence, working in air-conditioned offices, returning on predictably disordered public transport, returning to homes cleaned by their cleaner and receiving orders of goods from Amazon. I live like that too. Our worlds are predicable, safe, constructed and run by ourselves largely, so much of our existence produced by the arrangement of ourselves or our fellow man.

Sometimes, we will all slip from these worlds and often it's when we least expect it. A car accident. The sudden death of a loved one. A dreaded diagnosis from a doctor. But even then, these things aren't completely unexpected. We see these things happen to friends and family and it is not completely unforeseen when they happen to us – unwanted, tragic, devastating, but not unusual.

But I have been to places in the world where villagers know that something dark, something evil has stalked through their village. Where neighbours have picked up new arguments and old machetes and have slaughtered, maimed and raped those they once knew peace with. I have found men tied to trees, their penises severed and put in their mouths; people with arms missing; children left blind in a ditch because someone stole their eyes to sell. These people know that the Devil passed through their lives, they believe in the darkness that can feel tangible, real, not a childish horned cartoon, not an expression of human failings, but of an inhuman presence. A thing.

I felt it again. In that room, when Gary was crying on his knees, asking for forgiveness he wasn't going to receive. Aleksander was clearly an evil man, bent only on greed, but it wasn't his evil that I felt.

But when he had died, and there was only me and Destiny, I didn't feel it then. It had gone. It left us to deal with what was to come.

So when the police pointed a gun at me and told me to lie face down on the floor with my hands on my head, and Destiny started screaming and pointing at me, screaming again and again: 'She killed him!' I felt calm. I inhaled the smell of the filthy cement, its cold pressing into my forehead, and knew only peace.

Saturday
08:18

Jenni

I stood, handcuffed by the booking desk. The custody sergeant was asking me questions and I answered them. 'You understand,' he continued, 'that you've been arrested on suspicion of murder?'

'I killed Aleksander,' I told him, 'but not Gary.'

The portly sergeant with the kind eyes told me to save it until I had a solicitor. When we'd finished his paperwork, he told me I was going to a cell. 'Is there anything you need?'

I thought about asking him to phone my father, but reconsidered. I rarely saw him at the weekend, so he wouldn't worry if he didn't hear from me. And it would be so much better if he heard it from me in person. If it looked unlikely that would happen, I'd call him then. Then I thought about my job – how were they going to manage? I felt tension work into my shoulder muscles. They'd have to arrange cover for me: it was going to be a massive inconvenience for the poor sod who would have to work out what to cover. 'Can I send an email to my employer?' I asked. And the cost of an agency, of course. I'd saved Destiny but it would explode George's budget. I knew though that when he understood I'd saved Destiny from being trafficked, he'd consider it worth it.

The sergeant shook his head.

I'd have to phone then, but the thought of telling George, the thought of his face as he heard the news, almost – but only almost – made me regret the whole thing.

I'd half expected a strip search, but instead they showed me to a cell and let me have a cup of tea. It was too milky and therefore it was too cold, but I appreciated their kindness. I sat down on the joyless bunk and sipped my drink. I thought about what Destiny said and I thought about the sound that Aleksander made when he died. I thought about Gary crying and how perhaps I should've have saved him instead. I thought about what would've happened if I had saved Gary but then hadn't been able to save Destiny. I thought about the girl who had been shackled in the basement who had got away and where she might be now. I thought about the two men that had been part of the gang and had legged it. But most of all, I thought about Destiny.

Saturday
10:47

Jenni

'For the purposes of the tape, this interview is conducted by Detective Sergeant Anna Fields, speaking, and . . .'

'Detective Constable Simon McManus,' said the young too-skinny man next to her.

I looked at DS Fields across the interview table and decided she had intelligent eyes. About thirty, she was a little overweight and when she spoke, her voice was low and reassuring. To the tape, she introduced my solicitor, a youngish man called Jim Boyce.

DS Fields gave the time and asked me again if I wanted a cup of tea. She'd already asked me twice and I declined again. I nearly accepted because she clearly wanted me to have one, but I'd had several teas and not a hot one among them. Coffee I could drink if cooled, tea no. And at the risk of sounding fussy even to myself, the coffee was too cheap to want. I figured that where I was going anyway, it'd do no harm to give it up now.

I'd declined legal advice, but they'd pushed and I'd conceded to having a duty brief. I'd spoken to Mr Boyce before the interview and he understood it was important for me to say I was guilty. The advantage to me, he'd conceded, was that I could get a reduced sentence.

'Jenni, I wanted to do that because we see a lot of ... I'm pausing, trying to get the right word ... we get a lot of scum. Lowlifes. But I don't think you're like that. I think you're some-one who tried to do the right thing.'

'I didn't try to do the right thing; I *did* do the right thing.'

She pulled a face to suggest it wasn't true.

'What would you have done?' I challenged. 'Would you let a girl be sold for prostitution, lost forever to goodness knows where, just so your life isn't inconvenienced?' I looked directly at each person in the room, directly in the face.

'You broke the law.'

'Everything in context.' I let them think about that for a moment. 'I've killed many times. But the permission I've had means it's legal. You drive too fast in your cop cars; you break into houses to arrest criminals; you assault people when you arrest them. But the permission you've had means that it's legal. If I had waited for legality there would've been no one to save. Fuck context – I did the *right* thing. Now there isn't a girl being injected with heroin in a hovel in Amsterdam or Frankfurt or Rome, before being raped by a never-ending queue of scummy men who don't give a shit. You might choose to look the other way, but I won't, not just to keep myself safe.'

Credit to DS Fields, she nodded as if what I had to say was totally expected and thoroughly reasonable. 'Jenni, is it all right if I call you Jenni?' I nodded. 'Let's go back to the beginning, shall we?' And she did. She went through my job in some detail, before going back to my life in the army. She asked about my regiment, about my medals, about what my assignments were. I told her what I could, and what I couldn't she accepted with grace. We talked about my breakdown after Billy's death and about my being discharged and I didn't hide anything.

We even talked about my father. I started getting agitated at this point. Even at this early stage, I had started to accept that I wasn't going to get out, that my life now had changed for ever and that I would no longer be a teacher, I would no longer have hard-boiled eggs for lunch every day with him, that I would no longer compete in the Ironman contests. I needed to tell him. My agitation may have become a bit much but I settled when she told me that I could call him whenever I wanted. She even thanked me for my cooperation.

'Are you sure I can't get you a cup of tea?'

'Can I tell you something without you thinking me difficult?'

'Of course.'

'I love my tea really hot, which is really easy when you're making it for yourself. Everyone here is so busy, they're kind to bring me a cup of tea. But it's always cold. I don't like cold tea.'

DS Fields got up. 'I'm going to make you a cup of tea myself.' She didn't offer anyone else – she left the room and came back after a few minutes. The whole time she was gone, nobody said anything.

She came back in with two mugs of tea and restarted the interview. Mine was served in a mug that said *I love Disneyland Paris*. I drank some. It was hot. 'It's perfect. Thank you so much.' I even managed a smile.

Perhaps it was going to be all right. Sometimes people didn't get prosecuted because they did the right thing – like killing a burglar to protect their children. Perhaps this would be like that.

Saturday
16:06

Jenni

After several hours of nothingness, we were back in the interview room. I had just decided to ring my dad, when the skinny constable came to get me with the custody sergeant. I was a touch irritated; I knew that I had got into the right mindset to speak to my father and now I wouldn't be able to. Besides, I couldn't understand why they needed to interview me again – I had admitted guilt and told them everything I knew. It had been a long interview, nearly two hours, so I wasn't up to talking any more. I wanted to be charged formally.

I took my seat opposite DS Fields and waited for her to set up the interview tape again. 'Are you going to charge me?' I asked.

'We are still continuing our enquiries at this stage.' She sighed and met my stare with one of her own. 'Jenni, we've spoken to Destiny.'

'Why has it taken this long?'

'We had to wait for an appropriate adult.' She blinked, but did not speak immediately. Then she said, 'Destiny has made serious accusations against you. She has said that you kidnapped her and held her hostage in a hotel room.'

Now I blinked. 'That's not true!'

'She told us, that you,' she checked her notes, 'spilt your water bottle and for some reason, you thought the spilt water meant that that she'd wet herself. She said that you seem to have constructed whole conversations between you both in your head and that you would refer to those conversations as if they were fact.'

I didn't know what to say. I didn't understand why Destiny was lying. I felt lost for words.

'Destiny also said that you forced her into your car and drove her to an unknown destination. She said that she was forced to go along with your idea that she was being taken to an aunt – she says she's never had an aunt – as she didn't know how else she could get away from you when you refused to answer her requests to stop the car. She says the only aspect of what happened that she agreed to, was going to Hull. She admits she wanted to go there anyway, but by the time you agreed to take her there, she felt desperate.' She paused. 'Do you have a comment to make?'

I shook my head. I didn't know what to say. I understood she must be in shock; I understood that she must be deeply traumatised and I could understand that she'd be looking for someone to blame. She'd clearly got confused about her relationships with her captors – maybe that's to be expected. But to lie about me?

I remembered what someone had once told me about an idea held by many therapists – that in the end, all victims will turn against their rescuers and will persecute them. Destiny was the victim, I was her rescuer and now she was persecuting me. I put my head in my hands, feeling empty. I wished I could feel sadness, instead of this vacuum. But I did feel cheated. I could go to prison knowing I had done the right thing, but it felt different now. Now I felt robbed of my sense of strength and pride in having stepped up to do the right thing when so many people in my situation would not have. I had shown bravery taking on an armed gang on my own. Yes, two of them had died, but the right people – the young girls – had lived. It had felt like a success. Now I felt like a failure. What must Destiny think of me to turn on me this way?

'In your statement,' DS Fields continued, 'you said that there was a young woman at the address in the basement room. You were concerned for her because,' she looked down and consulted notes, 'she was unconscious to begin with, and had handcuffs on her wrists and ankles. Is this correct?'

'Just one wrist and one ankle.'

'Wrist and ankle – noted. The woman was Caucasian, had long dark hair, was approximately five foot six tall, slim build and aged approximately sixteen; wearing blue jeans, no shoes and a grey sparkly top. Is that all correct?'

I nodded.

'For the purposes of the tape, Jenni Wales has nodded. I have to tell you, Jenni, that in interview, Destiny has denied ever seeing a young woman at the property.'

I rubbed the bridge of my nose. 'She didn't see her. When she came down with Aleksander, I had already taken the woman to safety by removing the cuffs and getting her out of the basement window.'

'Which you did,' DS Fields said, again consulting the notes, 'with the help of a Gary Bridges. Gary Bridges was found dead by police on entering the property, with the presumed cause of death, loss of blood from three gunshot wounds, one in each kneecap and one to his stomach.'

'Yes. That's correct. I didn't kill Gary. Aleksander did that. Did . . .' I almost didn't want to ask the question, 'Did Destiny say I killed Gary too?'

'No. She says she was unaware about what happened to Gary Bridges because he was already dead when she went into the basement. She said it could've been you, she didn't know.'

I breathed out with something close to relief. The world I thought I was in, was no longer real. I started to see the news headlines. I'd never imagined them, but they would no longer be: *Teacher saves pupil*, but now: *Teacher kidnaps pupil*. 'Do you believe me that I took Destiny for her own good?'

DS Fields didn't say anything.

'I *had* to take Destiny. She was in danger. If I didn't, she would've been taken by bad people.'

'Are you a bad person, Jenni?'

'You don't believe me.' I thought for a minute. 'What about the social worker? Social services will confirm that they didn't send a social worker out to the school and my school will confirm that an imposter arrived and spoke to Destiny. If I have made all this up in my head, it doesn't explain why that would happen.' DS Fields didn't say anything, but she did look at her colleague and write something down. 'Also,' I continued, 'if I made it up, how come she met me outside the school in school hours? How would I have known to do that?'

'She said she had already had permission from the school to leave early yesterday for a dentist appointment. She suggests you knew.'

'No.'

'Perhaps it was on the school computer system. We'll check.'

I shook my head. 'No, that's not true. She came to me. She wanted my help. She said she didn't have to go far and I thought I would be back at my desk by four thirty.'

'Yet you weren't back at your desk by four thirty. Instead you ended up with two dead men in a basement two hundred and fifty miles away.'

'Because Destiny changed where she wanted to go. I've told you that. What choice did I have? I had made a commitment to save her by that point. I had to see it through. Sometimes . . .' I felt an ache in my throat, which for a second wrong-footed me, 'Sometimes if you deliberate about something too long, the moment has passed and the decision is made anyway. Sometimes, to not decide to do something is the decision to do something.'

'I don't follow.'

I threw my hands up, frustrated. 'If someone can't make up their mind to stop smoking and they don't make that decision, they are making a decision *to* smoke. If I hadn't made a decision to save her, then the decision would be to condemn her.' Nobody said anything. 'I had no choice.'

'Because she was in danger?'

'*Yes!* Yes, we've been through this.'

'But she wasn't in danger.'

It was the way she said it that made me say nothing.

'Those "strangers" were not strangers to Destiny. The man who you killed was her cousin.' DS Fields paused. 'Of sorts. It seems that social services were slightly misled by Destiny's mother, Simone, who insisted Aleksander and Destiny were cousins. For an unspecified time, Simone was in a relationship with Aleksander's uncle, and I suppose some people do apply these terms more loosely than others. Aleksander has known Destiny for years. She says that she asked him to get her and that they were going to go via her dentist appointment and then go back to the north-east area. Her social worker admits this is a regular occurrence for Destiny to go away at the weekends. They've tried to stop it, but have, albeit non-officially, given up. They recognise that as much as they don't approve of her relationship with Aleksander, they acknowledge that she always returns on a Sunday night and that she's started to do other things required of her, like treating staff better, doing her homework and other compliance issues that they've struggled with prior to the relationship becoming serious.'

'Relationship?'

'Aleksander was also Destiny's boyfriend, Jenni.'

Sunday
09:09

Jenni

I'd barely slept. I sat on my bunk watching the door, expecting someone to come in. I was held in Iraq, briefly, but I didn't want to think about that now.

I wasn't going to think about that now.

Instead I watched the door.

And finally, after about ten minutes, someone came through it. They took me back to the interview room and told me that they wanted me to run through everything again. I did. Then I had a few questions of my own. I knew they didn't believe me, and if they did some fact-finding, they'd realise I was telling the truth. I was still going to prison, but this wasn't that – this was about the truth of what I'd done. 'What about the girl I saved? The one from the basement? Have you found her yet?'

'We're still looking.'

'Well, what about the school CCTV? It'll show they were hanging around the area, that Aleksander came right up to the door – it might even show his gun.'

'We have contacted the school but recognise that it may not be possible to speak with the facilities manager until Monday.'

I sunk in my chair. 'So George knows?'

'George is ... unavailable. We spoke instead to the deputy head, a Steve Fullers.' She stared at her notes as if they were entertaining. 'He doesn't like you much, does he? Your head of department as well, isn't he?'

I said nothing.

'It sounds like he couldn't distance you further from the school if he tried.' She paused. 'He says that if you did take Destiny—'

'I didn't.'

'—if you did, then you're in breach of your contract. It sounds like you're about to be fired.'

She had snares in her voice and I realised she was trying to goad me. She didn't realise I'm not goadable; I just can't feel it. She watched me for a few seconds and perhaps she saw this in me, because her face tightened instantly like someone's turned a screw somewhere and everything has become more pinched.

'What about my boss, George. Why isn't he available?'

'He's in hospital.'

'Why?'

She paused, stretching the moment out like a fish takes a line. 'Apparently, he was beaten up so badly, he has been in a coma since Friday evening.' She stared at me without blinking, waiting for my reaction.

'I'm really sad for George.' I didn't sound it, I thought, but I knew this was the type of thing I was meant to say. 'Who beat him up?'

'Reports say it was a random attack at a service station. Apparently there's still the risk of permanent brain damage.'

I thought of the way his chin wobbled when he laughed; the way he tried to keep it jolly on a Monday morning. He was a good man. I knew I would never work with him again and I wished things were better for him.

I thought about the call I had finally made to my father. How I'd heard him answer in a bright manner, pleased to get a call during the day. I know he'd been in the sitting room watching the racing. 'Hello?' he'd answered, giving his telephone number as he did. I'd tried to get him to change that, but he never had. I'd said: 'Hello, Dad,' and with that he'd known that something was wrong. I don't know how, as I sounded the same, but he simply said, 'What's happened?'

Then I'd had to tell him about the arrest, what I'd done and why I'd done it. It'd felt ugly, brutal and I knew as I said it, things would never be the same again.

He'd listened silently throughout it all and at the end, had only the perfect words of support. But when he spoke, he sounded so old, the frailty in his voice broke the strength of his words.

So my dad knew, but there was no hero's tale to give him. And there would be no gratitude lighting Destiny's face in return for breaking his heart: instead just accusations, recriminations and condemnation.

I wouldn't answer any more questions, I just insisted on going to my cell. I had some thinking to do. I needed to know what I was going to do next. And that wasn't easy given my options were so limited.

I felt beaten.

Sunday
13:22

Jenni

Earlier, my solicitor asked for some time.

I agreed.

He asked if he could have my consent for a psychological assessment. He explained in detail what it was for and what it would mean, but I stopped listening.

He obviously didn't know that the reason I left the army was because I had refused to have a psychological assessment. Instead, I said I would consider it. Then I asked to go back to my cell.

Now I was here, I didn't know what to do. I placed my hands on the painted breeze-block wall. It was cold under my palms and it calmed me.

I breathed in and out.

I ran through the facts. I could cope with the future. I could cope with going to prison. As soon as I started on this path, I engaged with the reality that this is where it might end. I'm not concerned by this.

What did concern me, I realised, was this question, again, of my mental health. This question that refused to go away. I didn't know why this was.

I did two hundred sit-ups and felt more in control. Panting, sweating, I felt better. Even though I was running out of options, I still felt better. I had never been afraid of consequences; I'd lay down my life for the right cause, but this nothingness, this nowhere to go, the possibility that I'd let Destiny down was hard to accept. Was it possible I'd got it wrong? I couldn't accept it, because I knew my own mind, I knew what had happened – I was there.

I had to hold on to the truth.

I found a way of gripping the air brick that was only inches from the ceiling. With a good grip, I could do twenty chin-ups.

Afterwards, I felt exhilarated, until I realised that two of my nails were ripped and bleeding. I stared at them, sucking on the blood and wondered why I hadn't felt the damage.

Monday
11:04
Six months later

Jenni

I understand now: I imagined it all.

Destiny

I hang my legs over the cliff edge and look over so I can imagine your broken body lying on the beach below. I never tire of sitting here. I come even in winter, when the storms seethe, forcing me to grip the scant grass, because I feel that I could die here too. I like that. I watch the crashing waves below, beating against the bluff, pushing and pulling the flotsam and jetsam, relentless, relentless, relentless.

Then I do my own falling. I uncork a bottle and for a while feel the raw pain of my loss.

Walkers have approached me in the past; they see my solo picnic of wine and the inches between me and certain death, and think I'm going to jump. The police have been here too. Twice they've arrested me under section 136 of the Mental Health Act, determined to get me assessed. But my last psychiatrist intervened. He said that I push all of my grief and guilt onto the clifftop, as a way of maintaining my real world. He's wrong. I told him nothing about what happened. I go to remember because no one else cares.

As I sober up at home, I spend the night staring at my bedroom ceiling while the world sleeps. I stare and think about my choices, questions writhing like worms in my mind. I replay everything, everything I did and didn't do. What it caused; about the people who got hurt. Who died. I remember blue eyes locked on mine, eyes filled with the pain and the nearness of death. Then the peace, after.

I know I am guilty.

And then, when I tire of my self-hatred, I wonder what would've happened if we hadn't come together like a planet spun from its orbit into the path of the other. How different my life would've been. And that's what I can't get over – that's why I cannot know peace.

I turn over what happened to us in my mind, the memories getting no less worn through the constant re-examination. Relentless, relentless, relentless.

I don't need this clifftop to remember you or what happened that Friday afternoon in May three years ago, when everything that I'd ever loved would be gone before the sun rose on Saturday.

I think and I think and I think; thoughts of what I'm going to do next, beating relentlessly into the shallows of my mind.

Monday
06:59

Destiny

As I watch the sun creep through the too-thin curtains I realise I don't even remember coming back or going to bed. I'm not surprised and I don't try and remember. I am tired of thinking because it doesn't change anything. Instead I will change it myself, but before I get to Wednesday and pull the plug on this stasis, I have to get through today.

I sit up in bed and grab my fags. I light one. My social worker said, 'Dee, move over to a vape.' I told her, 'Why would I do that when they don't kill you?' She asked me if I wanted to kill myself and I had the sense to say no. I have always had the sense to keep my mouth shut about what I really think.

I light my fag and lean back; I can't smoke lying on my back, so I lie in a recumbent position and think about the days ahead. Tomorrow is my last meeting with the social worker. I run my finger down the dirty mattress. She's not coming here. If she was, I would've got a bed sheet from Primark, as I know she thinks I'm not taking care of myself enough. Last time she was here, she actually looked in my kitchen cupboards and saw

I was living on noodles. 'You're already too thin,' she told me, so I told her she was body-shaming me. That shut her up.

But she's not meeting me here today; she won't want to know that I'm not taking care of myself properly as that would mean that she would have to do something about it. She won't want to do something about it, because as of today, I am eighteen and therefore, finally, an adult. They just want to pass my case over to the next team so they can forget about me.

My hand moves over my ribs and I count them. I wonder if the social worker will get me a birthday card. I bet she doesn't. Their budgets have been slashed. But she's nice, I think as I pull on the fag and decide she might feel sorry for me; she might get me one out of her own money.

I grind my fag out in the overfull saucer. I wonder if I might be the only person turning eighteen who doesn't get a single birthday card. I wonder if that's not true, if there are others who have no one to buy them a birthday card. Perhaps I'm just the only one who doesn't care.

It'll all be over soon anyway; I only have two days of this life left. To leave it, will be a relief. Wednesday is the big day. It can't come quickly enough.

I fall back on the mattress, too apathetic to get up, even though I am short on time now. I stare at the cracked ceiling and am pleased that I only have two more nights where I stare into the night and not sleep. I check the clock: I don't even have that as I've got to be up in a couple of hours to catch my train. Big day.

I twist a lock of my short bleached hair; it will need to be washed. Normally, I just gel it back which looks hard, but I can't do that for my meeting tomorrow, and I can't when I go to work. It occurs to me that after today, I will never gel my hair again. I think of Aleksander and how pleased he would be that I can't do it any more. He would've hated it. He used to love my long hair. He used to love to fan my hair out on a pillow or brush it for me after the shower. He bought me a Mason and Pearson hairbrush, which he said was the best you could get. He loved to take the tangles out. Once Ollie came in and laughed at him. Aleksander threatened to shove the hairbrush up Ollie's backside and Ollie never said anything about it again.

Thinking of Ollie makes me want to read the clippings one last time. That gives me the motivation to get up and have my shower.

Today is my birthday; I can't believe it. It feels so surreal – how is it that I am only just an adult? I feel like I've been grown up all my life.

My bedsit is small; part of me is sorry to go because it has felt like a real home. But I'd have to leave it anyway, because at eighteen I am too old. I want to fucking laugh: *too old*.

This place will be filled with another hard-to-place kid in care by next week. He or she will know nothing of me, of my life. I've told the managers that I'm moving in with a friend. They're supposed to do checks, but they haven't, because if they had, then they would know that I'm not moving in with a friend, because I don't have any.

Living here was better than being in care. They let me come here when I was sixteen. They knew after Aleksander died that I wasn't doing well. After four months in a mental unit, they found this place for me instead. There are twelve bedsits and we are all allowed to live pretty much as we want, as long as we are in by eleven at night and we don't let guests stay over. The guy who runs it, Robert, is pretty nice. He tries to get me to go to church but I tell him that God won't want me. He says that's bullshit and that God loves me no matter what. 'Destiny,' he said, finding me a picture of a super-cute fluffy white puppy on the internet, 'if this pup was yours, what would you call it?'

'Lexi,' I said, not telling him that I always wanted a daughter called Lexi.

'So Destiny, say you had Lexi and you loved her so much – you would love her, wouldn't you?'

I looked at the puppy's eyes and yearned for her. I would love her more than she could bear.

He continued: 'Say you came home one day and Lexi had chewed your furniture and pooed on the floor, would you throw Lexi out? Or would you clean up and continue to love her?'

I stared at that picture on his phone. I wished I could believe it's true, but God will know what I've done even if Robert doesn't. Once I nearly told Robert, but I figured I like living here and I wouldn't want to do anything to ruin it.

My bedsit is pretty tidy; Robert and Marlena, the deputy manager, can come in and inspect it anytime they like so I do the minimum; I keep the mud-brown carpet clear of stuff and just shove everything in the wardrobe. There's only the one room with the kitchen at the far end but it's got a balcony, which I love to sit out on. If I angle my chair just right, I can get the sun on my face all afternoon. There's a big tree right outside and the wood pigeons coo, and they sound so close, I like to imagine that I can reach out and pet them; it's the most lovely sound in the world.

I take a shower, staring at the pale blue tiles. This was the only bit of the unit I didn't like when I moved in; the shower tiles reminded me of being on the psych ward. Being on the ward reminds me about how it felt to watch the blood come out of Aleksander and my future slip away.

I use soap today and scrub like I can scrub that memory away, but I know I can't because I've tried before. That time I didn't use soap and that's why I ended up in hospital with bleach burns. Most of the bleach damage is gone now, there's just some discolouration on my left thigh and a patch on the inside of my forearm. I feel sad when I look at it: my poor body has been through too much for only eighteen. It has been to places it never should've been. I almost start to remember, but tip my face under the shower spray. I remind myself that I don't need to remember – the suitcase has been packed for the last time. I'm glad: I don't want to think any more.

I am tired of myself.

I dry myself and think that if I have another bad night, I might struggle to get up before six thirty and I've got to be on the ward by eight. I've worked for the hospital for over a year if you include the voluntary work, but only got a transfer to Willow ward last week and since then I've been late twice.

I would've thought that since I got the transfer I would've behaved impeccably, but the bad dreams and sleeplessness have been getting much, much worse, and I struggle to get up and get in on time. I know they're not too happy about it. Still, it won't matter soon.

I dry myself not thinking about anything much. When I come out of the bathroom, I see someone has pushed a card under my door.

I stare at it while I get dressed. I dress in jeans and a hoodie, still staring at the white rectangle on the matt. It holds such promise.

I went through a phase last year, before I got a job at the hospital, of buying lottery tickets. I became a bit obsessed. I loved that feeling of holding them just before the numbers were announced, the exciting promise of what I would do when I won. I never thought it would be a possibility, more a certainty that I would definitely win big one day. I could see it so clearly in my mind's eye. I imagined making the call, what they would say when I told them I had a winning lottery ticket; what I would do with the money. I saw a house in the country, an amalgamation of the wonderful country homes I had seen with Aleksander. And I was never alone in that house; I had filled it with dogs and cats and fabulous friends, who would want to know me. Who felt I was worth something.

But I never won.

One day I just gave up. I just suddenly got that it would never happen for me, that I would never be worth anything.

I understood that I had been born unlucky. I learnt then that the absence of hope is a terrible thing.

Looking at that envelope reminds me of those lottery tickets. If I don't pick it up and open it, it's like an unchecked ticket: it still holds that intoxicating possibility.

I make a cup of tea first. Then I can't put it off any longer. When I pick it up, I'm surprised that my hand is shaking. I hate my mum for making me feel like this. How can I, after all this time, still care? Why, when I don't even like her, do I still get that lurch in my stomach, with the slight possibility that she might have got in touch with me? That's why I hate those PPI calls on my phone – I see a strange number and I think it might be her. I wish I could think something else, but still, despite the therapy, despite me trying to train myself, I am still pathetic. And I do it now. I have that hope.

Then I turn the envelope and see just my name written in blue biro: *Destiny*, and nothing else. No stamp. No address.

Of course it isn't from her.

But I still think, maybe she came here and popped it through the letterbox, but I don't believe it, not even a little bit, I'm just trying to stop that crashing sick feeling in my stomach. My mother wouldn't remember; she hasn't remembered my birthday for ten years. She doesn't even know where I live. Well, I guess now she doesn't have to feel any guilt. Today I am officially grown.

I rip the envelope open. It's a small card. The picture is of a painting; it's of a seagull flying over the ocean. Inside are cheery messages from Robert and Marlena. They want me to have a special day. Of course they do – they're nice people. As kind as they are, my sigh is still audible in the silence of my flat.

I look around the small bedsit and wonder where to put it. I decide on the bookshelf. I balance it on top of books I bought when I still thought there was a point to buying and reading books. They are fiction: ephemeral crap, thrillers and romance I devour to distract me, hip and shoulder to the classics I savour. I pull out my favourite, *The Great Gatsby*. I balance it on top of the others like a shelf, and then stand the card on it. Robert and Marlena won't understand the reference when they find it, but it's there in case they are smart. The stupid, romantic part of me, thinks that they might possibly care enough to want to know why I did what I did; that they might want to look for clues. Perhaps they will see that this book has been pulled out, selected above others. Perhaps they will read it and possibly understand how we are all helplessly pushed back into the past, unable to escape our actions. I am as trapped as Gatsby chasing Daisy. But my Daisy is dead.

Or maybe my mother is Daisy. I shudder. Unfortunately, she is still alive.

I stare at the card, a little freaked that it depicts of all things, a gull. I expect they buy these cards as a job lot to keep in a desk drawer ready for a resident's birthday, but *even so*.

The only animal Aleksander ever cared for was seagulls. He once broke Ollie's cheekbone when Ollie kicked one, hurting its wing. He had a thing about them, said they were survivors, like him. A couple of times we even fed them, down in Hastings. He said no one liked seagulls, said that to some people they were

Monday
14:31

Destiny

Hastings to Hull is five hours. I missed a connection so I'm here so much later than I thought. This level of hassle is why I don't visit my mother I tell myself. I know it's a lie. It's not that long ago I used to run away from care to come back and see her every weekend, but it was a habit, with Alek's help, I could break.

Until now.

As I walk towards the nearest thing I had to a childhood home, I pull my coat around myself like it is cold – but it isn't, in fact it's the opposite: there's a heat in the air that's more like August. The sky is a pretty blue, but it doesn't touch me. I can't feel anything here: I have to be careful. This place is dangerous to me.

I haven't been here in so long. It feels important coming back here today. Cars line both sides of the street; other than that it's featureless, no trees, nothing of interest except the two long stretches of small terraced Victorians. In some ways, it reminds me of the road where we had our last party house. Despite the warmth, I dig my hands deep into my coat and rub my knuckles with the thumbs. My fists explain that I mustn't remember that place.

Once, maybe, this street might've been a salubrious area, but not now. A fridge has been dumped outside one house; rubbish has been dropped all along the gutter. I stand for a moment, looking at a pile that looks like someone picked up their bin and emptied it in the street. A broken mug; a couple of barbecue skewers; a pile of fag butts from an emptied ashtray; a stool with only two legs. How can people bear to let their lives be so publically displayed?

I walk until I get to number 232. I haven't been here since I was fourteen.

So much has happened since then, I almost expect my old house to look different. But I stand in front of the door and it looks the same. The door is the same – dark navy, the same as all the properties in the street owned by the local authority. It's dirty with the exhaust from the cars who use this street as a rush-hour rat run. I look closer – there, I can see a dent. I breathe. I needed it to be there, the marks the police ram made when they bust down the door all those years ago. The drugs raid was the last night I spent here as a legal ward of my mother's. I couldn't bear there not to be a sign of the catastrophe it caused, a memorial to the final death of my life with my mum. But it's here: it's all the same as before.

I can't believe I'm here again. I know it will only hold disappointment – and pain. But I came with a purpose, a duty, even: I feel I should say a final goodbye.

But as I stand here, a small voice inside whispers what I don't want to hear. Yes, I can convince myself that I am here for duty – to do the right thing – but I know that it is something different. I still want her to hold me, to love me, to change my mind. Even though I'm an adult today, it seems I still can't quite kick the childish habit: today, on my birthday, I still want my mum.

Angry with myself, I rap the door hard.

My knock pushes the door open. It opens right back as if anyone has the right to cross the threshold here – all comers, come and take what you want, it's all yours, just come in and help yourself.

Inside, the house is as dirty as the outside. The hallway still has the same pink carpet I remember. It was worn threadbare in places, but now it's also been sullied to grey. The house stinks of cigarettes and something else, something that could be cat shit. I can also smell something else, something chemical. I know that smell and know that my mother has moved past heroin. Of course she has: I've been off the drug scene for a while, but I will bet all I have that fentanyl would've found my mum and my mum would've found fentanyl. What a twisted romance.

Despite the sunshine outside, the house is dark: the kitchen at the back has blinds pulled down and the door to the front room is shut. I glance at the staircase. I wonder if my old bedroom has changed at all. I've got no desire to see it. I remember that the social worker I had at the time stood in the doorway while I packed my stuff up; his name was Malcolm or Martin or maybe even Mark, and when I started to throw things around, the sympathy in his face dissolved to fear.

'Hello?' I call out into the silence.

A black cat springs out of the shadows to weave between my ankles; the sudden movement makes me start. I want to pat it to reassure myself that it's OK, it's only a cat. But I don't – I'm suddenly afraid. I can feel myself being watched. There's a gap in the door to my right. My heart is beating hard and I can't breathe. I push it open.

Inside, it has changed. The sofas have gone, the TV too. Everything, in fact: the room has been stripped bare. The heavy framed mirror my mother liked so much has gone from above the fireplace. There's not even a shadow to suggest that it was ever there. There is only the dirty pink carpet and a mattress where the sofa used to be. I can't delay it any more; I finally look down.

She is lying on the mattress with the thinnest, dirtiest of duvets across her.

'Hello, Mum.'

Monday
14:56

Destiny

'Well, lookee here at what the cat brought in,' she says laughing at her own joke. We look at each other for what feels like a long time. I wish she would sit up, not lie like that, half-slumped. She has new angles on her face but her dark hair is still long. She only looked at me with the vaguest surprise despite not seeing me for years. I thought she would get out of bed. I didn't expect her to bring out the teapot and the bone china, but not to get out of bed . . . I check myself, fingernails digging crescents into my palm. *Stay real*, I remind myself.

It's my only defence. Even when I was in hospital after Aleksander died, those long months when I wanted to die, she never came to see me. I think she was the only person I wanted to see, but I don't know. Maybe I didn't want to see her. I don't remember a lot of that time, so perhaps my needing her is me projecting back onto that time as if it was fact when it wasn't fact at all.

Maybe I just thought about Aleksander; perhaps it was only him that I missed. I almost wish I could remember.

Her grey eyes stare at me with the cold look I have seen before. 'What do you want?' When I don't answer, her face softens and she looks at me speculatively. 'Have you got any—?'

'No. I have no money,' I say automatically.

Instantly her face hardens and she looks away, her thoughts elsewhere from me. I can't reach this woman, I think desperately, I've never been able to. Nothing will change. Not ever.

The cat leaps on her and her hand snakes out, twisting over its body in a way that makes it shudder and twirl beneath her. They like each other.

'How have you been?' I ask, wanting to scream: *it's my birthday, it's my eighteenth fucking birthday today. Why can't you remember for once?*

But I don't.

'You know,' she says with a shrug.

Her hand trails up the cat's body, revealing the maggot holes of her track lines up the inside of her grey-skinned arms. One foot has fallen out from under the safety of the cover. It's almost skeletal, but with half-grown-out red nail varnish. She made some effort a few weeks ago. But I also see the tell-tale black punctures, surrounded by bruising. Her veins are no longer her ally. Like my life, they are collapsing.

'It's my birthday today,' I say. I did not want to say this.

She turns sharply. 'I haven't got anything.'

'I know,' I say, punching my fists back into my coat pockets, hating myself for still – after all this fucking time – wanting to make her feel OK for her shortcomings. She should have some-thing for me, even – no, most of all – I'd like a dry, listless kiss from those lips who give so freely to so many for so little. But she is already looking away.

I remember that next door was rented to a woman with schizophrenia. I remember she used to shout crazy things at all times of night. It was a long time ago since I had that sort of detail about my mother's life, about who bothered her, or who made her laugh. We did have that once; the best of it was when she dated Jakob and I Aleksander. We shared a world.

She looks back at me with tiredness. I see new creases then around her eyes; the lines around her mouth more drawn. I see then that she has jowls – this woman who once traded on her good looks is losing them. What will she have then?

The expression on her face shows something I can't read. 'Destiny, why are you here?'

Because. I want to say, because you're my mother. Because I wanted to see you on my eighteenth birthday. Because I wanted to come or perhaps because you wanted me to be here. Finally, I say, 'Because I came to say goodbye.' I lift my chin and I hope my eyes are as hard in the receiving as they are in the giving.

My mother was a fine-looking woman, once. Dark like me, small-boned like me, but a different class. I know I am attractive with my high cheekbones and well-proportioned face, but my mother was, once, something else all together.

She scrabbles on the floor, her hand a scorpion looking to pounce. She finds a box of cigarettes and the other hand finally stops fussing the cat and reaches for a cigarette. She pushes it into her mouth with surprising determination. She rattles a lighter from the pack and lights her cigarette, all the time her eyes staring at me. I sink to the bare floorboards opposite her in this empty, empty room.

'What do you want, Destiny?' she asks again, after she has taken several deep inhalations.

I want you. 'I don't want anything.'

'You've always wanted something your whole damned life.'

'No. Nothing,' I insist. *I want you.* 'I only came to say goodbye.'

'Got that big job in New York then?'

For a moment I don't know what she is talking about. Then I remember. A lifetime ago, before the last time I had been taken into care, before she had started dealing drugs and was still only dealing her body and I was living with her after being in foster care, I remember telling her I was going to do better than she had done. She had provoked me into it and, because I was childish and young and wanted to make her listen, I lied and told her I'd been asked to model in New York City and that I would never return. To remember my childish hyperbole shames me. Even more so that this is what she has remembered, after all these years. This woman who can't remember her only child's birthday can remember this.

'Not New York,' I say, thinking: ask me where then? Where am I going? Ask me: why am I saying goodbye?

Instead she inhales so deeply, she draws the cigarette to a sharp, hot, fiery point. She blows out slowly, looking at me. 'Are you still with that Polish prick, Aleksander?'

'Yes.' I'm surprised that I've said this; my lie makes me edgy. I thought I'd moved past pretending things.

'He still owes me forty quid,' she says, coldly.

'What for?'

'We went to the Golden Lion and he said he'd pay for the drinks, but had left his wallet somewhere. I stumped for him,' she drags her hand under her nose, 'and I never saw him again. He still owes me. Tell him that. Tell him I want it back – I need it.'

I force myself to take a breath. Stupid Destiny: stupid, stupid, Destiny. Fancy thinking it would ever be any different.

'Tell him?' she prompts again, eyes narrowed on me. 'Or maybe you can pay?'

I pull my own wallet out. I emptied my account today. I left it overdrawn by two hundred quid. I wanted everything I could.

I open my wallet. She leans forward, like she's hungry and I'm presenting a five-course feast in front of her. She is almost salivating. My fingertip flicks over the notes, pathetically enjoying her interest. She is only wearing a vest top, one strap has slipped over her shoulder. There are dark shadows under her collarbones. She might be even thinner than me, I realise with alarm. 'I'll pay you what Aleksander owes. He wouldn't have wanted – he doesn't want to owe you anything.' I pull fresh plastic tenners from my wallet. They are immaculate, smooth and innocent in this room where nothing else has been for a long, long time. I count them out: one, two, three, four.

She takes them and secretes them beneath the duvet. She lights another cigarette from the tip slumbering on the dinner plate ashtray. After a moment, she points the packet at me. 'Want one?'

I reach out with trembling fingers and take one. They are not my brand, but my mother has offered me something and I want it.

I light it quickly from the outstretched flame. Something young in me likes this ritual that we used to share when I was younger, the giving of flame, drawing us together, uniting us in a shared experience. The other experiences in our lives shouldn't have been shared and when they were, it only stained us.

But this is only a fag. I draw it in and let my thoughts hover above the stinking mass of what is us. My mind darts across the top of memory after memory of us as if it is a mosquito looking for somewhere to rest and draw blood. But there is no memory I can pause on to feel good. The best times were with Aleksander and Jakob, but I am no longer able to think of that.

'Can you buy us some booze? The newsagents is only down the road and I have cash.'

My cash. I shake my head. 'I've got to go soon.'

'So how is he, Aleksander?' Her eyes narrow sharply.

'Aleksander,' I say, faltering as if to speak about him is to evoke him into the room, 'is doing really great.' I say this with conviction, because if he was alive, he would be.

She wrinkles her nose in a sneer. 'I let you have him. It was all down to me.'

'It was *not* down to you!' I shout, my flash of anger surprising the cat, who suddenly bolts from the room. It was not down to her, what Aleksander and I had was what we created between us. We took two broken worlds and put them together to create our own universe. It wasn't a good place, but it was better than what we had when we were apart.

She leans back against the wall, her eyes widen slightly. 'Is he here?' she says, her eyes drifting to the door as if she expects him to walk in.

'I came on my own.'

'Why? Why did you come Destiny?'

There is so much hate in me. I can no longer live with it – it has to do something. It is too strong, too immense to simply lie dormant. It occurs to me that the hate I live with started here, in this house. I thought it was because of all the things that have happened to me in the last four years: being taken, Gary's death, losing Aleksander. But perhaps this hate started with her. Perhaps, even when I was only two years old, it was in me. Or perhaps younger, perhaps even when I was a baby. Or perhaps even before that, when I was in utero, a curled foetus, forcibly intoxicated as I took her filth down my umbilical cord, perhaps I began to hate then.

But despite that, despite the hate I feel, I know that I love her too. It's a crazy dichotomy that I can't process. It meant that even when I was away from her, feeling safer even in the children's home, I missed her so much. I am crying now, because I feel so sad for the little girl that was so muddled because she missed her mother, yet hated her, yet still missed her. That little girl is me. It's still me today. And I'm here because I've got to pack that girl up and be something different.

She watches me cry and lights another cigarette. 'You've got cash. I could score us some Friend. Fentanyl,' she says patiently, the voice of a parent explaining phonics to their little one.

I look down on this spider of a woman: thin, dangerous, her eyes even now watching my wallet, rather than me. I'm about to leave, then something occurs to me, something I didn't know that I wanted to know. 'Mum, what was your mother like?'

She looks away. She doesn't like me calling her mum. She used to say it made her feel old. She pulls hard on her cigarette, blowing the smoke out like an old movie star. 'She was like you, Destiny.'

'Me? How was she like me?'

'For a start, you've got her temper!' She laughed but it sounded brittle. 'You never had to fear my hand, like I had to fear hers.' She pulled on her fag. 'When you've lost it, nothing can touch you, nothing. I made sure I kept sharp things out of your way. She was the same. My brothers and me would run if ma reached for the kettle.' She screeches a laugh: 'She'd throw the hot water and then send the metal hob kettle after us! And she was a whore; just like you, just like me.'

I feel stung. 'I am not and I never will be!'

She laughed again. 'You really think I don't know what went on? I know Aleksander is dead and you're standing here, lying to me, to my face, like I'm stupid. All that publicity about that teacher who took you, don't you think it was all people could talk about when it was in all the papers? Ollie and Jay up on charges, but not you? You acted all innocent like you were the *victim*.'

Her hand jabbed her accusation at me. 'Destiny, you're no victim, you never was. I know you would've been right there with that gang taking those girls out of the country. The gang was busted and Aleksander got banged and you got all doe-eyed like you were a lost Disney princess.

'But you're just like your nan and just like me, and don't think I don't know you, girl, because I've been knowing you all your life. At least we had the decency to only sell our own twats. You sewed yours up like Snow bloody White and got your dwarfs to do your very dirty work for you. And trust me honey, there's no dirtier work than yours.'

When I leave, I'm breathing heavily, gulping the air in as if I'm drowning. I stumble in the hall pulling the sitting-room door behind me hard. *Click.*

The sound of the clicking latch or perhaps the smell of my mother, takes me back.

I'm in my bedroom. The light comes through the slated blinds, throwing stripes against the My Little Pony duvet. Where it's bright, it's shining bright; where the shadows are, it's dark. Somewhere I can hear a bird outside: cheep; cheep; cheep. It sounds like it's talking and I wonder what it's saying. Outside of this room it is quiet, except for the bird. Perhaps it's because everyone else is at school. I think of my teacher, Mrs Hampshire, she is nice. I wish I was sitting on the carpet with her and I wish she was reading a story. I like stories.

I watch bits of dust tumble slowly through the air. They cut in and out of the light. When they are in the light I can see them move. In. Out. In. Out. In. Out. The movement makes me feel sick.

They turn slowly. I pretend that they are fairies; I watch them dance like they are drunk. All the time I'm doing that THING,

I watch them. I think about where the fairies are going – I like to think about where they will end up. They are not coming to see me, I know that. They've come here by mistake because they got lost. Sarah at school told me about the tooth fairy – perhaps one of them is the tooth fairy, going somewhere to deliver some money in return for a new brick for her castle. She doesn't come to see me. I don't blame her: my mouth is too dirty for my teeth to be nice. I try every time to put a new tooth under my pillow but in the morning it is still there and no money. She doesn't want my teeth.

I don't want my teeth.

I don't want to be doing *this*.

I watch a piece of dust tumble and change direction; perhaps that is her – perhaps the tooth fairy is trying to get to the window. She wants to get away and be somewhere else. She doesn't want to see what I am doing, it is scary. I wish I could help her, open the window and set her free. But I won't be allowed.

He changes how we are and the air must change because of us, because the tiny thing busts up suddenly and moves towards the window as if she is flying really fast.

I watch this and wish I was her.

My bedroom door opens. My mum is standing in the door; she has her blood eyes on. For a million years she stands there, and I watch her hand on the door move like a crab. I hear my heart: I am scared. But I hope she will save me. *Please save me, Mummy. I don't want to be doing this.* She stares at him, then at me.

I stare at her.

I can tell in my mouth that he is worried.

I am worried; my cheeks feel hot. I stare at her and wonder if she is worried. She might be mad with me; I know I shouldn't be doing this and she might be mad with me. I don't want her to be mad with me, I don't want to be doing this, but I do want her to save me.

Then she sways a little and I know.

She looks down and goes back out. The door shuts. She was not worried and she did not save me. The sound of the sticky-out-bit of the door clicking shut, is louder than my heart. It is the loudest sound in the whole world.

I carry on being a GOOD GIRL, but now I don't see the fairies and now I don't hear the bird: now I can only hear the sound of the door shutting and his breathing getting faster and faster.

I hear the click of her front door shutting, I remember what I never forgot: she never saved me. She was right about one thing: I ain't ever been Snow White.

I fall from her house, into the warmth outside. But there's no comfort in the sun. There's no comfort in anything.

Tuesday
10:10

Destiny

The current social worker is called Val; she looks like a social worker. She wears ethnic-inspired fashion, is overweight with arms that, when she lifts them, swing underneath. She wears earrings made of coral. She smiles at me now like the nice mum she probably is to some lucky person and she does it at every opportunity, and not merely because it makes her face pretty. 'Dee, did you have a nice birthday yesterday?'

'Yes, thank you.'

She beams at me and drinks her tea. 'So ... did you do anything nice?'

I think about telling her that I went to see my mum, but I know she has a thick file on my mother and she'd know that no good would've come from it. If only I could've had her insight I could've saved myself the train fare, the forty quid and the memories.

'My friends took me out for breakfast.'

She beams and I'm pleased I told the lie. I'm also pleased I'm here.

When I left for this appointment, Robert and Marlena stopped me at reception, where they'd put a *Happy Birthday!*

silver helium balloon up for me. They insisted because they didn't catch me yesterday. I'm sure they tried, but I took the fire door when I left the building, which I thought was a metaphor for how I felt. But they really wanted me to see the balloon and afterwards, Marlena insisted that I took it with me. They'd bought a carrot cake from the Co-Op, because I once said I liked it and they made me stop and have a slice. 'We didn't think that we should get you a candle now you're all grown up,' Robert told me, after they both stood and sang 'Happy Birthday' to me in voices clarion and bright like trumpets.

The sweetness of the cake made me gag, but I was more glad of the song than I would've like to have admitted; I knew they were trying to make an effort and I wondered if they will miss me. It must be hard for them when someone moves out. I know they're a little worried about me, about the lack of things like cups and plates that I've failed to amass. I did get some vouchers to spend on things I would need, but they don't know that I gave them to my neighbour instead. 'Don't you want them?' she'd asked. I told her that I didn't need them where I was going, but she didn't hear as she had already started to shut the door in case I changed my mind.

'So, Dee,' the social worker said, 'this is our last meeting. I've got a little checklist I've got to go through and some leaflets about the after-care team. They'll continue to keep an eye on you until you're twenty-one.'

'I know that.' I put my hand up to show I don't want the leaflets. 'You've already given me some.' She's always trying to give me leaflets; I know it's because she wants to help me and all she's got to offer is her over-bright smile and the leaflets that signpost me to other services that might have enough money to offer me help.

But they can't help, because I still have the loss of him. My life stopped when he died and I've never been able to find the answer of how to get him back in any conversation, any therapy session, any leaflet, because there *is* no way of getting him back. There's only one possible thing that I can do to make me feel better and I'm going to do it tomorrow. Wednesday.

After she's done her checklist, I think that's it. I'm already half out of my chair. I don't like goodbyes and I think Val is the type of person that might try to hug me. I'm small and I guess, since I'm too thin, that I look to some people like I need a hug. Or maybe they do it because they feel guilty that after a life in care, nothing good ever happened for me, that I failed all my exams despite the predictions of nines in most subjects – because how could I think of measures and *Macbeth* and molecules when I was dead with grief? – and now I'm the no-hoper that they always feared I would become.

'Dee,' Val says, 'stay for one more tea.'

I can't argue, because she's playing me at my game and is already out of the chair and across the office, putting on the kettle. I settle back in the chair and accept that I've got nowhere else to be today. The fact that I wasn't working on my birthday, or today, is a coincidence; I would've been happy to turn up to work, but it was not to be as I was rostered three days off after a nine-day run. That's why I am sitting here. I should've been in this meeting last week but Val was off sick. As she makes my tea, she apologises again for this, and the fact I'm here after my eighteenth birthday. She obviously believes my crap that I've got better places to be.

She puts the tea in front of me. 'Of course you're all grown up now.' She regards me like I'm something interesting under a microscope. 'Maybe that means we can have a different kind of chat.'

I take the mug and sip. I have to hand it to Val, she knows how to make a fab cup of tea. 'What do you mean?'

'I mean that, as of yesterday, technically you're no longer my case. You're an adult now, so I wondered if we could have a talk.'

'About how I'm different?'

She gives me a polite smile. Her gentle eyebrow raise suggests she doesn't understand me.

'Now I'm grown up,' I explain. 'Now I've left my past behind.'

She looks at me and it's an analytical look as if she suddenly sees me differently; perhaps she finally sees *me*.

She purses her lips. 'I'm going to be frank,' she says as if she's suddenly decided an approach which was different to one she had thought of before. 'I'm going to come at this issue straight on.'

I shrug like I don't care. I guess I don't. 'What issue?'

'I wanted to talk about what happened to you when you were fifteen.'

I shrug again, but this time it feels jerky to me; I wonder if she noticed. I don't speak in case my voice gives me away.

'That was quite a thing you went through back then.'

She makes it sound like an obstacle course. I nod when it becomes clear that she's expecting some sort of response.

'A terrible thing, being taken like that.'

I drink my tea. 'It's difficult for me to talk about.'

'I understand that. That's why I've never mentioned it to you. Nor did Norma before me.' She's talking about my previous social worker who was a drip and was always breaking appointments. The only reason Norma wouldn't have mentioned it to me was because she wouldn't trust me not to break her nose if she did.

'I had therapy.'

'Was that successful, do you think?'

'Yes.' I say this because this is what you are supposed to say. The NHS rarely pay for the type of therapy I had, but my psychiatrist felt that nothing else had worked, and as I was still trying to kill myself, I think they were becoming desperate. They splashed out on me because I was in care. Guilt money. You have a shit life, so take this. Afterwards, I made sure I smiled more. It was easier because I had developed my plan – in a funny way, that's how I got my plan because my therapist asked what I needed.

What do you need, Destiny?

I'll tell you what I need, but you won't like it.

'Why do you say that, Dee?'

I blink, coming back to her. 'Why do I say yes?' She's surprised me – she's gone off on a tangent I hadn't expected. 'Because it worked?' But I sound hesitant, like I've asked her, because I don't know myself.

She smiles and nods, coral earrings swinging in pudgy lobes.

When she doesn't say anything, I feel compelled to add, 'Because ... because ...' but I falter, because I don't know what to say. It didn't work, because if, by working, I'm meant to be different or better, an improved version of myself, then it's not true and she knows it's not true. Because I weigh six stone and I cry every night, and if I can afford it, I smoke and drink until I pass out and if I can't, I climb into a hot bath and sink under the water leaving my nose above the water-line, before slowly dipping under, feeling the water edge closer and closer to my nostrils, fantasising that I might not come back up. But it's hard to drown yourself in the bath. There's an automatic choking point where I end up spluttering and coughing and crying with the failure of living and the failure of trying to die.

And then yesterday I find out that I'm just like my mother. And her mother before that. No doubt I'm from a long line of fuck-heads. So this isn't upbringing: this is fate. Then I understand there's no escape. This is what Shakespeare wrote about; this is destiny. Me. I'm not just star-crossed: I'm star-locked; star-imprisoned.

I'm star-fucked.

And I guess, when my mother gazed down at me and named me, she knew that all along.

The social worker doesn't say anything, but at least she can read my mood enough not to smile. Smiling would not work for me right now. Instead she reaches for my hands and takes my right thumb where I have been digging it into my left palm. We both look at the deep mark I have left and she says: 'You mustn't let your anger drive your actions, Dee.'

I pull my thumb free from her gentle, but firm grasp. All this is bullshit.

All that happened when I finished therapy was that I thought *up yours, world* and formulated my plan. A plan I have been putting into action ever since. One that could've taken several years, but instead has only taken a year.

She doesn't know about this plan. How could she? I only doubt it for a minute because she's looking at me like she's got me worked out. I can see she's smart – not regular smart, but possibly super smart and definitely smarter than I gave her credit for, which is stupid of me because smart people can tell other people are smart, too. Average people don't notice if other people are smart because they don't know. But smart people are in this little secret club of understanding. It's like we can smell each other.

I wonder why she ended up in this job if she's as clever as I suddenly suspect. 'How come you're a social worker?' I ask, trying to divert her with my new train of thought.

'Because I had a tough childhood, Dee, and I wanted to help other people.'

I blink, disconcerted. 'As tough as mine?'

She pulls a little face as if she's considering it. 'Well, no one can know how tough someone else has had it, can they?'

'You've read my file,' I challenge.

'Yes, of course, and there are lots of similar features you share with my childhood. I can say this now,' she reminds me, 'because

I've finished your paperwork, so I'm no longer your social worker' she checks her watch, 'and this is now my lunch break.'

'You don't have to talk to me?'

'No. Does that surprise you?'

Of course. No one talks to me unless they are paid to talk to me, like Robert or Val, or when I'm at work and I am paid to talk to them. A conversation with my own mother costs me forty quid. But I don't tell her that agonising, humiliating fact. Instead, I say nothing.

She sips her tea. 'I realise that, and I feel like I should be transparent, which is why I say it. But I do want to have this chat with you and I won't write down what you tell me. We are simply two adults talking about the things we have in common. And most people don't have the things in common that we do, do they, Dee? Which, I hope like me, you're jolly pleased about.'

I nod. This is true. All my life I've been on the outside. Locked out of the world that other people live in. A world where only moderately shit things happen to them, if at all. I don't know what it's like to only have moderately shit things happen. The best metaphor to describe my life is that I stand alone in the cold shade watching everyone else enjoy a picnic in the sunshine, all laughing and chatting together. But maybe Val has been standing in the shade with me the whole time and I didn't even notice.

Maybe that's why she smiles at me the whole time, because she knows that we stand together.

I've finished my tea. 'Can I have another one please?'

She beams like I've pleased her and gets up. She finds a biscuit tin and takes the lid off. 'Help yourself.' She pats her stomach.

'The more you eat, the less I do and trust me, you need to help me out.'

I hesitate, thinking of the carrot cake. But I suddenly fancy one. I take a chocolate digestive and realise as I eat it, careful to catch the crumbs in my hand, that I like this, sitting talking to someone just because. Even if the subject matter feels dangerous. Or maybe *because* it is dangerous. It feels real, like it's important, rather than blandly commenting on the weather or how late the trains are, those things that people say to each other to fill the silence they're afraid of.

She gives me another cup of tea.

'How was your childhood the same as mine?' I ask her.

Val speaks and now she isn't smiling. I feel bad for doing this, but I don't want to stand alone in the shade any more. I've done it my entire life. Even though I've lived in care homes with other kids, we didn't talk about the bad stuff. Or if they did, they didn't with me.

'I was put into care at two, because my parents either didn't want me or because they couldn't look after me. I don't know which, because I never met them.'

I'm surprised by this bald statement. She hasn't tried to dress it up.

'I went to a care home that was very abusive. I'm nearly sixty. I've never got over it. But . . .' she looks at me very closely as if it is me saying something interesting, not her, 'I have learnt to live with it in a way that I have peace.' When I don't speak she adds: 'There's no thunder in my heart any more. Only blue skies.'

I don't say anything for a while, then: 'What is your life like now?'

She smiles again. 'After I found a therapist that worked for me – you see, if the first one doesn't work, you can try again with someone else, a different approach, a different time in your life, and that can make all the difference – I found I could move on. But the real difference was meeting someone, falling in love and having my babies.'

'You have babies?'

When she laughs and tells me, 'My babies are twenty-five and twenty-three now,' I feel a little foolish.

'I was in love once,' I tell her. Now I'm on dangerous territory. No one knows about me and Aleksander now – no one but Ollie and Jay, and Ollie is in prison for drug dealing – the only charge that stuck after a kilo of resin and several ounces of white was found in his flat – and won't be out for another six years. They found the modified van, which told a story, but by the time they got to it, Ollie and Jay had washed the inside of it with bleach and stuck it through a car wash several times before dumping it. It was registered in Aleksander's name and he was dead.

Jay went to court on charges of drug dealing and trafficking, but the evidence was thin on him as his brother refused to squeal, and so Jay walked. The rabbit never saw the brothers, so there was nothing to link them to her. I still watch Jay through my fake Facebook account; he moved to Cornwall last year and married an Australian woman, retrained as a plumber and spends his free time surfing off Newquay, so I don't think he's ever going to care about any of it.

I stuck with my story that I was another victim and was treated like that. The rabbit was found and at first she tried to blame me, but in the end, all she knew was I was another girl at the party and rescinded her accusation. By the time she stood in the witness box, my name wasn't even mentioned.

'"Once" suggests that it's in the past.'

I bite my lip. I want to tell someone. I want to have a proper conversation. I'm tired of living my life. I take a deep breath and remind myself that it's all going to change tomorrow.

'He died.'

'Dee, I'm so sorry.'

'The worst thing is that he didn't have to die. There's someone whose fault it is and I can't get over that they are still alive and he's not.'

'That sounds very painful.' She pauses. 'Dee, did this happen before you had therapy?' When I nod, she continues, 'Did you share any of it then?' When I shake my head, she adds, 'Do you think that's why the therapy didn't work?'

I hesitate, ready to fib and tell her it did work – *what are you talking about? I'm cured!* – but I don't. The shade is too cold. And it's so fucking lonely. 'Probably. I just wasn't ready to talk about it. But now I've decided what to do, I feel like I can.'

'What have you decided to do?'

This is the question I cannot answer. Instead, I say, 'Can I tell you about him first?'

She smiles and nods. 'I would love to hear about him.'

I close my eyes as I remember. 'He was handsome and strong. He had a terrible sense of humour – he couldn't understand my

jokes at all, but he wanted to, and that was what was so endear-
ing. I love that he wanted to, wanted to be better, wanted to
always improve himself. And he used to really encourage me,
too, he found out about degree courses for me through the Open
University, and told me it didn't matter if I didn't do well in
school, I could still do my degree in English Literature.'

'He sounds amazing. And of course that's still true, you could
do that and get a good job.'

'I never wanted to do that,' I say, not keeping the disgust
out of my voice. 'I didn't need to get a normal job, as he had
got his own business in trade and I was his partner and it was
doing really well. He used to say that he was a true capitalist,
when most people didn't understand what that meant. He said
exploiting the market stopped the market exploiting you.'

She purses her lips at this.

I felt the need to defend him. 'He was going to do a degree
in business and economics, even though he was a natural. He
was going to move into new avenues of trade and in five years
we would've been raking it in as well as trading in new things,
which would've meant we were one hundred per cent . . .' *legit*, I
was going to say. 'Independent,' I say instead. 'He wanted good
things for us.'

'Dee,' she spreads her hands out in front of her on the desk,
fanning her fingers. She stares at them for a moment as if the
answer is in the gaps between them. Then she snatches them up,
decision made. 'You may not have been told this because of both
your age at the time and because of the frailty of your mental
health, but the police wanted to bring charges against you.'

I don't move. I don't even breathe. I did not know this.

'The CPS wouldn't take it forward – insufficient evidence, they said, as it was only Oliver Forth-Standing's word against your statement of events.'

I don't even swallow, blink or breathe. *Ollie, what did you say?*

'The police alleged that you were part of Aleksander Baranoski's gang – the man who your mother said was the nephew of a former boyfriend of hers and one of the men who died at the scene where you were found.'

I can hear in her careful selection of words that she wants me to know that we are both talking about the same person – my lover and Aleksander. She knows.

'Oliver Forth-Standing alleged that you were an essential part of the gang; that you helped lure girls to the gang who were then trafficked out of the country. He even said it was you travelling with Aleksander that made it possible for him to cross the border multiple times. Customs are less likely to suspect a young couple. As, I suppose, girls are more likely to be trusting of other girls their age.'

I'm so stunned, I cannot speak. So Ollie did rat me out. I feel nauseous: he tried to fit me up.

I wait for her to say something else – a direct accusation, perhaps. Perhaps she wants me to deny it. But I couldn't deny Aleksander. I wouldn't deny him or the world we created.

Somewhere a clock ticks and a phone rings in a different office.

'You look different when you talk about him,' she eventually says. I see the twinkle in her eyes. Although her skin crepes with age, I can see the intelligence and youth in her eyes.

I realise I'm breathing again. 'It's nice to talk about someone who was and still is, so important to me.' This is my badge of loyalty to him. 'I haven't talked about him in a long time.'

I'm unprepared for the avenue she has led me down. 'So, Dee, what's changed now?'

I can't tell her. She'll never let me leave her office without calling for the police and a psychiatrist if I did. Instead, I put down my tea cup and stand, holding out my hand.

She shakes it, her smile replaced by a slight frown. 'Stay in touch, Dee, please let me know how you go.'

I smile back, not wanting to make promises I can't keep.

Her frown deepens. 'It's not too late, you know.'

'Too late for what?'

'To do that degree. To fall in love with someone else. To find a new life. To have babies of your own.' She smiles a little, but it doesn't reach her eyes. 'To fly free, Destiny. That's what I want for you.'

I feel my throat thicken with threatened tears.

She stands up and glances towards the door like she wants to run to it, to stop me going through it. 'You're so, so young.'

I'm so, so old.

I walk out without looking back.

It feels good to be eighteen. Yesterday I left my childhood behind. Leaving my, now ex, social worker's office when it suits me is my first independent act as an adult.

Tomorrow will be my second and final one.

Wednesday
01:02

Destiny

I can't sleep. I'm thinking about Jenni. I'm thinking about what's going to happen to her. I'm thinking about how she got away with it all.

I remember I was going to take one last look at my cuttings album. I pull it out from under my bed. I turn the first page. It's from the *Mirror*, front cover: 'Teaching Justice'. I read the paragraph next to the headline. 'Jenni Wales, 40, single-handedly exposed a child-trafficking ring. Jenni, a decorated ex-soldier, foiled the gang, which ended in a bloody standoff, when Jenni killed the gang's evil ringleader.'

I turn the pages.

I'm briefly distracted by my nails – they look so clean, milk white against baby pink. They are the nails of someone who has done nothing wrong. They surprise me.

I read how in a later article that: 'Hero Jenni Wales, 41, finally got acquitted of all charges following the nationwide campaign to recognise her work in putting a stop to a criminal gang's sleazy activity at selling snatched girls abroad.'

An inside spread from *The Sun* sees Ella in a bikini and the headline, 'Jenni is my hero', and then the text tells: 'How Jenni single-handedly pulled her from a nest of viper-like villains, who'd handcuffed her and pumped her full of drugs. Cruel kidnappers had snatched natural beauty, Ella, 17, chaining her in a cellar, ready to sell into a lifetime of work in the sordid sex trade. Innocent Ella was only saved when national hero, Jenni Wales, pulled her from the building, teaching the villains who really was boss.'

The next page saw Jenni putting her hands over her face as she was papped. 'Tragic hero, Jenni Wales, 41, has been admitted to a psychiatric hospital following a mental breakdown. Jenni, who became a national treasure after her heroic actions saved the lives of numerous future victims, has said before in an interview that she did not manage to save the girl she tried to.'

I know she was talking about me. I still want to scream at the cutting that I didn't want her to save me, that I didn't need to be saved, but I'm now too tired.

I drop the scrapbook and collapse onto the mattress, pulling the coverless duvet over me.

In the dark, I think about what Val said about the police wanting to prosecute me and about how Ollie tried to blame me. I think about this, turning it over in my mind like a new stone that shows promise of something more interesting, perhaps more precious than its origins first suggest. I do remember that witnesses remembered the brothers inviting people to the party. At the time, I thought that a party invite had been too far a reach to get the trafficking charge to stick. But now

Wednesday
06:30

Destiny

I put my uniform on for the last time. It is pale blue, with a loose-fitting top and trousers that match. I brush my hair in the mirror, careful not to look at my reflection. I brush it slowly back, still amazed by the short bleached hair that makes me look so different. I add eye liner, nothing else.

I get out my coloured contact lenses and my irises change from blue to brown. I take out my earrings and put them down on the bathroom shelf.

I cannot resist. I pick one up again, turning over the gold stud in my palm; Aleksander bought them for me and I'm amazed that I will never see the earrings again. I can't wear them at work, otherwise I would wear them now and of course I'm not coming back here ever again, so they will just sit here on this shelf until someone packs up my belongings. But I can't help but feel a pang of regret and wonder if there isn't something more appropriate I can do with them. It should be something significant. I wish I had someone to leave them to, someone who would care about them for me, so there was a sense of their importance going on, going forward. But there is no one.

I think of Val and her babies. I wonder if, when she is gone, they will treasure her earrings. Confused at my sudden rush of disappointment, I put it down, making a little *chink* sound as it touches the glass shelf.

I sit at the table and on the note pad I bought especially for the occasion, I write a letter to Robert and Marlena. I've decided since talking to Val that Robert and Marlena might deserve more than some abstract guessing game. I realise that just because they are paid, doesn't mean they definitely don't care. Perhaps they know what it's like to watch everyone picnic from the shade too. So although I keep it short, I am clear about why I've done it.

When I've finished, I put it in an envelope, writing their names on the front with a short instruction. I put it in the kitchen cupboard, lay it on the layer of dust that has been there since I've arrived; I've already decided that that is the perfect place to put it as they will only clean out the kitchen when I'm gone, ready for the next fuck-up.

Destiny

Now the patients' lunch things have been cleared away, many of the staff take their own lunchbreaks. I go to the hospital canteen, while many of the patients doze in high-back chairs. There's another nursing assistant in the queue in front of me and she has started a conversation with me about the chips as we wait in line to be served. 'Your first week on Willow, isn't it?' she says.

I nod. 'Although I worked on Sycamore for six months.'

'Got a transfer?'

'I really want to work in rehab.'

She nods thoughtfully and tells me it's good. 'And better than working round all those zonked out on ECT.'

After she's been through the till, she waits for me.

We chat about the differences of the wards as I follow her to a table. She looks at my lunch – fish and chips, mushy peas – and I asked them to give me the biggest they could and they shoved a mountain of chips on my plate too. I also took an apple pie and custard.

She looked me up and down and then back at my lunch as I take things off my tray. 'I would've thought you'd have eaten like a bird.' She's about my age and my height, but not thin like me.

'I thought I'd treat myself as it was my birthday on Monday.' I don't tell her it's because I will never eat in this canteen again.

She claps her hands with a childish delight. 'Your birthday! How old?'

I smile in spite of myself. 'Eighteen.'

She squeals and looks round like everybody else should be sharing such a thing. 'Your eighteenth! You should be off all week celebrating!' Her face is so comic, I have a strange desire to shove a chip in her open mouth to make her laugh. But I remember I don't know her. I don't even know her name.

'They let me have the weekend off and that was enough,' I say, giving her a wink.

She catches the point. 'Def. Where did you go?'

I say the name of some club in town. I eat a big piece of fish in batter; it tastes great. I should eat this more often, I think, then I remember what's happening later today. She's waiting for an answer. 'I got a limousine to take us there, me and my school buddies.'

Her eyes widen, she's impressed. 'Awesome. Next year, invite me. I'm Charlotte, by the way,' she says, sticking her hand forward.

I try her name. 'Charlotte.' I like the sound of it in my mouth again. *I had a sister, Charlotte.* I remember telling Miss that. I never told anyone about my lost family, not until her. My lost sister will probably be living in America still, but this Charlotte looks almost as nice. I can almost, holding her hand and looking in her eyes, imagine what it would be like to have a friend like this girl. My life would've felt different if I'd had a single friend who wanted to spend my birthday with me. 'Next year, *Charlotte*, I will.'

A bit of me almost wishes it could be true.

Wednesday
13:49

Destiny

This is what I've been waiting for. I'm standing in the crowded ward office as the senior nurse is divvying up duties for the afternoon. They call out patient names and then staff are allotted the duties. I check my nails again to make sure they are clean as I wait for the names to be called. Then I put up my hand. Everyone looks at me – it's not a hands-up situation. Besides, I'm still so new that no one here, except Charlotte next to me, really knows who I am.

'Can I be the escort? Please? I . . .' I hadn't counted on the staff looking at me like I was the strangest thing in a mental health ward. 'It's my birthday and I fancy the fresh air.' Everyone looks to the window, where rain hits the glass. Almost comically, they all look back at me again.

'If it stops raining,' I add. 'Otherwise, I'll push them around the corridors . . . if you think that's better . . . but I don't mind going out . . .'

They like them to go out in all weathers. There's no such thing as bad weather, only bad clothes, apparently. This is bullshit, of course.

For a long second, I imagine this woman will say no. *You will have to do something else. Or, yes but stay indoors.* And I will feel that rage again. The rage of not being listened to. The rage of people doing what the fuck they want no matter what it means to me. I imagine them staring at my rage and then taking control just like they do with their patients, just like what happened to me when I had my bad time.

Charlotte is looking at me with a question mark in her expression.

I force a smile. It might look worse.

I imagine having to go back to the bedsit, to walk past reception and say hello to either Robert or Marlena, forcing myself to smile so they don't get concerned.

I am so consumed with living the crushing disappointment that I don't realise that the woman has already answered me and has moved on to allocating a different patient to a different member of staff.

I turn to Charlotte and whisper, 'Did she say yes?'

Charlotte doesn't take her eyes off the woman but nods, whispering, 'Yes.'

I breathe deeply, my palms flat against the wall behind me. After all the planning, it is now happening. Charlotte is asking me something in a whisper but I don't even bother to try and hear.

It's all come true for me, finally.

I am taking Jenni.

Destiny

I can barely breathe. Jenni is sitting in front of me and I am standing there holding her coat. She doesn't look at me, but instead stares at a patch by my feet. She looks the same, unlike me. Her face is the same, her hair is the same, she is the same. Although I notice that her clothes are different. I was used to seeing her as a teacher: shirts under blazers and smart trousers. She always wore the same shoes every day – black lace-up brogues, polished to a high shine. We used to notice stuff like the same shoes every day. Then, the teachers weren't real people, they were only teachers. But Jenni Wales became a real person to me. Now she has on tracksuit bottoms and a T-shirt. But apart from the clothes, she looks the same.

A second glance tells me that she's not the same. Her face is slacker and she's a bit fatter around the middle. She knows I'm standing here, because her eyes glance up, but move across me as if I'm as much a part of the ward as the table or the bed. But then I am taller now, in uniform and I've lost weight, leaving my face even more angular. And of course my hair and eyes are a different colour. I've been careful to think this through.

I'm nervous to speak in case she recognises my voice. Aleksander had paid for a few elocution lessons for us both; it was part of his plan. Now I realise how incredibly unusual he was – he truly cared about making himself into something else. I know that, given the chance, he would've done it; he would've become something different than he was at birth. It seems to me that is what is the problem with our country: nobody can become different to what they already are. If people try to be different, they are sneered at or laughed at. How dare they try? Who do they think they are? People agree that one should better one's education; it's better to try and say 'one' not 'I'; to take exercise classes to improve fitness; to learn a language. Do that: be thinner, smarter, richer, healthier. If you don't, you're a failure. But don't try and be a better class. Never do that.

But Aleksander knew what he was and he wanted to be different. He wanted to have children who wouldn't struggle like we had: we both wanted that. Our children would've gone to the finest private schools. We were going to be fantastic parents. We would both have cut-glass accents and a successful, legitimate job of importing European goods. Our start-up position would've been far behind us. Our children would never have known that we both grew up poor: in Aleksander's case, beaten and hungry; in my case, unwanted and abused. They would only look out from a huge window, across a huge garden, and know what it was to have loving parents.

Wednesday
14:05

Jenni

As Destiny searches for my shoes, I can see that her hands are shaking. This means that what I have been waiting for is happening now. I'm glad.

She had stood me up, got me into my coat and then into the wheelchair, even got me into the corridor before she realised that I wasn't wearing any shoes. I'd wanted to tell her to be helpful, but it's so long since I've wanted to speak, I'm not sure I could.

I think I've been better a while. I'm not sure when exactly, but certainly for a little while.

It was George and Sal that made me realise I was back. They come every two weeks, my only visitors since Dad died, but I went from seeing them but not properly, like a projector image that's not clear in the strong sunshine, to them actually being there. I must have absorbed them before, poor image or not, because I knew that they visited me. I know the patchwork quilt on my bed was made by Sal and I know that she makes lots of them and her church ships them abroad to the poor. I know that George's face is noticeably different since his jaw had to be operated on and I even know that it was Aleksander who did it. He must have told me all this, but I don't remember him telling me. I don't remember the visits. All I know is that they were always there in the most distant of ways and then they came into focus and they were sitting and talking to me and I was there with them properly and I thought that I might actually talk back to them, I just didn't get round to it.

But I do remember the visit I got from Billy's girlfriend Maddie, when I hadn't been here long. I recognised her instantly.

She sat opposite me. I realised, then, how bad I must've been. The nurses here all talk to me like I'm having a normal conversation with them, their faces giving nothing away. But seeing Maddie was like looking in a mirror. It's like I could see how I looked by her reaction to me. I could see her shock.

She left soon after, leaving a box of fruit jellies on my table. As she left, she turned and said: 'Thank you. Billy always said how . . . you were always nice to him.'

And then she went and she never came back.

And that was all I was left with, the knowledge that I had been nice to him. It didn't seem enough then and it still doesn't now.

I used to like jellies but they sat there until someone took them away. I was relieved when they went because my head hurt a lot back then and the sight of them made the pain in my head, which sounded like the old transistor radios when trying to find a station, much worse.

But as time has moved on, I've spent a long time thinking. I looked out of the window and stared at a bird feeder. I watched the sparrows and blue tits and other small birds I didn't know the name of, and I thought that I was nice to Billy – enough for him to tell Maddie. I thought about that a lot. Perhaps I always will.

But then I got better. The thinking had been enough for such a long time, but then it wasn't any more. I started to feel restless. I began to be aware of my body again and I wanted to move. Not in the way I did before – the days of competing are behind me. I'm glad. For me, exercise was a way of not thinking. But now I've had this time to think, I understand things about myself that I didn't know before. I now understand what happened to me and about what happened to my family. I've finally given myself time to grieve. And now I think I might be ready to go home.

I think my dad would be proud of me.

I was thinking of telling the staff about going home, when Destiny suddenly turned up on the ward. She looked different: a little taller, her hair shorter, and her eyes, I don't know if it's my memory, but her eyes are now brown.

I know enough to know she's been here a few weeks. I know she knows who I am. She never comes over but I've seen her watching me. I know something else too, I know from the look on her face that she hates me.

She's right to hate me. I know she's here because she's going to kill me.

And I know that I will let her.

Destiny

I wheel Jenni towards the ward entrance. This is the tricky bit. When I worked on Sycamore ward, I brought patients in all the time to Willow where most of the rehab goes on. I already had my plan from the day I started volunteering at the hospital. I did several months as a volunteer before getting a paid job here. I've been watching all that time. Waiting.

Now I've got Jenni in a wheelchair. Even though I am supposed to be doing this, I can still feel my heart thumping. I push her up to reception. The ward reception window opens and the nurse looks at Jenni, 'Hello, Jenni!' she says brightly like she expects Jenni to answer.

She doesn't.

I've not read Jenni's notes because I wouldn't be allowed to. But I know that she's here because she's had a breakdown. From guilt, apparently, for taking me against my will. For forcing me into her car. For letting Gary die. Aleksander. She has blood on her hands. She deserves her guilt.

I sign Jenni out after showing my pass card.

We are free to go. I leave and push Jenni towards the door; the door buzzes. I do a neat 180 and push it open with my back.

I'm through.

I push Jenni through the corridors, my senses on hyper alert. I'm expecting someone to call me back. That they would suddenly see that my bullshit of getting voluntary work in the first place because of my own mental health problems was only that: bullshit. How the work led to paid work. How the paid work led me here. I can't believe that no one would realise the connection between us. But why should they? The HR woman who processed my application may not even have read the case and if she did, would she recognise me now? No one remembers the names of people in the news from three years ago, and they definitely don't if, like me, your name was not reported. My criminal history check was clear as I have no convictions. My appearance was different. That heart-stopping moment when Val told me that the police wanted to charge me for my involvement in the trafficking ring would have meant that I would've never got this job. But they didn't and I did.

And now I'm pushing Jenni down the corridor towards the exit.

I could hear every step around me. Hear every conversation. See every movement or glance my way. All the time assessing: are they looking at me because they know what I am doing? Do they know where we are going?

But no one stops us.

Of course they don't: we are supposed to be going outside. I am supposed to be taking Jenni for her daily fresh air. Every day, someone does this with Jenni: today it is me. Later, an OT and an assistant are expecting me to take her to her exercise where they expect to encourage her to stand up, walk around and get moving. But I am not taking her there. By the time they realise we've not turned up, we'll be long gone. And I think they won't realise for ages because they are understaffed at the moment and struggle to get through the workload. They will think that Jenni is on the ward and the ward will think that Jenni is in OT.

I pause by the front office. The nurse slides back the glass screen. 'Are you new here?'

I've cleared the ward, but I need to clear the hospital reception too. I try to give her a smile and force my voice to sound confident. 'I'm Dee.' I show her my I.D. 'I've been transferred to Willow over from Sycamore. I'm interested in doing my OT training,' I add. This lie about becoming an occupational therapist is the guff I gave as the reason I was pushing for a transfer.

'Well, you look after Jenni for me; she's a big hero in our family and my sons take a special interest in how she's doing.'

I feel a spear of paranoia. 'Why?'

'Because of her army background.'

This isn't what I'd feared, but I have to know. I step up close to the counter. 'What do you mean?'

She tells me to bring Jenni into the front office and pats the seat in front of the computer. I sit and she googles Jenni. I've searched her before, and brought up pages of the kidnapping articles praising her actions for standing up to Gary and Aleksander and saving Ella's life.

But the nurse's search includes 'army' and 'bravery'. She brings up an article I've never seen before. I read it.

I sit back, shocked. She is beaming at me as if she's just shown me her prodigal tap-dancing two-year-old. I struggle to find the words. 'I didn't know that,' I say, eventually. I stare at the article which show photos of Jenni being awarded the Conspicuous Gallantry Cross.

She looks epic in her uniform. I can't stop staring at her. She looks so heroic, so smart, so brave. For a brief moment I think, *I wish I was like her.* Then appalled, I shove the thought away.

I've been staring so long, I feel compelled to say something. 'I can't believe it.' The nurse smiles at Jenni. 'You're very impressive, Jenni, don't you forget that.' She turns her attention to me. 'My sons are both serving in the army and they send her stuff. Obviously, soldiers like my sons, have a whole lot of love for those who get PTSD from being in service.'

'PTSD? Why has she got that when she did so well?' Again, I feel the creep of paranoia. It's imperative that they don't know about me.

'She couldn't save someone.'

Me. She couldn't save me. 'Who couldn't she save?'

'Well, you've seen that she saved two soldiers in a rescue operation but there were others she couldn't save. Maybe it hit her harder than she let on. Dr Shanklin says she can't get better because she won't forgive herself for her mistakes. Make sure she gets a good spin round the block. After all, we all make mistakes, don't we?' She turns back to Jenni, 'Half of life is learning to forgive yourself.' Then to me she adds, 'Shut the office door after you, will you? I hate the draught.'

Dismissed, I push Jenni out of the hospital's front doors.

It has stopped raining. I look behind me to check that no one is watching and when it is clear that no one is around, I push her, not towards the gardens, but towards the car park.

Wednesday
14:24

Destiny

I am breathing hard, urgent breaths. Although I am pushing her fast – not too fast that it is obvious that I am up to something – but pacy, and while I want to get to my car as soon as possible, my laboured breathing is not from the effort. Nor is it because I am breaking the law; I have broken it before and never looked back when I did it. Nor is it because I know how this day ends – I'm not afraid. But I am fearful of being stopped.

This is so important to me: it is all I have thought about, worked towards, for three long, lonely years.

My car is purposefully parked next to the path, by the hedge. If I am going to get caught, it is now. If someone sees me on the CCTV, they will realise that I am breaking the rules. But it is possible that they won't. Not all the wards at this hospital are locked wards, many are open for patients who have chosen to come here. Besides, I remind myself, I've already passed the two points of security. Now we look like a patient and staff from the other wards, where patients are taken out regularly; trips to the shops, trips out with family. I have thought this through – I think I can do this.

I park her next to my old Peugeot. I already have my car keys in my hand: I press the fob. 'We are here,' I tell Jenni.

I feel a flutter of something I can't place. It feels strange to directly address her again. When I thought of this, I thought of Jenni but it was a cardboard cut-out version, something not quite real. But she is here now and real under my touch as I reach out and take her arm and it occurs to me – suddenly, how did I not consider this? – that she might not comply. She is too big for me to force. Panicked, I keep my voice sunshine bright. 'We are going out for a day trip in my car! Isn't that wonderful?' She doesn't move; she doesn't even blink. 'But we have to be quick! Let's get going! Upsy daisy!'

She stands up and beneath the mountain rock of relief, I am also surprised by her height. I'd forgotten how tall she is. I open the passenger door and help her in. I am struck by this reversal of our situations, me helping her into my car, a strange mirror image of only three years ago. I realise I even bought a blue Peugeot. I feel a bit sick that I did not grasp this at the time.

Jenni gets in and I put her seat belt on. She hasn't spoken to me, only looking into the vague distance. I wonder what goes on in her head, if anything.

I walk round the car and get in. With shaking hands I turn the key. I imagined this going well and now it is, I can't quite believe it. I drive slowly out of the car park and turn onto the road.

In only twenty minutes we will be there. And there it will end.

Wednesday
15:10

Destiny

I follow the winding roads that weave through green fields filled with sheep. The sky is blue and huge, the type of perfect cornflower blue that inspires poetry and postcards. We have left the bad weather behind us. I love that about here – how the sea wind and the cliffs pull the bad weather away up and over the over side of the Downs. That's why the Victorians headed to Eastbourne for their health.

Seeing the sky gives me an odd feeling – it takes a moment to place it and I realise that I want to write a poem. There was a time when I liked poetry, feeling the quiet thrill when we covered it in English classes. Even in the children's home, I would secretly write a few stanzas of my own. Then when I was with Aleksander, I wrote him love poetry; he loved it, declared me a genius and found a place where he could publish my own booklet, or pamphlet as he called it. He said my work deserved it. At first, I'd pushed the idea away, but he persisted. I was choosing my favourites for the collection when he died.

Aleksander would've loved a day like this, skies so blue, the open clifftop. We used to come here together. If we were together now, I'd write a poem for him.

I almost want Jenni to say something, to comment on the endless sky, just so I don't feel so lonely. But she says nothing.

What happened to her, I briefly wonder, thinking of the medal. I grip the wheel. *Shut up, Destiny.* Even if I insist on others calling me Dee when I'm cross with myself or upset, I still can't help but call myself Destiny. Shut up because you know what happened to her. *You* happened to her.

I think again – what did I do that was so wrong? What did I do that caused all this? She had a good thing; I had a good thing. She was a maths teacher and I had an amazing relationship with Aleksander – the only relationship I'd ever had where there was only kindness and no disappointment. He never let me down.

I blink against a different memory of him. No, he *was* perfect, I force myself to think. I will only remember the good times. I grip the wheel. He *was* perfect, he was; he gave me a future. Without him I have none.

I pull up to the clifftop car park. There's a few cars here, day-trippers, people with dogs, walkers and birdwatchers with binoculars or long lenses.

I check my rear-view. Nothing behind us. I yank up the handbrake; it makes a crunching sound and Jenni turns to look at it.

Jenni.

Sitting here in the car reminds me of what I had forgotten. That she wanted to save me. But I didn't need saving – not from Aleksander.

Fuck her, she was crazy. Crazy, crazy and sucked me into her madness with her.

Perhaps, an irritating voice whispers, perhaps she thought she was doing the right thing.

I pause, then, not wanting to feel the confusion, get out. I walk round the car to the passenger door. My feet crunch against the chalk rubble of the car park. I inhale ozone, sea-salt, the freshness of the wind. I love the smell of the sea.

I get her wheelchair out and open her door. Without saying anything, I grab her arm. I pull her and transfer her into her chair.

I push her across the car park to the sea, to the clifftop. We keep going. It's hard; a struggle. The ground inclines in places and Jenni is a dead weight in the chair. But I'm strong, determined and the ground is hard with only sparse grass, so the tyres push over it easily with me as the brute force behind it.

The wind picks up as we head towards the cliff. I have dreamt of this moment. We move in silence, my knuckles white against the handles.

Wednesday
15:38

Destiny

Most people stick to the path that edges the cliff, but we go beyond. Beyond that is the edge. I know this place well. I always come alone – except for today. Today is the day I have planned for.

We approach warning signs, with pictures and words shouting about rock falls and crumbling edges. The signs tell us to stay back. Other signs are from the Samaritans, offering a listening service to those who are suicidal. We pass them and leave them behind.

Only then do we reach the cliff.

I park Jenni next to the edge. I put the brake on. We won't have long before someone approaches us. A chalk rock dislodges and falls, bouncing down the white cliff face; to lean over to see where it lands would mean we would follow. Danger is here: we are five hundred feet up and the waves crash below. The wind has picked up, an occasional cloud now crossing the sky. Most people would baulk at this – but Jenni doesn't even seem to notice the height.

I stand behind her chair. Jenni's feet, in the foot plates, are inches over the edge. If she notices, she doesn't say anything.

She is fearless, but then again, she always was. An army hero. I consider this and suddenly feel a swell of admiration for this woman. Was there nothing she couldn't do? So why couldn't she suddenly cope? Why did she have a breakdown?

Perhaps I spoke this question aloud because she answered it, her voice rusty like an old hinge: 'Because I took you.'

I'm standing behind her, ready to push her over the edge. I always knew that I would have to go to prison for killing her, but I have no life to walk away from. I am content that if I am not seen doing this, I will hand myself into the police straight after. I want to be punished for killing Jenni; I will do it for Aleksander, for his memory. I want to give my life to avenge his.

I am ready.

I had my childhood, then I had my time with Aleksander and then I've had this dead zone of time being alone. I can't wait to move into my next stage, where I will leave my life as it is and go to prison. It will be fair that I go there and there I will fulfil my natural destiny – perhaps my mother always knew I could never escape it. And there I won't be alone. There I will not have to try any more.

But her sudden voice, its clarity, surprises me. She knows it's me! This is no catatonic woman – she knows what she is doing. Has she been fooling them? Fooling me? The wind picks up and as though this is my first time here, I'm suddenly acutely aware of how far up we are. How precarious our situation is – how precarious my situation is. 'Is there nothing wrong with you?'

'Yes there is.'

'They told me you didn't talk.'

'It wasn't them I needed to talk to.' I see her swallow, trying to work her throat. 'I've been waiting for you.'

I swallow against the dry of my throat. I've imagined sitting here with Jenni over and over, but I did not imagine this. 'Why have you been waiting?' I thought I had been so smart – finding out where she was, blagging my way into a position of trust, waiting. But all the time, she was waiting for me.

'Will you . . .' her voice breaks even more: 'Will you sit next to me? Please?'

I do. I hang my legs over the edge of the cliff and I breathe deeply. I should've pushed her by now, but everything is different to what I'd planned. I have to know. And as I sit looking out across the sea that continues endlessly into a distance I can't see, I know it will end.

Very soon.

Tuesday
15:50

Destiny

She puts her hand on my shoulder; it feels heavy. I feel the proximity of her. There's nothing behind us and nothing in front of us and only hundreds of feet of indifferent air to fall through before hitting the hard, stony beach and cold water. 'I'm sorry,' she says.

'What for?' I say angrily, snatching my shoulder away. I don't want her hand on me, I don't want an apology – I don't want anything from her.

I expect her to say lots of things, but I don't expect her to say what she did. 'Because I shouldn't have let you kill your boyfriend.'

I hold my breath. I could hear the sound of the sea smashing its steady current against the shore. I could hear the roar of banging blood in my ears.

My first thought is: *did anyone hear?* I look over my shoulder, but no one is near . . . yet. Only me and Miss know the truth. I've always known that one day she will get better and then . . .

But if she is dead, then it will only be me and then perhaps it will be like it's not real any more. Perhaps when there is only me to change things to being how I want them to be, perhaps that becomes the new truth and the only one that matters.

'I should've moved quicker,' she says, her words a tumble. 'I was unprepared. I let you down. You were a child. You shouldn't have had to live with that.'

A bruised cloud covers the sun; we are cast into shadow.

I want to say, *No.* I did not kill Aleksander, *you did.*

But I don't say that. I let her put her hand back on my shoulder and this time I don't move away. Instead I think of the nurse saying, *We all make mistakes.*

I thought of Val saying: *You mustn't let your anger drive your actions, Dee.*

I remember my mother saying, *When you've lost it, nothing can touch you . . . I kept sharp things out of your way.*

But the gun was there with nobody to keep it out of my way.

Tears are rolling down my face. Of course I know this. I was there.

I remember the searing anger when I found Gary dead. Aleksander had ignored my pleas to leave Gary alone, ignored me just like everyone else had always done. The surprise was like being dropped into a deep snow drift. My whole life, Aleksander was the only person who didn't ignore me and then when he did, it felt horrific that he was like everyone else and I realised that everything I thought we had was all fake because he was going to do anything he wanted and when people did whatever they wanted to, it was never any good. Not for me. And I looked down and it wasn't good because Gary was bleeding out.

He was on his front and too heavy for me to move, but I managed to cradle Gary's head so the hard floor didn't hurt him and although he was heavy, it meant he could look at me. He gave me this look I shall never forget: he really saw me.

Me.

Then he'd gone. Gary had been my friend: my only one. It was horrible seeing his dead eyes, his beautiful blue eyes no longer staring at me but at some place behind me, somewhere I couldn't go to with him and the blood from his legs and stomach had slowed to a leak, like there was no real force behind it any more, because of course there wasn't, he'd already left me. And the gun had been knocked within my reach as Miss fought with Aleksander.

And I just did it. I wasn't even thinking: I was just so angry. So I shot Aleksander.

And that's why I hate her. 'It *is* all your fault. Aleksander and me were happy. If you hadn't have taken me . . . my life would've have been so different. And I wouldn't be alone now.'

I get up, feeling the fire in my soft tissue, my bones, my blood. It will be so easy to finally put an end to it. She has accused me and it occurs to me that perhaps that's what I needed to hear: the truth.

I know I've never been able to get better because I can't admit the truth to myself – let alone a therapist or a psychiatrist. That's why I could never make a friend. I could never risk telling someone.

I have to live with so much: stuff I've done; stuff I've chosen to do; stuff I was made to do. To live with so much already, how could I live with killing the person I loved most in the world?

I could not be that person. It is too much.

The cloud moves away from the sun and the light hits the water, sending diamonds scattering across the sea towards me.

I thought of Charlotte, of the promise of a different life, where people want to come to my birthday party. How things could be different for me, perhaps.

I feel it, but I push it away and get up. My legs feel shaky and I feel the wooze of standing so close to the edge of such a high cliff. I come here so much that normally I am used to it, but perhaps it's the sudden standing that makes me feel the danger.

I rest my hands on Jenni's back and she knows what I am going to do. She's a foot taller than me and several stone heavier. She could push me off, but she doesn't. I realise then exactly how brave she is. How she will accept this. But of course she's brave: she risked everything for me. It cost her everything. And even when she'd given everything she had, she kept my secret for me. She took the blame, risked a prison sentence and then let her own mental health crumble as a consequence. She is a hero. She was before, fighting for her country, and she is now, fighting for me.

I tense my fingers and press my palms against her back.

I will have to live with this too, I think, not just all that went on before. This – killing this woman – will simply be one more weight pulling me down under the water. I am only a fraction above the water as it is – perhaps this will be the thing that pulls me under. It won't be absolution – it will only be more shit in my life. Or maybe it will be the final thing that drowns my life.

I consider this, and know I am tough enough not to be broken. But then I think about my overburdened suitcase. What if she goes down screaming? Will I hear that noise too late at night while I stare sleepless at the ceiling?

No. I have to stay firm. I have given so much to get to this point.

In my mind, I have held firm that she killed Aleksander because even if she didn't pull the trigger, she created a situation that pushed me to do it. She was the change: before her, we were happy and we were building something. Believing that, keeping a tight grip on that, meant that it's been the truth in my head. Like a river that wears a deeper and deeper path in sand, the more I thought it, the easier it was to believe it.

But now it isn't. Now it feels confused. I did not expect to waver; I have always felt so decisive about this.

I think of my mother. The way her nose wrinkled with disgust; her, a drug-dealing prostitute who let men go after her little girl, but not thinking of that as she looked at me with condemnation, and pointed her grimy finger as she said: *there's no dirtier work than yours.*

No dirtier.

That means I am the dirtiest of all.

And it's true. Despite the filth of the accuser, she is still right.

It occurs to me, as the wind ruffles my hair, that perhaps it wasn't money I was after. I thought I wanted it because that was what Aleksander wanted – to him financial security meant safety. I thought we were the same, but perhaps we weren't. Perhaps I needed something else. Perhaps all I needed was love.

I've never thought of this over the last few years; I've not allowed myself to think of anything other than avenging the ruination of my life. But this feels true: now I've thought it, I instinctively recognise this is right. I needed love.

I've had so little of it over the years and what I had been given had always been at a price. Under my thumbs I feel the material of Jenni's coat; it's padded, silky, but synthetic. It's not the coat of someone who has money. It occurs to me that perhaps she is the only person who ever gave me something of themselves with no price attached. She gave it all up for me: she gave up her pay cheques; her anonymity; her profession. Why? Why when nobody did anything for me they didn't have to, did she? I ask her this: 'Why?' I hear the truculent teenager in my own voice.

She pauses before giving a little shake of her shoulders and head. She doesn't know. Or if she does, she hasn't got the words.

'Do you regret it?' I ask, unable to help myself.

'No.' This sounds clear and determined. 'It was the right thing to do. Children's safety should always come first.'

'But I didn't need any help!'

'You were doing bad things, Destiny. You were a child, still. You had been groomed.'

Groomed! That was for sexual exploitation. I start to think of Aleksander, always on me and not always in a kind way. *No!* I don't want to think like this. I reach for the nearest accusation. 'You make it sound like I didn't know my own mind.'

'You didn't have any choice about what you did,' Jenni says, so softly I nearly missed it.

When I realise what she's talking about, I feel a bolt of anger. 'Not true! I had a—' but my argument stumbles over the word. Choice. It turns over and over and over in my mind. *Choice.*

I think of a time before, not long after we'd started the business. I was fourteen. Aleksander and the boys had taken care of the first couple of rabbits, but then Aleksander decided I should be in on it. 'You're not a proper business partner unless you can do it all.'

'Doing it all' meant following him upstairs. I don't remember that particular party house, but I remember that the treads creaked a warning with each step I took.

I remember my fingertips trailing against the banister, and me watching them fascinated and afraid, as if they weren't really mine, as if I knew they were hands that were going to do new things. Bad things.

Inside one of the bedrooms was a girl only a couple of years older than I was. I knew she was there – I'd helped drug her. But seeing her now, naked, thin, arms held behind her back, showing breasts so small and innocent, felt shocking. Just looking at her made me feel queasy. In my mind I'd imagined her in the room as I saw her the night before – still confident in boots I wanted for myself, still wearing an easy grin following an even easier swig on her booze. But there was no party now.

'Hit her.' Aleksander goaded. It was only me and him – and her.

I didn't want to and I told him that. She stared at me with frightened eyes, watching our exchange.

'Do it,' he said, always so easy with the imperatives.

I stared at her, her jaw biting down on the gag, as if antici-pating me changing my mind. 'I don't want to.'

His voice came low, like a warning, 'Destiny.'

But I shook my head, my eyes squeezed shut against the brewing storm.

'I can't do it,' he said. 'I never hit women or girls.'

No, you find other ways to make them cry, I wanted to say. Instead I kept my eyes and mouth shut. I felt a twang of long-ing for some other time before, somewhere when the world didn't hold choices that were not really choices. But in that moment, I couldn't think of one single time.

Not one.

I heard him rush across the room; I felt the movement of air around him move on my face. I flinched.

The door banged open. 'Gary!' he yelled.

Gary? I felt a sliver of concern.

Only seconds later, I heard Gary's heavy footsteps on the stair. 'Yes, boss?' he said coming into the room. I kept my eyes closed.

'*Destiny.*' Aleksander's voice was low and heavy with warning.

I opened my eyes.

Like a conjurer, Aleksander now held a metal bar. 'I will make it easier for you, this one time. You don't have to use your hands, you can use this.'

I shook my head. I think I said no.

Aleksander turned to Gary. 'Lie down.'

'Boss?'

'Lie down.'

Immediately, Gary lay down where he stood, still halfway in the doorway. Something about his decision to be half in and half out of the room, bothered me.

In one easy movement, Aleksander raised the bar above his head and brought it down, hard, on Gary's leg.

Gary cried out in pain, but struggled back tears.

Aleksander did it twice more. As Gary dragged the air into his lungs, Aleksander wordlessly held the bar out to me. I understood. Aleksander knew that Gary was my only friend. He knew I'd do anything to protect Gary.

I turned towards the girl and for a moment the girl's eyes met mine. I knew then that she understood it too. Maybe she even forgave me a bit.

Maybe.

Then I think about afterwards, how Aleksander held me close and kissed my eyelids. He told me he loved me and that I was his queen. Then I remember the time after that he didn't need to hit Gary.

The wind picks up. I'm starting to get cold. I've never done it – never wanted to, but I imagine now where those girls are. Perhaps it might amaze someone – someone sane who's not had my life – how I have *not* thought of them before, like all the time. But I don't.

But now, for the first time in my life, I actually choose to look in my suitcase. I choose to remember.

I think of the girls I took; as the wind lifts my hair, I count them. One, two, three, four, five . . .

There were thirteen.

I don't remember them all. What I do remember is the hovels we operated out of.

We moved nine times and in four places we netted two rabbits each go. Thirteen. Unlucky for them.

I let the suitcase fall open. I try to think of their faces. I try to put what I have together – places; names; faces; experiences. Anything I have. I go through them one at a time and say to their memory: I took you. I also took you. I took you too.

One of them sticks in my throat like a fishbone: she was small like me, dark like me, wrists a wind could snap, the same as mine. I wonder where she is now. *No.* I don't want to know. Yes I do want to know.

For a moment – the briefest of moments – I imagine her, tethered by her foot to a brothel bed, a trail of full stops up her arm, punctuating her reality like caesura.

I did that. I put her there. She followed me. She didn't follow Gary or Aleksander or Jay or Ollie. She followed me because she looked into my big blue eyes and saw something that wasn't there – that's never been there.

No. I decide, I don't want to think about that – I can't. Because I can't change it now. Those girls are lost, like blown seeds into a sand storm.

As much as I am unwilling to turn the reality over and examine it for what it is, I could still see it wasn't Miss who was wrong – it was me. The most grown-up thing I have ever done is to accept that is true.

I. Was. Wrong.

The realisation of that, the implications of that, are huge. I teeter on a cliff edge and feel it in my mind as a different, worse, precipice. Who am I?

At least before I had a future. What do I have now?

For a moment, the wind lifts. My right foot is slightly over the edge. I am so close to falling. For a moment . . .

Then a seagull lands next to us. It stands on the scrubby grass, before stepping towards me and turning its head to one side; it fixes its strange yellow eye upon me. I stare at it, expecting it to go. I think of Aleksander and his love of seagulls; I think of my birthday card; of Val telling me to fly free.

And it turns and flies away.

I stare at it as it flies into the blue; I think of a puppy called Lexi and I think of forgiveness. I would like forgiveness, I decide. I stare into the sky and hope that it can be mine.

As the gull disappears towards the horizon, Jenni tells me again that she is sorry. I can hear the emotion in her voice and feel the shudder of her shoulders, so I know she is crying. A piece of rock breaks free and bounces down the cliff front and drops somewhere down, far out of sight. I know she means it.

I think of my mother telling me that I am not even as good as her. I look at my clean, white nails. I think of her dirty, needle-tracked skin and I know it is true.

I also know that I can't kill off my past, it will always be with me. Because of me, I think of those who don't have a future: Aleksander; Gary; the girls I took. I look down at Miss – poor Miss, perhaps even her. I rest my hand on her shoulder as I think of the nurse who said: *Half of life is learning to forgive yourself.*

And I could, I realise, be like the seagull. I too could fly free. I still have a future, not one that has to be spent behind bars, but the opportunity of a purposeful one. A good one. I could just leave all I have done and all that has been done to me, and just . . .

The wind blows on my face and I think of all the possibilities this holds . . .

And eventually, finally, I decide.

I put my other hand on Jenni's shoulder, bracing them.

I take a deep breath. 'Jenni,' I say, after what feels like an eternity, 'It's time.'

She turns and looks at me from over her shoulder. Her eyes are searching, suggesting she's not sure what's happening. But I am.

'Let's go home,' I tell her and she nods as I pull her chair away from the edge; together we both turn from it and in doing so, I hope, turn away from our pasts and perhaps, *perhaps*, I think as we journey back to safety, the wind behind us now, pushing us forwards, we have the chance of finding a future with something new.

Something better.

Acknowledgements

There are many people I'd like to thank, but perhaps I should start with you, dear reader, for your investment in this story, because if you got this far, you stayed with Jenni and Destiny until the end.

The queen of this book is undoubtedly Katherine Armstrong. I first met her through The WoMentoring Project, when she showed great generosity working on a previous project of mine. With this novel, she has shown both faith from the start and editing finesse and has my enduring gratitude. We all need a fairy godmother and she is mine. Thank you also to the rest of the team at Zaffre who have developed this novel with flair, skill and zest, with particular note to Jennie Rothwell. Thank you also to Micaela Alcaino for the stylish cover and Susanna Scutt for my author photo (and cinnamon buns).

I feel blessed to be agented by the superb Jane Gregory whose wit, energy and expertise meant she was always my dream agent. So thank you to Jane and her editor, Stephanie Glencross also, who saw the earliest draft and help shape it.

A large thank you is owed to Alan Kingshott, who served in the British Army for many years. He was recognised for his service by becoming the Chief Yeoman Warder at the Tower of

London, an eminent and highly trusted position which reflects his professional career. Any accuracies of army life are his; inaccuracies remain mine, with my apologies. Additionally, I'd like to thank Jack Nunn at *Stop The Traffik*, an organisation that works tirelessly to stop human trafficking in all its forms. He helped me understand 'the boyfriend model' which presents a real risk of grooming, particularly to vulnerable young girls. Please take the time to read their material, because much can be done if people understand who might be at risk. Again, any liberties taken with the facts are my errors. I've spent two decades working with vulnerable people whose childhoods, sadly, inform this story. I have much to say on this subject, but perhaps through this novel, I've already said a little.

A big acknowledgement must be for all those who work in education. I do myself, so I see daily the ways teachers and support staff rescue children in ways – thankfully – smaller than Jenni's, but often no less significant. They don't just educate, champion and encourage, they also do their best to keep our children safe against the myriad of modern and less modern dangers, and do so on a shoestring budget.

I've referenced The WoMentoring Project, so would like to acknowledge the project's creator, Kerry Hudson; although we have never met, she created an opportunity that fundamentally changed my life. Kerry, I hope to be able to buy you a drink one day.

I'd like to thank my writing buddies; the world of publishing is a warm one, but I'd particularly like to mention those who've supported me for over a decade: Vashti Hardy, Hattie Gordon,

Clare Nias and Tracy Hind. Your friendship and support is a powerful thing.

There are other cultures who are more at ease with thanking God than our own, but since much can be learned from the wider world, I would like to, because if there is anyone who has had to listen to my woe at being an unpublished writer, then it is Him.

I would love to individually acknowledge all of my friends who encourage me, but I am fortunate that the list of lovelies is too long, and I hope you know I appreciate it and each one of you. I will just note Dorrie Dowling, whose wisdom and optimism uplift me greatly and deserves a hooray all of her own, as does my sister, Juliet Hunter, who has always been first reader and only gives me just enough advice to make a draft better, without popping the balloon of belief – a judgement in itself. I'm fortunate to have a wonderful extended family who are all very dear to me, but for reasons of brevity, will only pause on my immediate family: my always engaging brother James, with particular reference to my parents, John and Jenny Elton, who are both unfailingly encouraging, loving and full of conviction. Thank you both of you – it really helps. I'm also championed by my wonderful sons, Cooper and Casper, bringers of sunshine. Finally, my incredibly patient husband deserves the last word. He has spent many years in my company, whilst I have been tap-tapping on my laptop, really somewhere else, but he has only ever encouraged me. Thank you Brad, I got published in the end, *phew* – but it certainly took a while, didn't it?